DOWN & DIRTY: DEX

Dirty Angels MC®, Book 8

JEANNE ST. JAMES

Jeanne ST. JAMES

Editor: Proofreading by the Page
Cover Art: Susan Garwood of Wicked Women Designs
Beta Readers: Author Whitley Cox, Krisztina Hollo, Andi Babcock and Nessa Kreyling

---

www.jeannestjames.com

Sign up for my newsletter for insider information, author news, and new releases:
www.jeannestjames.com/newslettersignup

Keep an eye on her website at http://www.jeannestjames.com/or sign up for her newsletter to learn about her upcoming releases: http://www.jeannestjames.com/newslettersignup

Author Links: Instagram * Facebook * Goodreads Author Page * Newsletter * Jeanne's Review & Book Crew * BookBub * TikTok * YouTube

Down & Dirty 'til Dead

CHAPTER ONE

Dex had a fucking half-chub. He grimaced because he needed to adjust it, but if his sister caught him doing so, she would give him shit. He glanced over his shoulder through the large picture window into the pawn shop's office where Ivy sat working in front of a computer.

Fucking hell.

Then his neck twisted once again to stare at the woman who was wandering around Shadow Valley Pawn pretending to check out the items for sale.

She was faking it and he wanted to know why.

It was possible she was just trying to pass the time. Maybe she'd been sent here from that asshole rival MC, the Shadow Warriors, to case the joint so they could wreak future havoc.

They hadn't heard from those outlaw nomads in a while, so it was about time for them to show their bastard faces.

But no matter why the woman was here, Dex couldn't ignore the fact that the woman was fucking dick-hardening sexy.

Smoking hot.

Tall. Leggy. And tits that made his mouth water.

Fuck.

Now his half chub was a full-blown hard-on.

Fuck it. He reached down and yanked it to a more comfortable position.

Fuck Ivy. She could bitch all she wanted.

If he was lucky, she hadn't noticed.

Now that he wasn't so uncomfortable, he leaned back against the counter behind the glass display case and crossed his arms over his chest as he continued to check the "customer" out.

Her hair was like a strawberry blonde. He was pretty sure that's what chicks called it. Not as red as his sister Ivy's and not as light blonde as Emma's, Dawg's ol' lady. An in-between.

He could imagine the woman on her knees in front of him, his dick in her mouth, his fingers wrapped tightly in her hair and her head bobbing up and down.

Fuck yeah.

His dick twitched, and his balls pulled tight as he wondered if the carpet matched the drapes.

For fuck's sake, he never wanted to lick a carpet as badly than he did at that moment.

He needed to see the color of her eyes. He wanted to imagine what they would look like when she tipped them up toward him as he blew his load into her mouth.

He groaned. Then groaned again when she ran her fingers over a marble sculpture that reminded him of some ancient dildo.

Yeah, that's it.

When she circled the base of the sculpture with her fingers, a soft whimper escaped him before he could stop it.

Fuck. He was going commando today and his dick was making a mess in his jeans. He shifted, then shifted again as the denim scraped the sensitive head.

He might have to go back into the storage area, lock himself in a closet and relieve the load in his balls.

He checked over his shoulder once more to make sure Ivy was doing whatever she did. Her head was down and she was busy typing away on the keyboard.

His gaze shot back to the *sex-on-a-stick* who was now running her thumb over the crown of the...

It was a fucking sculpture!

Why the fuck did Ace accept that pawn? No one in their right mind would pay a grand for a marble thing that looked too much like a dick.

Maybe this chick would since she seemed fascinated by it.

He pushed off the counter, adjusted himself one more time, and strode over to where she stood fondling the...

"Hey." He winced as his voice cracked. He cleared his throat and dropped his voice an octave. "Hey, you need any help?"

Glancing up from running her finger up and down the smooth veiny marble, she pinned him in place with...

He couldn't tell what color her eyes were. They were blue, but not a typical blue. Like a grayish blue, sky blue, slate blue, whatever. He had no fucking clue since they seemed to keep changing the longer he stared at her. Maybe it was because of the lack of blood to his brain.

"What are they?" he asked as if in a trance.

"What?" she asked softly.

"Your eyes. What color are they?"

She raised her brows and tilted her head to study his face. "Do you ask all of your customers that?"

Just the ones that make my dick hard. "Yeah, it's a requirement."

"Like a credit check?"

"Somethin' like that."

Her lips twitched, and she shrugged. "They're blue."

Simple enough. Those *blue* eyes met his and he pictured himself pumping his cum down her throat.

She jerked her head toward his now throbbing dick. "Do you always sport wood when you talk to your customers, too?"

Dex smiled, but kept his hand from creeping down to touch what she was looking at. "Depends on who the customer is."

"You know that's sexual harassment, right?"

He frowned. "What is?"

"Undressing me with your eyes the moment I walked through the door, staring at my tits, standing this close to me with a hard-on."

"Well, maybe you shouldn't jerk off a marble dick."

Her gaze bounced to the sculpture, and she removed her hand. "Is that what it is?"

"Dunno. Don't care. Just know I'd like to be in its place."

She clicked her tongue. "I guess you didn't hear what I just said."

"Nope." He grinned. "Haven't touched you yet. When I do, you can warn me again about my bad behavior."

"Or misbehavior."

Dex shrugged. "Just wanna let you know, I like what I see."

"So, the marble sculpture turns you on?" Her eyes crinkled at the corners.

"You touchin' it did."

"No filter, huh?"

"Whataya mean?"

"You just say," she waved a hand around, "whatever's in your head."

"Yep. Pretty much."

She laughed and shook her head.

Damn, that laugh didn't help the little problem in his jeans. *Fuck that*, his *big* problem.

"I guess you work here?"

"Yeah," he grunted.

She jerked her chin at his cut. "Is that a uniform all the employees wear?"

"Some of us." At least Ace and Dex wore the Dirty Angels MC colors. Ivy didn't wear her ol' man's cut. And Ace had a couple of part-timers who worked in the pawn shop, but they weren't a part of their club. "Ain't a uniform. It's a cut."

"I know what it is," she answered.

Dex pursed his lips and ran his gaze over her from top to toe. Sexual harassment be damned. Did the Warriors send her in?

Would those fuckwads even know a woman who looked like her?

She wore jeans that hugged her thighs and hips, brown high-heeled boots that went up to her knees, and a tight long sleeved-top that... *yeah*, emphasized her rack. A brown leather coat was tossed over her arm.

"Don't look like a biker chick," he murmured.

"What does a biker chick look like?"

Good fucking question.

The buzzer went off, indicating the front door to the shop had opened, and Ace stepped inside. His uncle's eyes immediately landed on them and Ace shook his head.

As he passed, he gave Dex a pointed look. Ace didn't like Dex flirting with the customers. He'd warned him time and time again not to turn into Pierce, the former DAMC president, who was a total dick and liked to take advantage of women by...

Sexually harassing them.

Fuck.

He shuffled his feet, hoping Ace didn't spot his hard-on, and cleared his throat again. He was supposed to be helping customers and making sales, not chasing them away.

"So... you wanna buy that... thing?" He cocked an eyebrow toward the sculpture.

"For a thousand bucks? I could buy a Rabbit cheaper."

"What?"

"I said no."

That wasn't what she said. He had no idea what a rabbit was, besides the kind that hopped. But maybe he should find out.

Later. When he was alone.

"So, if you don't want it, what are you here for? What are you lookin' for?"

"My father."

. . .

The guy was handsome... sort of. In a bit of a rough biker way. But he wasn't bad. He didn't have a beer gut. Yet. And he didn't have a long beard. Yet. Unlike the older man that had just entered and walked through the pawn shop in worn jeans, heavy biker boots and wearing a similar cut as this one's.

Brooke's gaze went over to where the man stood behind the counter. Could he be him? Her father?

"Who's your father?"

Her attention was drawn back to the man before her. Colorful tattoos spilled over his forearms, from where his long-sleeved thermal shirt was pushed up past his elbows, down to his wrists. He sported a small gold hoop in one ear and a couple fingers were encircled by clunky brass-colored rings. A wide band of leather wrapped around his left wrist. So typical of a biker. "Trying to figure that out."

He had good teeth, though, and he looked clean. Well, except for his leather vest. The patches were dirty. But then it wasn't like he could throw his cut into the washing machine. A white rectangular patch over his right chest said "Secretary."

"Why would you come here, though? Gotta have a reason."

Brooke moved behind the biker to read the back of his cut. She reached out and brushed her fingers over the top rocker of his colors. "Because of that."

He twisted his head. "What?"

"What your patches say."

He spun around to face her. "Fuckin' speak English."

She shrugged. "Okay. Like I said, I'm looking for my father."

His dark brows furrowed. "And what does that have to do with the DAMC?"

"I'm pretty sure he's a member. Or was. At least when I was conceived. Not sure if he still is."

Brooke watched a look cross his face. It held a mixture of disbelief and surprise. Her gaze dropped to his name patch. *Dex.*

She wondered what that name meant. Surely all bikers had a nickname. "Dex."

"Yeah," he grunted, then turned to yell across the shop to the older biker behind the counter. "Ace, you got another kid you don't know about?"

The older biker's eyes widened, then narrowed as they landed on Brooke.

"What the fuck you talkin' 'bout?" this "Ace" grumbled as he rounded the long glass display counter and headed in their direction.

"A kid. As in, you knocked up a bitch an' didn't know?"

Brooke sighed. She should take offense at this Dex calling her mother a bitch. Hell, she should take offense at the way he fucked her with his eyes.

Ace was pulling on his long salt and pepper beard as he approached and eyeballed her up and down. Almost as if he was trying to see if she looked familiar. She did look like her mother, at least before the cancer turned her into nothing but a shell.

Ace's voice was gruff and worn like his cut. "How old are you?"

Some women would also take offense to that question. But she was here for a specific reason, so it would be smart for her to answer. "Thirty."

Ace snorted and ran a hand over his brow as if he was wiping off sweat. "Ain't mine. Janice had me neutered after Diesel came outta her like a wreckin' ball."

Brooke should feel relieved that this biker wasn't her father. But she wasn't. Disappointment crept in before she could knock it away. Because that meant she had to keep looking.

"Also, haven't fucked anyone other than Janice since Hawk was conceived on the back of my sled. Knew right then it was true love." He shot her a wide grin and then leaned closer like he was about to tell her a secret. "Yeah. Tight pussy over a Harley. Nothin' better than that."

Dex whacked Ace on the arm. "True, brother. Maybe good head's a close second." His eyes landed on her lips.

Brooke tipped her head down to hide the roll of her eyes. She needed to keep them on the topic at hand. "I'm sorry. I just know he's a biker and might own a business in Shadow Valley. I asked around town, and there seems to be a few businesses owned by bikers, so I'm stopping at them all. This just happened to be the first one on my list."

"Well, the only bikers workin' in this shop are me an' Dex here. An' this boy might be a horny fucker but doubt he knocked anyone up when he was two."

Brooke fought the twitch of her lips. "Are you two related?"

"Uncle. An' club brothers," Ace stated, then tilted his head. "Sure your pop was an Angel?"

"Pretty sure."

"How come you're only lookin' for 'im now?"

"My mom passed away a couple months ago, and when I was going through her things, I found out my father wasn't really my father. Or at least he wasn't my biological father."

Ace regarded her for a long moment. "Got a name?"

Brooke shook her head. "Nope. Just found some things hidden away in the attic. Some of it mentioned your MC and it was dated about the time I was born."

"You think she hung 'round the club thirty years ago?" Ace asked her.

Brooke shrugged. "I don't know. I'm not sure how involved she was with this biker. Might have been just a one-night stand since she *was* married when she got pregnant with me. Whatever happened, she never talked about it, never told me the truth. I always just assumed my father was... my father. His name was even on my birth certificate."

Dex shifted next to her. "So, why do you think he ain't your father?"

She regarded him for a moment. "Besides the stuff that I uncovered? I found it curious that I never looked like him. I never looked like my brother or sister, either. I just didn't fit in." Though, she looked like her mother, she looked nothing like her father, while her younger siblings did. Brooke had always wondered about that, but never got a good answer. So, she let it go. Until she began to wonder again as she cleaned her mother's house out, and came across a few things that made her question who her real father was.

"D'ya ask your pop?" Ace asked her, hands on his hips.

She shook her head. "No, he died from a heart attack when I was a teenager."

"Damn. Lost both your mom an' pop. Sorry to hear that," Ace mumbled. "But still don't get why you'd think your biological father was an Angel. Just a few mementos, or whatever, don't indicate shit. Been a member of this club forever. Hell, I was born into it. My pop was a foundin' member. So, I know everyone who's come an' gone an' has worn our colors. Had to be a brother who was 'round my age or older. Unless..."

"Unless?"

Ace shrugged his broad shoulders. "Unless it was a hang-around or prospect who didn't pan out. Ain't too many members left from back then. Rocky an' Doc's in prison. As for the rest, quite a few of 'em got taken out when shit began to get hot an' heavy with the Shadow Warriors."

"Grizz," Dex mentioned.

"Who's Grizz?" Brooke asked.

"One of the oldest members," Dex answered. "At least not in prison," he added quickly. He glanced at Ace. "Could it be Grizz?"

"Fuck. Don't even say that out loud. Momma Bear would have his balls on a spit an' be servin' 'em up at The Iron Horse lickity split."

"Is The Iron Horse one of the club's businesses?" Brooke asked. She didn't remember if that one was on her list. If it wasn't, she needed to add it.

"Yeah," Dex answered.

"Who runs that?"

Ace snorted. "My son, Hawk. He definitely ain't your father, either."

"If it ain't Grizz, then who?" Dex asked. "One of the members the Warriors killed?"

Ace pulled at his beard slowly and frowned. "Could be."

"How 'bout Rocky?"

"Dunno, boy. He's old enough to be." Ace regarded Brooke. "Question is, if you find 'im, then what?"

That was a damn good question. She hadn't thought that far ahead. She figured she needed to find out who he was and if he was still breathing, then...

Then depending who it was...

"If it ain't you, an' it ain't Grizz. Might be Rocky."

"Could be anyone, Dex. An' she don't even got any solid proof. Not even a fuckin' name."

"Maybe she could talk to D. Maybe his crew can help 'er out."

Ace scowled at Dex. "For what?"

"To help her figure out who 'er pop is. What the fuck, Ace?"

"Why do you fuckin' care, boy? Why do you wanna bring more drama into this damn club? Ain't we got enough? You just wanna stick your dick in 'er, an' think she'll give you a little grateful pussy if you help 'er. Keep your nose out of it. For all we know her pop could be the same as yours since that deadbeat took off, leaving your fuckin' mother with three little ones."

"Ace."

"No." Ace threw up his hands. "Don't be stickin' your dick in 'er 'til you know she ain't your sister. For fuck's sake! That's all we fuckin' need." He stalked away grumbling.

"Um," Brooke began, heat crawling up her neck.

"Yeah," Dex muttered. He raked his fingers through his dark hair which was a little on the longer side. Not quite shaggy but not trimmed tight, either. His dark brown eyes landed on her. "Sorry 'bout that. Kinda killed my fuckin' boner, too."

Brooke's gaze automatically dropped to where his hand landed, then she closed her eyes and cursed herself for doing just that. But Ace was right, they could be siblings. She shuddered as she thought back on how Dex was staring at her earlier.

A knuckle grazed her cheek and she opened her eyes. "Ace is

wrong. Ain't my sister. My pop was no longer an Angel when your mom got knocked up. He got on his sled, took off an' never came back."

"Are you sure?"

"Yeah, babe. 'Cause that woulda sucked."

"Why?"

"'Cause I'm gonna buy you a fuckin' beer."

She wasn't sure if that was supposed to be a pick-up line. Because it if was, it sucked. But she had to admit, the man had a lot of confidence. "I don't drink beer."

"Whiskey, then."

"We could still have a whiskey together even if we were related."

"Yeah, but couldn't do the rest of the stuff I have planned."

Her eyebrows shot up her forehead. Maybe what she thought as confidence was actually cockiness. "Oh?"

"Oh, fuck yeah," he whispered, then licked his lips.

Well, now his confidence was bordering on creepy. She needed to get the hell out of there.

"Dex!" Ace yelled across the shop. "Leave 'er alone an' get the fuck back to work. She needs to get gone."

That was one thing she could agree on.

Dex's lips twisted in a frown. "Guessin' you ain't from 'round here."

Brooke shook her head.

"Where you stayin'?"

"I..." Why the hell was she even going to answer his question? "Nowhere, yet."

"Need a place to crash?"

"Are you offering?" she asked in disbelief.

"Gotta room above church. Bed's too small. Was hopin' you had a motel room or somethin'."

Or somethin'.

"Church," she repeated. She knew that didn't mean what it should. She had done some research on MCs before hopping in her car and heading to Shadow Valley. But she couldn't remember what church meant in biker speak.

"Yeah. Was gonna move into the apartment upstairs, but D's a stubborn fuck an' thinks he'll be raisin' his kid up there. Jewelee's havin' a shit fit about it."

She shook her head, lost on who he was talking about.

"Don't matter. You end up bein' a part of the DAMC, you'll meet 'em all eventually. This club's like a big dysfunctional family."

Her plan wasn't to join the MC. Her plan was to find her father. Ask some questions. Take care of business and go the hell home. She wasn't here to settle in with a bunch of bikers like they were long-lost family.

"How about if I just meet you somewhere?" She quickly added, "For that whiskey." She certainly wasn't meeting him for anything else. But she wouldn't mind getting together with him and asking more questions since he seemed willing to help. Maybe get a chance to meet more of the club members. Try to find out who her father really was.

Or is.

And why she should even care, she hadn't figured that part out yet, either.

She had loved the father who raised her, whether he was blood or not. But when she dug through that shoebox and found info in it to make her wonder who she really was, something had pulled at her.

Curiosity.

And maybe he would understand the meaning behind some of the things her mother had written down in the diary that had been buried under some old newspaper clippings. Maybe he could clarify some of the cryptic scribblings.

But no matter what, it wasn't like she needed an actual relationship with her biological father. She just wanted to know who he was. At thirty, she didn't need any type of "daddy."

Especially not the type that stood in front of her.

Wanting to buy her a whiskey.

CHAPTER TWO

Dex downed the shot of whiskey Linc had placed in front of him only seconds earlier. He winced until the burn subsided, then tapped the shot glass on the bar. Linc shot him a frown since The Iron Horse Roadhouse was busy for a Friday night. He snagged the bottle of Jack Daniels and slammed it down in front of Dex.

"Ain't fuckin' here to serve you," Linc growled. "Do it yourself."

"Gonna tell Hawk you're treatin' his customers like shit."

Linc flipped him the bird as he moved down the busy bar. "Since when are you a customer?"

"Whatever, dude," Dex yelled out and snagged the bottle. "Hey, I need another shot glass!"

"Get it your fuckin' self!" Linc shouted from the other end of the bar as he poured a draft.

"Work all fuckin' day, can't even relax an' get some service 'round here," he muttered to himself.

He pushed from the stool and rounded the bar. He found clean shot glasses and grabbed one. When he glanced up, he spotted *her* coming through the front door of the bar.

He wasn't the only one who spotted her. A muscle began to

tick in his tight jaw when he noticed almost every male in The Iron Horse straining their neck to watch her cross the floor.

For fuck's sake.

Yeah, it was fucking December and, yeah, women wore jeans because it was cold out. But, *fuck*, how many women could look that smoking hot just by wearing skin-tight denim which clung to fucking long legs that looked like they could wrap around his waist twice. And worse, those high-heeled boots made her legs look even longer...

Fuck. Fuck. Fuck.

He needed to get his own place and move the hell out of church. His shithole upstairs wasn't a place to take a woman of this caliber. No, it fucking wasn't.

She stepped up to the bar, leaned into it and he forgot all about her legs. Now her tits were on his radar, since she wore some sort of deep V-necked thing that showed her *very* generous cleavage. This was not the top she was wearing earlier. Though that was hot, this was *blazing* hot. All that cleavage was framed by the little brown leather coat that hugged her curves perfectly.

But it was her breathy, "Hey," that almost took him to his fucking knees.

He opened his mouth to say it back. When nothing but a squeak came out, he grimaced. *Holy motherfuck!*

Then she *laughed*. A throaty sound that came from deep within her that went right to his dick. He had to grab onto the bar to keep upright.

Her slate blue eyes dropped to the bottle of Jack sitting on the bar. "Are you going to pour me a whiskey? Or are you just going to stand there looking like you just shit your pants?"

His spine snapped straight and he grabbed the bottle, twisted the cap, and poured her a double.

After sliding it in front of her, he refilled his glass, too.

"Dex," she said softly.

Goddamn, she remembered his name.

Then he remembered his name was sewn onto the front of his cut. *Shit.*

"Dex," she said again.

Holy fuck, she could say his name a million times in that tone. He'd never get sick of hearing it.

"Dex! Yo, dickwad, get the fuck out from behind the bar," Linc yelled at him. "It's busy an' you're blockin' me an' Jester from gettin' shit done."

"Dex, what the fuck you doin' behind the bar?" Hawk came up behind him and clapped him hard on the shoulder. "You ain't a bartender. Get gone."

"Linc's a rude motherfucker," he muttered.

"Yeah, but he gets shit done an' he's good at keepin' the money flowin'. An' I need that green since I got a kid on the way. Right now, you standin' there's fuckin' him up. So, get gone."

Dex rounded the bar, his eyes never leaving the woman. Then he realized he'd never found out her name!

But he knew how to remedy that. As he stepped up next to her on the customer side of the bar, Dex said, "Hawk, this is..."

The woman held out her hand to Hawk. "Brooke."

Hawk's gaze dropped to her outstretched hand, then he looked back up at her face. "So?" His gaze landed on Dex. "Since when d'you start introducin' your pussy?"

"She ain't my pussy."

Yet.

Hawk's dark eyes narrowed. "What is she, then?"

"She's lookin' for her father."

"Yeah?" Hawk's attention went back to Brooke.

"Yeah," she answered softly.

"Did you lose 'im?"

"Never had him to lose," she stated.

Hawk stared at her for a long moment. Dex could tell his cousin was trying to figure out if she looked like anyone familiar. "Think he's here at The Iron Horse?"

"She thinks he's a part of DAMC." Dex added, "Or was."

Hawk cocked a brow. "Why's that?"

"Because of something I found in my mother's attic."

Hawked lifted one broad shoulder. "Ask your ma, then."

"She's dead."

"Fuck," Hawk muttered and scrubbed a hand over his mohawk. "That sucks. So, who's your pop?"

"That's the million-dollar question."

Hawks brows rose. "Don't have a name?"

"No."

"Well, good luck with that shit," Hawk replied and moved down the bar.

"That's Ace's son?" Brooke asked as she watched Hawk talk to Jester.

"Yeah."

She took a sip of her whiskey. "And you're his..."

"Cousin."

"Cousin," she repeated slowly as if she was trying to build a family tree in her head. "Are all of you in this MC related?"

"No. Doc an' Bear were the foundin' members of our club. Most of us were born into the club, but there were two distinct trunks of the tree. Now? Not so much."

"Why's that?"

"The tree's kinda gettin' a bit twisted." He downed his double shot, hissed, and wiped his mouth with the back of his hand.

"Like incest?"

He slammed his glass onto the bar. "No! Fuck no. Like... look if I told you, you'd get confused. But back to your question, no, everyone ain't related. Plenty of members who didn't come from Doc or Bear's blood." He lifted his chin toward Linc. "Linc for one. Prospected an' got patched in. Jester's still a prospect an' should be patched in soon. Neither are related to any of the rest of us."

"How many members are in this MC?"

Dex shrugged and poured himself another double. "Haven't counted lately. Enough to keep the club's coffers fat."

"With these businesses the MC owns."

"Yeah."

"Do these businesses support everyone?"

"Pretty much. Everyone's gotta do their part."

"Or what?"

"Or you're out."

"I didn't think it was easy to leave an MC."

"It ain't." He sighed. He wasn't going to get into club business with her. Even the women of the DAMC didn't hear all the business. It wasn't for women's ears. "Look, got a private bar on the other side of this buildin'. Let's head over there where we can talk easier."

"We're talking just fine here."

Dex glanced around the bar. "Too many eyes on us." Truth was, there were too many eyes on Brooke. He wasn't sure he liked that. No, he was sure. He definitely didn't like it.

"So?""

Dex gritted his teeth at her stubbornness. "Wanna get to know you better since you might end up bein' a club sister."

"Club sister? Do you look at all your *club sisters* like you did me at the pawn shop, or how you did when I walked into this bar?"

Dex frowned. "Fuck no. I'm related to some of 'em."

"But not all of them."

Damn, this woman didn't miss a thing. She was sharp. "Grew up with the rest. Same shit." He grabbed the bottle of Jack and jerked his head toward the double doors leading to the kitchen that separated The Iron Horse and church. "C'mon."

"Leave the Jack here," Linc shouted. "There's enough of it over there."

Dex scowled at Linc. "Fuckin' Linc. Don't know what's been up his fuckin' ass. Wouldn't have voted his ass in if I knew he was gonna be such a dick."

"Maybe he's having a bad day," Brooke suggested.

"Just probably needs to get laid."

Brooke smirked. "Sometimes we all need that."

Dex's head spun to consider the woman in front of him. *Damn.* "Yeah, we do. Some of us more often than others."

With not even a twitch of a reaction to his words, Brooke pushed away from the bar. "Okay, let's go."

Dex placed the bottle on the bar and stared at Brooke in shock. He picked his jaw up from the floor. "Let's go? To my room?"

Brooke's gray-blue eyes widened. "No! To the other side of the building like you said. To talk."

Ah, fuck. She got his blood boiling there for a second. "Yeah, right. That's what I meant."

"Lead the way."

Oh fuck no. She needed to lead the way so he could appreciate everything about her. But... damn, she had no idea where she was going. He sighed and held out his hand.

She stared at it. "What's that?"

"My fuckin' hand."

"What do I want that for?"

"So you don't get lost."

Her eyebrows knitted together. "I need to hold your hand so I won't get lost? Is it far? Through a maze? I mean, you think I could be lost forever as we walk through one building?"

Dex's lips flattened in annoyance as he shook his hand. "Just take it."

She shook her head. "It doesn't work like that."

He frowned. "What doesn't?"

"You telling me what to do and I do it."

Dex heard a loud snort and noticed Hawk leaning against the bar, thick arms crossed over his chest as he watched the two of them. "This is gonna be good."

"Fuck," Dex muttered under his breath and dropped his hand. "Whatever. Let's fuckin' go." He turned on his heels and headed toward the kitchen, hoping she was right behind him. He refused to turn around and check.

Though he wanted to.

He pushed through the double doors and held one open for her. And, yeah, she had followed him. He bit back his grin as she passed by. He fought the urge to lean in and smell her hair. He had a feeling he might end up sporting a black eye if he did.

And the whole bar would see her sucker punch him. Something he'd never live down.

He released the swinging door, then placed a hand on the small of her back to guide her through the kitchen. Surprisingly, she didn't bitch. When they got to the swinging doors that lead into church, he held the door open for her again.

This time when she passed by, she paused and turned her head to hold his gaze. "That's how a man should treat a woman. Not be demanding or crude by undressing her with his eyes." With that, she walked into church.

His eyes dropped to her ass. *Fuck*. Those cheeks in those jeans...

She glanced over her shoulder and he quickly raised his gaze, pretending he didn't just appreciate her ass.

But it was hard not to appreciate it.

Fuck, and now he was hard, too.

She stopped a few steps into the club side of the building and Dex realized why. Church wasn't as busy as The Iron Horse, but there were way too many people hanging out, drinking and shooting pool for his liking.

They needed to go somewhere more private. He doubted she'd agree.

She wrinkled her nose. "This is your so-called church?"

For fuck's sake, she acted like she walked into a meth-den or something.

"Yeah." He pushed past her and moved behind the private club bar. He did a chin lift to Grizz who sat at the one end in his regular spot, nursing his endless beer.

Dex grabbed a bottle of Jack off the shelf behind the bar and found two clean shot glasses.

"Do you mind getting me a bigger glass with some soda in it? I normally don't drink whiskey straight."

Dex eyeballed her for a moment. Then his gaze swept the common area of church and noticed—once again—that his eyes weren't the only ones checking Brooke out.

He really needed his own place.

Diesel and Jewel needed to move out of the apartment over the pawn shop and find a bigger place, before Jewel popped out D's kid. Which was probably going to happen soon. A two-bedroom, one-bathroom apartment wasn't ideal to raise a family.

But he really thought D was still in denial when it came to the fact that he was going to be an actual father. With an actual kid. One that wore diapers and cried and shit. However, if they moved out of the apartment and bought a house, reality was going to hit him like a two-by-four. Like that positive pee stick did.

Dex grinned when he remembered how D passed out at the news that Jewelee was pregnant. His big, badass cousin had hit the ground hard.

Unlike Hawk, who was happy when his ol' lady got knocked up.

Dex was fine with letting his club brothers continue to pop out kids, because he wasn't ready for that himself any time soon.

Though, if the woman in front of him right now got on her knees and begged for his baby, he might be willing to give it a shot.

Damn, that woman had rattled his brain.

He poured some Jack into the bottom of a tall glass and topped it off with the soda gun as Brooke settled on a stool at the bar, glancing around the common area.

"Is your clubhouse always this busy?"

"No. Depends on the night. Depends on if there's a party or not."

"Is there a party?"

"Nope. If the weather holds, goin' for a run on Sunday. Pig roast after that."

Her brows knitted together. "A run?"

"A group ride," he clarified. He hoped the mild early December weather held, because it was most likely the last run of the year. Once winter hit, not too many of the brothers rode their sleds. And they certainly didn't take them out on long runs.

"Ah. On your Harleys."

"Yeah, our sleds."

"Right. Sleds." She accepted the glass of Jack and Coke and took a sip. "Will everyone be there?"

"Probably most of us." Anyone who wasn't afraid of a little cold weather.

"How does one get invited to go along on a run?"

"Why?" His eyes narrowed because of her question, but then his gaze dropped when her cleavage bounced as she shrugged.

"Just curious."

"You wanna check everyone out."

She cleared her throat, drawing his attention back up to her face, framed with her reddish blonde hair, and those gray-blue eyes. "Yeah, maybe. Could be a good way to figure out if my father is still in your club."

"Why you determined to meet him?"

"Wouldn't you be curious if you just found out your father wasn't really your father?"

"Actually would be fuckin' happy if he ain't."

"Why's that?"

"Fucker took off leavin' my mom with three small kids an' no money. Cleaned out their account, got on his sled, never to be seen again."

Those amazing eyes of hers widened. "Really?"

"Yeah," he breathed.

"You never talked to your father again?"

"Never talked to him ever. Was too young to have a fuckin' conversation with 'im before he split."

"So, you're in the same boat as I am."

"Fuck no. Know his name. Ain't lookin' for his deadbeat ass."

"Like you don't have members in this club who aren't deadbeat dads."

Dex's head jerked back at that. "Fuck no. The DAMC's a family. Family's fuckin' important. Blood or not. Got me?"

"But your dad—"

Dex cut her off. "He split."

"Right, but—"

"He fuckin' split. 'Nough said. Ain't nothin' thicker than DAMC blood. Nothin'."

"So, if my father's still in this club and he knew about me..."

"Don't think he is."

"Are you sure?"

"Most of us ain't old enough to be your pop. Already had this discussion. Grizz an' Ace ain't it. Doc an' Rocky's been in prison longer than you've been alive. The only one left who..."

No. *No fucking way.*

"The only one left who... what?"

He wasn't even going to say it out loud, because it couldn't be him. "Nothin'. Thinkin' your pop's long gone. That's all. Or you're wrong an' your blood father ain't an Angel."

"I don't think I'm wrong."

"How do you know for sure?"

"Because of what I found under some old newspaper clippings that had to do with your club."

"Which was?"

She hesitated a moment. Then after another long sip of her drink, she said, "Her diary."

"Yeah? An' it didn't mention a name?"

She shook her head, her long hair brushing along the skin of her exposed collarbones. Skin he wanted to sink his teeth into as he was nailing her to a mattress.

"No. No name. I think there was a reason for it."

"Why's that?"

She took another sip of her Jack and Coke, avoiding his gaze. "I'm not ready to discuss details of my mother's diary."

"But you want info from me," Dex stated with a frown.

"Yes. And some of your other club 'brothers,'" she admitted.

Right. "Don't work like that."

She placed her glass on the bar. "Why not?"

"'Cause we don't just spill shit to anyone who asks."

"I'm not just anyone."

"So you say. Don't know that for sure."

She turned slightly on her stool and surveyed the common room once more. "Maybe I just need to hang out with your club for a bit and get to know some of you better. Seems like you all don't mind women hanging around."

Dex glanced over at the sweet butts who were hanging all over Crash and Rig as they played pool. His eyes slid over to Tequila grinding her crotch against Rooster as they danced to some music being piped through the speakers from The Iron Horse. She was doing something she shouldn't, like normal. Rooster knew better, too. Prospects couldn't do sweet butts since they were off limits.

But right now, he didn't give a fuck. It didn't matter to him since he wouldn't touch Tequila with a ten-foot dick. He had a feeling she did anyone in the club, prospects and hang-arounds alike. If Hawk, Z or Diesel caught her, her ass would be outside looking in.

"Ain't one of those," he muttered, then downed his whiskey in one swallow.

"What does that mean?"

"You ain't one of those," he clarified.

"One of what?"

He lifted his chin toward the pool tables. "Those."

"Those women?"

"Yeah."

"Why's that?"

"You just ain't."

"Are they sweet butts?"

He kept his expression blank, but he was surprised she knew the term. "How do you know about 'em?"

"Read it on the internet. Is it true? Do they just hang around and fuck any of your club members who want them?"

"Yeah."

"Do you do any of them?"

Dex glanced over at Destiny and Roxy. He grimaced. Yeah, he had done them. In fact, one night he did both at the same time. "Nope."

"You're such a liar," she whispered, shaking her head in disbelief.

Sure was, because he wasn't fucking stupid. He wanted the woman who sat at the bar, not the ones hanging off Crash and Rig. He would be a fool to admit he'd done those sweet butts when they were standing not far from them. Right in Brooke's view. So, fuck no, he wasn't admitting to shit.

All that was in the past, anyway. His future sat right in front of him. Or at least his "future" which meant maybe tonight and the next few nights. If he was lucky.

Beyond that? Fuck no. He wasn't looking for anything permanent. And he doubted Brooke wanted to become anyone's ol' lady. Or even a biker's regular piece.

But right now, he was shooting high and hoping to hit the target.

"So, can I come along on this *run* Sunday?"

"The only bi... *women* who come along on our runs hafta earn a spot."

She paused with her glass halfway to her lips. "What do I have to do to earn a spot?"

"More like who."

She put her glass down on the bar without taking a drink. "You want me to sleep with you so I can go on a motorcycle ride? You're fucking out of your mind."

"Like I said, that spot has to be earned. Gotta be a regular piece or an ol' lady. Three ways to get there."

"I don't think I want it that badly."

Dex shrugged and poured himself another double. He tossed it back and slammed the shot glass on the bar. "Suit yourself. But everyone's gonna be there."

"You said there's three ways to get there but only mentioned two."

That he did. The third was an invite. Normally, just inviting some bitch to come along on the back of your sled was frowned upon. The runs weren't for the women. They were for the brothers. Any woman who wasn't a regular piece or an ol' lady could wait back at church, or wherever they wanted to sit their ass down, until the run was over and the pig roast started.

"Yeah."

"Are you going to share the last way?"

"Nope."

She lifted a shoulder. "So, I'll come to the pig roast afterward."

"Gotta be invited to that."

"I already have my invite."

He cocked a brow. "How's that?"

"You invited me."

Dex shook his head. "The fuck I did."

"I heard it."

"Need your ears cleaned out."

"You asked. I accepted."

Goddamn, this woman. "Now you're lyin'."

She gave him a big smile and tipped her head toward the pool table where Destiny and Roxy were. "Just like you did about fucking those women."

He shrugged. "Just snatch."

Suddenly, Brooke's face changed from friendly and joking to dead serious. She slipped off the stool and grabbed her purse, which was sitting next to her drink.

"And you're just a dick."

Dex blinked. Then his feet felt like they were in quicksand as she marched back through the double doors of the kitchen, slamming them open with her palms.

"Fuck," he muttered, then finally found he could move. He rushed after her and caught up as she slammed through the second set of swinging doors into The Iron Horse.

He didn't bother to check to see if they were being watched or if they had an audience. Or if he looked like a fucking fool. He grabbed her wrist and pulled her toward the front entrance of the bar.

She jerked her arm, but he didn't release her. "Let me go."

"No."

"I don't need you to walk me out."

"Ain't walkin' you out."

She jerked her wrist again, but he just tightened his grip. "Then what the hell are you doing?"

He pulled her outside into the dark, cold night, slamming the door behind them, then hesitated. "Which is your car?"

"Let. Me. Go."

"Fuckin' answer me. Which is your fuckin' car?"

"If you let me go, I'll show you." She jerked her arm one more time.

He released her wrist and raised his palms up. "Show me."

She hurried through the dark parking lot. Since the lot was full, she had to park at the very edge along a line of shrubs. She was digging in her purse at the same time taking lengthy strides with those mile-long legs of hers.

But he had no problem keeping up. She was tall but he was still taller than her. Still had more weight behind him. And he was a fucking man, goddamnit.

She stopped at a four-door BMW and hit her remote. It was too dark to tell the color but the lights flashed as the car unlocked. He snagged the remote from her hand before she could get around to the driver's side.

"Hey!"

He hit the unlock button again on the remote and heard the locks release on the rest of the doors. He yanked open the back door and pointed. "Get in."

Even in the dark, he could see her eyes widen.

"What? No."

"Get the fuck in."

"You have this misconception that you can give an order and I'll listen."

"Yeah."

Her head jerked up higher as she stared at him. "Yeah?" He watched as she took a visible breath and her spine straightened. She pointed into the back of the car. "Get the fuck in the car."

What? She was giving *him* orders?

"You want to play this game? This *let's-see-who's-more-dominant* game? I can play it." She leaned in close. So close he could feel her warm breath across his lips. "I fucking eat that shit for breakfast. Now... Get. The. Fuck. In. The. Car."

Dex's heartbeat thumped heavily in his chest. What the fuck was going on here? He should be worried that this woman was crazy, and could shank him. Maybe she was going to do just that. Get him in the back of the car, tear his heart out with her bare hands, and drive away to go dump his body in some far away field.

She crossed her arms over her chest and tapped her booted foot.

Fuck. His dick was rock hard thinking about her dominating him. Making him submit. "You gonna fuck me?"

"Get. In. The. Back. Seat."

She didn't say no. *Fuck yeah.*

The forcefulness of her tone, the hard look in her eyes from what he could see in the limited light...

All that shit turned him the fuck on.

He shrugged out of his cut, since he couldn't wear it in the cage he was about to climb into. He leaned in and laid it carefully over the back of the driver's seat.

Then he climbed in, wondering if he was making a big mistake.

But, hell, he might be getting laid. And he needed to bust a nut. Like soon. So, if he was going to die, he was going to die a depleted, satisfied motherfucker.

Or he hoped that was the case.

He slid over to the middle of the back seat, leaving her room to follow. And, fuck him, if she didn't.

She threw her jacket onto the front seat, climbed in after him, then slammed the door shut behind her and put out her hand. "Remote."

He dropped it into her open palm and she hit a button that started the car and started blowing warm air.

Good idea since it was almost winter and he didn't want any shrinkage.

Then she hit another button and all the locks clicked, securing them in together.

Another good idea.

Then she was on him, facing him, straddling his thighs, taking his mouth.

He groaned when her tongue forced its way into his mouth, taking control.

Fuck yeah, was all he could think.

He grabbed her ass and squeezed as she rode up and down on his lap, both of them still fully clothed.

Then she bit his bottom lip so hard, he grunted and tasted blood.

"Mine."

What? What the fuck did she just say?

"Pants down. Hurry." She ripped her blouse over her head and tossed it into the front seat, then moved off him, unzipping and yanking off her boots, shimmying her tight jeans over her thighs and down her calves, over her heels. "You're not moving!" she yelled at him.

He jerked into action, his blood racing through his body, landing in his dick. He lifted his hips off the seat and unfastened his jeans, shoving them down as far as he could, which was only to his bent knees.

"You have tats on your chest?"

"Yeah."

"Shirt off. I want to see them."

This woman was crazy! And by removing his shirt, she was going to see something most of his brothers didn't know he had.

But fuck it. He was going to get his rocks off by this smoking hot woman. And he didn't give a shit what she saw.

He pulled his long-sleeved thermal over his head and threw it.

Then he grinned when her eyes dropped. She wasn't looking at his dick. As magnificent as it truly was. Fuck no, she wasn't.

She straddled his thighs again, her hot, slick pussy brushing against his twitching cock.

"Wasn't expecting that," she whispered, her voice so breathy that he almost came.

He tried to keep his voice from breaking when he asked, "Don't like it?"

"Love it," she murmured.

He grinned. Then threw his head back against the seat as she yanked on both of his nipple rings hard. All the oxygen left him on an "*aaah, fuck*."

Then she dropped her head and sucked one of his nipples in her mouth, her tongue flicking the ring.

He thrust up against her wet pussy. She grabbed his other ring and twisted it, causing his back to bow away from the leather seat.

"Fuck yeah, babe," he groaned.

Her tongue continued to tug and tease one pierced nipple, her fingers twisted the other harder. Almost to the point of pain.

But he wasn't going to tell her to stop. Fuck no, he wasn't.

His fingers dug into her ass as she rubbed against him, his dick sliding back and forth through her wet folds.

Fuck, he needed to come. But not on himself.

"Ride me," he groaned.

She stopped everything she was doing. Just shut it all down and pulled back. "You don't tell me what to do."

Holy shit, this woman was crazy. But he fucking loved it.

A string of precum was sticking to his stomach, and his balls were so tight, he was about to blow. So if she didn't do something soon, she was going to miss out on her chance to fuck him.

But maybe she didn't want to fuck him.

Fuck.

No. Would she do that to him? Let him blow his load all over himself, then just walk away?

That would be cruel and unusual punishment. Wouldn't it? Fuck yeah, it would be!

He went solid when she reached down and held him in place, his dick throbbing in her hand as she rose up and...

"No wrap," he groaned in a half-assed protest.

...sank down on him.

CHAPTER THREE

Brooke closed her eyes as he filled her. But only for a second. She only allowed herself one second to appreciate that fullness. Then she began to ride him hard.

She needed to get all the demons out of her. Frustration. Anger. Grief.

And the gall of this man to try to tell her what to do!

To hell with that.

No one told her what to do. Ever.

Her mother had always told her and her sister to never let a man get the upper hand, never show weakness. Always act like you're in control, even when you felt like you're not.

She had taken that advice to heart. Maybe even took it farther than her mother had intended. Not once had she ever let a man dominate her. Not once. She had always had control of her destiny. And she was successful for it.

But now Dex's hands were on her ass again, helping her rise and fall on his hard length. She didn't want that. Didn't need his help. Not in this case.

She snagged his wrists roughly and ripped his hands from her, pinning them to the back of the leather seat. She tightened her fingers around his wrists, the one with the wide black leather cuff, the other just his naked skin. His tattoos stopped at his wrists like a sleeve. They ran up his arms and over his chest just like he said. Her gaze landed on his nipple rings.

She had no idea bikers were into that.

Maybe they weren't. Maybe it was just this one.

Dex.

She still had no idea what that was a nickname for. Normally, it would be short for Dexter. But what biker was named Dexter?

Especially one with a bunch of tattoos and nipple rings. It was an anomaly.

Even in the limited light, she could tell that his lower lip was swelling from her bite. She couldn't help herself. She needed to give him a little reminder that he wasn't the boss of her.

Not now. Not ever.

This was the way she liked it. Being on top. Controlling everything during sex. Controlling everything. Period.

Most men didn't like it. She scared a lot away.

Sometimes she'd find one who'd tolerate it for a while. Until she intimidated them with her strong personality and her demands. Both in and out of bed.

They complained that she attempted to take away their "manhood."

No, that's not what she was trying to do.

This one, though... This one wasn't complaining. He was allowing her to pin him to the seat. With both her hands and her pussy. He didn't bitch about her biting him, actually drawing blood.

The harder she sucked on his nipple rings, twisted and played with them, the more his body reacted.

He liked this shit.

He ate this up.

He wasn't afraid of her.

He wasn't intimidated by her.

Yet.

If he could take everything she gave him and ask for more, then...

She stopped the direction of her thoughts.

Then, nothing.

She was in Shadow Valley for a reason. And it wasn't to ride some biker's cock. That may be a fringe benefit, but that was all it was.

Nothing more.

She'd only met him earlier in the day. She didn't even know his last name. Didn't even know his real name. And here she was in the back of her Beemer, fucking him.

But this would only last a few minutes, then she'd be done with him. Go on her way. Finish her quest to find whoever the hell her real father was.

To quench that burning curiosity.

To find out the truth.

Maybe confront whoever he was.

She had no idea what she would do. She figured she'd know when she found him. *If* she found him.

If not, she'd go back to her life. Her place, her job. Forget all about the Dirty Angels MC. Finish settling her mother's estate.

And simply fucking move on.

Right now, the man whose cock she rode was just a distraction. Maybe a tool in her search.

That was it.

That was all.

This *Dex*.

She fell forward, shoving her face into his neck, sinking her teeth hard into his throat. He tensed beneath her, but didn't pull from her grip. He allowed her to continue to hold him down. He was bigger, stronger, but he didn't use his strength or his size to take control.

No, he liked it.

Hell, he wanted it.

He was hard as steel as she rocked her hips, making sure her clit hit him in just the right way.

Right there. That was perfect. Just what she needed.

She released his wrists, dug her fingers into his hair and ripped his head back, arching his throat, stretching his skin along his delicate windpipe. Making him vulnerable.

He was breathing hard, his skin getting damp, his chest heaving, grunts coming from between his lips. She slammed down harder onto his lap, grinding against him until he could be no deeper inside her.

Yes, this was what she needed.

Just this.

She put her lips to his ear. "You like it like this."

He didn't answer at first, didn't fight the pull of his hair which she knew had to be painful. Because she made sure it was.

A few breaths later, he managed, "Fuckin' bitch, bring it."

Brooke smiled, dropped her mouth to his shoulder and bit him harder than ever. He cried out, his body tensing once again. She released his hair, found both nipple rings and pulled as far as she could without ripping them out of his skin.

She licked up his neck, over his cheek, sucked on his injured bottom lip, then took his mouth again. He tasted so damn good. She explored every recess of his mouth while raking her long nails over his pecs, over the hard tips of his nipples, down his stomach.

Brooke suddenly pictured him naked and bound spread-eagle on her bed so she could do whatever she wanted to him. She wanted this badass biker, this man who rode Harleys, wore leather and biker boots, to whimper, squirm and beg.

Her orgasm caught her off guard, throwing off her rhythm as she clenched tightly around him, then pulsated fiercely.

"Fuck!" he cried out.

She took his mouth again as she continued to ride him hard, picking up her pace again, holding his head still by using his dark hair to keep him in place.

She hadn't orgasmed like that in a long time. She needed another one. He needed to last just long enough for her to get it.

She pulled back enough to tell him, with her voice huskier than normal, "Don't come yet. Hear me? Not yet. I'll tell you when. Not before."

He didn't answer.

"Answer me," she demanded.

He closed his eyes, blew out a breath and dug his fingers into her ass. They were going to leave bruises, but she didn't care. She just needed him to last a little longer.

Just a little...

His fingers kneaded, squeezed and dug into her flesh and she swore she heard him grind his teeth.

She jerked on his hair. "Not yet."

He released a loud, long groan. "Gonna come."

"Not yet, damn it. Don't."

"Yeah, babe, gotta come."

"When I tell you."

"Ah fuck," he moaned. "I can't..."

"You can and you will," she said firmly, trying not to sound like she was losing it herself. Just a few seconds longer. That was all she needed.

She was right there. His cock was hitting all the right spots as she ground down on him, pressing her clit hard into his pelvis.

She needed his hands on her breasts, on her nipples. But she'd never took off her bra and she wasn't going to take the time now. She was so close.

And then... She. Was. There.

She threw her head back and screamed since this orgasm was even better, more intense than the first. It ripped through her, making her shudder, fall against the man who was still as hard as a rock inside her.

"Fuck, babe," he muttered, then shouted, "For fuck's sake."

She realized he was waiting for her to give him permission to come. *Whoops.*

Still panting, she put her mouth to his ear. "Now."

With a grunt, his hips lifted off the seat, almost throwing her off balance. She grabbed his shoulders to stay in place as he came fiercely inside her, his cock throbbing and twitching.

After a moment, he collapsed against the leather seat of her BMW, his eyes intense as they stared at each other, looked at each other almost as if in surprise. Shock, even.

Her heart did a nervous flip as something went unsaid between them. Some connection. Something that shouldn't be.

He was just a distraction. Nothing more.

He was just a means to an end. A way to find her father.

That was all.

A large fist pounding on the back passenger-side window had them both jumping.

"Fuckin' got an audience out here," Hawk yelled, his mohawk-topped, tattooed head coming into view as he stared at them with a grin.

"Fuck," Dex muttered as they both looked out of the partially fogged side window as Hawk's face disappeared. They certainly did have an audience. Some of the bar patrons stood around the car, big smiles on their faces. A couple of them even raised their beers as they hooted and hollered.

"Take your snatch elsewhere, brother, before the pigs show up an' charge you for lewd acts or some such shit. Don't need 5-0 here tonight, got me?" Hawk leaned closer to the window again and said, "Nice nips, Dex. Knew you were a fuckin' freak deep down." He straightened once more and turned to the crowd, waving his beefy, tattooed arms. "Everybody back inside. Fuckin' show's over. Give 'em a chance to cuddle for a bit in the afterglow." He howled with laughter as he forced the crowd to disperse.

Brooke held herself still, frozen on Dex's lap. She focused on the tattoo over his heart even though she couldn't read what it said clearly in the limited light.

"Gonna get off me?" his deep voice washed over her and she gritted her teeth. "Babe—"

"Don't fucking *babe* me." She closed her eyes, trying not to lash out at the man who she still straddled. It wasn't his fault. It wasn't him.

He didn't do it.

He wasn't even aware of what happened. Like his Uncle Ace had said this morning in the pawn shop, he might have been about two when she was conceived.

Conceived.

That made it sound so much nicer than it was.

"What the fuck's wrong with you?"

She opened her eyes and realized she was gripping his arms so tightly, he was wincing. "Snatch," she murmured.

His dark brows pinned together. "What?"

"Snatch! Snatch! My mother was probably just considered *snatch* to you fuckers. To the *Angel* who got her pregnant."

"Her choice to fuck a brother."

"No!" She shook her head. Then the truth hit her right then. Like a ton of bricks. Smacked her right in the fucking face. What she couldn't see clearly until that very moment. Until Hawk had called her snatch. "No. It wasn't."

His body went solid against her. "What are you sayin'?"

"It wasn't," she repeated as if those two words could explain everything.

"Brooke."

She turned stinging eyes to him. And she realized that was the first time he actually said her name.

"Brooke," he breathed again.

"What?"

"Are you sayin' an Angel fucked your mother without her say-so? That you were born from... that your mom was forced?"

She took a deep inhale and attempted to steel her emotions. Tried to dull all those raw nerve ends that snapped and crackled at the answers to his questions.

Those words in her mother's diary... She never quite came out and said who. Or what. Or why. Or even exactly where. But the pieces of evidence, the clues she left behind. Maybe not on purpose. Maybe in an attempt to clean her own soul of the filth. Those clues all made sense now. All those scattered words suddenly came together like a puzzle creating a picture Brooke could now clearly see.

Her mother didn't cheat on her father.

Her mother didn't keep the truth from Brooke to be mean.

Hell no.

Her mother was protecting her.

From the truth.

From knowing where Brooke came from. How she came to be.

Now she knew why she was in Shadow Valley.

And finding her so-called father was no more of a curiosity but now a necessity.

He shook her and growled, "Answer me."

Dex stared at the woman still on his lap, the one who wouldn't respond. His dick was still inside her, though that was about to change quickly. Talk of rape was like someone pouring ice water down his spine. With a frown, he slipped from her, leaving a mess and no way to clean up.

Another reminder of how they hadn't used a wrap. What a fucking stupid move that was.

With a ragged sigh, she slipped to the seat next to him and grabbed her purse. Digging through it, she pulled out a couple of single-use wet wipes and a travel pack of tissues. She slapped a couple tissues and a wet wipe packet onto his chest then proceeded to clean herself up before wiggling back into her panties and jeans.

"Good thing I'm on birth control. Wouldn't want a repeat of history."

His nostrils flared and he ripped open the packet, wincing when the alcohol on the wet wipe stung his dick. "Don't compare me to a fuckin' rapist. Didn't hear you say no once. Not fuckin' once. Don't throw that shit in my face." He threw the used wipe onto the floor of the car, then did the same after using the tissues.

"Sorry," was muffled as she pulled her blouse over her head and jerked it into place.

"An' you fuckin' took over. Rode my dick like it was a stripper pole. Probably will get an infection from all the bites an' scratches you gave me."

"I didn't hear you say no, either."

"No shit. Ain't stupid."

She shifted to lean back against the driver's side rear door and watched him as he yanked his jeans back up his thighs and over his hips. He didn't bother to fasten them.

She jerked her chin toward his chest. "What's with the nipple rings?"

Dex shrugged. He got them after he was done getting his chest ink. He didn't want Crow to see them while the man tattooed him since he didn't need to hear shit from any of the brothers about them.

He had told the sweet butts if they mentioned them to anyone, they would get kicked out of church for good.

But now that Hawk knew... He was screwed.

"Like 'em?"

"Fucking hot," she said, her voice low.

He smiled. "Yeah." He found his thermal and pulled it over his head, covering those nipple rings she liked so much. Hid her bites and scratches. He'd feel those for a while. Probably see them even longer.

They were worth it.

"Did I earn a spot on your run Sunday?"

What the fuck? Did she use him? He eyeballed her. "That why you fucked me?"

"No. But I'm thinking you might want to let me come along anyway."

"Why's that?"

"A little bit of this afterward?"

Damn. She wanted to fuck him again? He wasn't going to say no to a repeat, but... "Still could have you sit on my dick without you sittin' on the back of my sled."

"But you'll take me with you."

It wasn't a question. This woman had confidence oozing out of her fucking pores.

"Will have to think 'bout it."

"No thinking needed," she assured him. "What time is the run?"

"Damn, woman." He shook his head and blew out a breath. "Gonna make you a deal. Gonna help you find out who your father is. An' when we find out, an' if what you're sayin's true, that he took your mom without her sayin' yes, then I'm gonna flay the colors off his back myself. Got me?"

"So, you'll introduce me to all your members?"

"Ain't takin' you to Greene to see Doc an' Rocky, but yeah, everyone else." He had a feeling he was going to regret this. They didn't need any more drama in the club. And this shit... this accusation of hers, was going to bring just that.

"Greene?"

"Prison. SCI Greene."

"Oh. What did they do?"

What didn't they do? "Murder."

"Nice." The sarcasm was thick.

Dex lifted a shoulder. "Gotta do whatya gotta do."

"Right. Murder. Rape. Whatever. *Gotta do whatya gotta do*," she repeated.

His lips flattened out and his jaw got tight. "Shit has changed."

"Has it?"

She didn't believe him. "Yeah."

"No violence at all, then?"

She was mocking him. He sighed. "Gotta do whatya gotta do."

"Right. Thought so. Now I *gotta* go."

He didn't want her to leave. He wasn't ready to part ways with her. "Did you find a place to stay?"

"Yes."

"Where?"

"Around."

"Woman," he said in a low grumble.

"No. Don't even try dominating me. You won't win. You can try it on those women," she glanced toward the building, "in there. But it won't work on me." She opened the car door and turned back to look at him. "Can I give you a ride somewhere? It's the least I can do after letting me ride your cock."

He snorted. Goddamn, *this woman*. "Got my sled. But no. Live here."

"Where?"

He jerked his chin toward The Iron Horse. "Got a room upstairs."

"Above the bar?"

"Above church, yeah."

She leaned closer, sucked his injured lower lip into her mouth, then released him. "Then why are you still sitting in my car?"

He snorted again, shook his head, snagged his cut, then shoved the other door open. He climbed out, jerked his jeans up higher on his hips, and headed around the back of the building to church.

He needed a fucking shower.

And to get his head examined.

This woman was nothing but trouble.

He grinned. After a second, his grin turned into a smile so big he couldn't wipe it off his face, even if he wanted to.

CHAPTER FOUR

A pounding on his door had Dex cursing under his breath. He grabbed a towel and wrapped it around his waist. Who the fuck was bothering him this early?

They still had an hour before the run started.

Normally, he wouldn't get up this early. On Sunday runs, he'd roll out of bed, pull on the cleanest jeans and shirt he could find, grab a quick cup of coffee downstairs, hop on his bike and head out with his brothers.

This morning was different. He'd woken up at some goddamn fucked-up hour and couldn't get what happened in the back of that BMW out of his head. At least yesterday, he had to get up and work at the pawn shop, so that had been somewhat of a distraction. But this morning, he knew he had time and his brain was spinning with what Brooke had done to him on the backseat of that car.

That gave him the most painful morning wood. Which he happened to relieve twice, shooting cum all over his gut and chest. Because of that, he had to get up and shower.

He lifted his fingers to his lip, which was still fucked up, as someone pounded on the door again. *Fuck*. "Yeah?"

Crow's voice came through the door. "Get downstairs."

"Why? We havin' a meetin' or somethin'?"

"No. Somethin's down there that belongs to you."

What the fuck? He didn't order anything. "I'll be down."

"Soon."

"Get coffee started."

He heard an answering grunt, then Crow's heavy booted feet heading down the hallway.

He yanked open his top dresser drawer and pulled out his favorite Harley long-sleeved tee. He searched the floor for jeans until he spotted a pair that didn't look that dirty. After a quick sniff, he yanked them on. He slipped his cut over his shoulders, grabbed his boots that had a pair of socks peeking out of them, and headed downstairs.

As soon as he could see the bar he almost stumbled down the rest of the steps. He put out his free hand to catch himself on the wall, trying not to drop his boots in the process.

His gaze landed on something that shouldn't be.

Or more like, someone.

Brooke sat on a stool, facing the steps, leaning back on her elbows which were planted on the bar. From what he could see, she had jeans, once again, covering her long legs that fit her like they were painted on and a tight cotton shirt that not only hugged her tits but clearly showed everyone in the room how hard her nipples were.

Fuck me.

Crow was on the other side of the bar, a coffee mug lifted halfway to his lips, a shit-eating grin on his face as he watched Dex carefully descend the rest of the stairs.

Linc sat at the other end of the bar in Grizz's normal spot, nursing coffee as well.

Crash came through the double doors from the kitchen with a plate of what looked like scrambled eggs piled high. He stopped short when he noticed Brooke, then hurried to take a seat next to her, giving her a great big smile.

"Hey," Crash greeted her.

"Hey yourself," Brooke answered, turning her attention to him. She held out her hand to him. "Brooke."

Crash stared at it, wiped his hand on his jeans, then took it, shaking it firmly. "Crash. Were you invited on the run?"

"Yes," Brooke answered, ignoring Dex's glare.

"No," Dex yelled across the room as he made his way around the empty pool tables to the bar.

When he reached them, Brooke reached out and ran a thumb over his swollen bottom lip while she smiled. "Yes, I'm coming on the run."

Dex pulled his head back. "Said I'd help you, not that you can ride on the back of my sled today."

Crash swallowed a mouthful of eggs, wiped his hand over his lips, then said, "She can ride on mine."

Brooke shot him a smile. "Thanks. I appreciate that."

"You don't even know 'er," Dex hissed, dropping his boots by the empty stool next to Brooke.

"That could change real quick," Crash said with a smile and a wink at Brooke.

Crow leaned his ass against the back counter and chuckled.

Dex shot him a scowl and then faced Brooke. "Who let you in?"

"The door was unlocked."

"An' you just walked in?"

"Yes."

He shook his head, huffed out a breath, then headed toward the commercial-sized coffeemaker in the corner. He snagged a mug and filled it, inhaling the scent of fresh-brewed coffee. Crow made it perfectly almost every morning.

Thank fuck.

The day Crow moved out and got his own place was going to be a sad day for the brothers who relied on their caffeine fix in the morning. Especially after a heavy night of partying.

Crow was suddenly next to him, his voice low but amused.

"Was gonna ask if you hit that yet, but it looks like she hit you instead, brother. Bet she's a handful."

Dex gave him an "mmm," ignoring Crow's chuckle, and headed back to where Crash flirted shamelessly with Brooke.

As soon as Dex was in reach, she grabbed his mug and took a careful sip of the hot coffee. "Thanks."

His eyes widened. Crash's mouth dropped open. And Crow just about fell to the ground in laughter. He might have even heard a snort from Linc at the other end of the bar.

The back door to church was yanked open and Hawk walked in with a hand to Kiki's back. Dex noticed the club's lawyer was now wearing baggier tops to cover her slightly-rounded belly.

Crow came around the bar and pulled Kiki away from Hawk, placing a large hand on her stomach and an arm around her waist. "Goin' on the ride today, momma?"

Kiki smiled up at him. "Yes, I'm dying to go. I need to destress."

"Why? What's goin' on?" Crow asked her.

"Emma's former in-laws are fighting for visitation with Lily."

"Shit."

"Shit is right. Dawg and Em don't trust them and I can't blame them one bit."

Crow nodded. "Not when their piece of shit son stole her girl an' they helped finance it. But shouldn't be stressin' out the baby."

Kiki placed her hand over Crow's along her stomach. "It's Hawk's kid. Tough as nails. He'll be fine."

"He?" Crash asked. "You know already?"

Hawk moved over to the coffeemaker and filled two mugs, bringing one over to hand it to Kiki. "Yeah. We wanted to know," the club VP answered.

"Diesel doesn't," Crash said.

"No," Kiki agreed, "but he'll find out soon."

"Yeah, think Jewelee's about to pop," Hawk agreed.

"If D could, I think he'd put a cork in it. I don't think he's ready," Kiki said. "Unlike my ol' man who's eager to meet his son."

Jewelee happened to walk into church at that moment, her stomach leading the way. "Where's your ol' man?" Hawk shouted.

"On his sled. I had to take my Jeep since there's not enough room on his bike for him, me and," she laid a hand on her huge belly, "this kid."

"Why you here so early if you ain't goin' on the ride?" Crow asked, heading over to Jewelee and putting his hand on her stomach like he did Kiki's.

Jewel reached up and cupped his cheek. "Because I said I'd watch Baby Z so Sophie could go along. Oh, and Lily, too. She can help me keep Zeke entertained while we wait."

D barreled through the back door, saw Crow touching Jewel and frowned. "Brother," he warned.

Crow raised his palms up in surrender. "Can't help it. The ability to grow life amazes the shit outta me."

"Well, there's gonna be more," Jag announced loudly, coming in next.

All attention turned to him and Ivy. "Yeah?" Hawk asked.

"Fuck yeah," Jag answered with a big smile. "Finally."

Kiki and Jewel hugged Ivy as the men clasped hands and bumped shoulders with Jag.

"'Bout time you get it in the right hole," Hawk said, pounding Jag on the back.

Dex hugged his sister. "Couldn't tell me before everyone else?"

"It wasn't supposed to be announced like that," she told him. Her gaze slid to Brooke, who still sat at the bar by herself, sipping coffee and watching everything unfold. "Wasn't she in the shop the other day?"

"Yeah."

"What's she doing here?" Her green eyes narrowed when she noticed his mouth. "What happened to you? Her?"

"Yeah."

She snorted, then beelined over to Brooke. Dex followed since he had no idea what was about to happen.

Ivy stopped in front of Brooke, waving a hand toward Dex. "You do that to my brother?"

Brooke's gaze slid to Dex then back to the redhead standing in front of her. "Dex is your brother?"

"Sure is. You pop him in the mouth?"

"No."

"Oh, I was going to buy you a drink if you did. He deserves it sometimes."

"I wouldn't doubt it," Brooke said. She put her hand out. "I'm Brooke."

Ivy grasped her hand and gave it a shake. "Ivy."

Brooke gave her smile. "Congratulations."

"Thanks. Long time coming."

Brooke tilted her head. "The fun is in the practice, right?"

Ivy blinked. "Yeah." Then she looked at Dex's mouth again, more carefully this time. "That's a bite, isn't it?"

"Don't answer that," Dex said to Brooke.

Brooke shot him a grin, then answered Ivy. "Yes, it is."

Dex threw his hands up and, shaking his head, walked back to where the men were gathered watching Ivy and Brooke.

"You're so fucked, nipple boy," Hawk laughed.

Jag looked at Dex. "What does that mean?"

"Nothin'," Dex answered quickly, hoping Hawk would take the hint.

Of course, Hawk had to announce loudly, "Dexter's got these gold rings in his tits."

"Jesus," Dex muttered.

"How do you know?" Diesel asked his brother.

"Saw 'em. Those two were goin' at it in the back of her Beemer in the lot Friday night."

"Explains the lip," Jag said.

"Doesn't explain why she's here this mornin'," D grumbled as he eyeballed Brooke across the room.

"She's comin' on the run," Crow told them.

"Damn, Dex," Hawk said. "Got your balls in a vise already. Musta been some good shit the other night."

Ace and Janice walked in next, followed by Dawg and Emma. Emma's daughter, Lily, ran past all of them to go to Jewel, who was now standing at the bar talking with Brooke.

Fuck. He wondered what the women were yapping about. He shuddered at the thought.

Janice and Emma slowly followed Lily.

Ace came to a screeching halt next to Dex. "What's she doin' here?"

"Know 'er?" D asked his father, one eyebrow cocked.

"Was in the shop Friday mornin' givin' this one a hard-on that wouldn't quit."

"Jesus," Dex muttered again. Maybe he should just go back up to his room and back to sleep. This day was heading into the shitter already.

"Musta come in to buy somethin' an' got Dex's dick instead." Hawk said.

Ace frowned. "She did?"

"Yeah, boned her in the back of 'er Beemer," Hawk confirmed.

Fucking Christ, he was never going to hear the end of that.

"What the fuck, boy? Told you we don't need trouble hangin' 'round our neck."

"What trouble?" Diesel asked, pulling himself up to his full height.

Ace glanced in the direction of Brooke, then back at his son. "She's lookin' for her father."

"So?" D grunted.

"Thinks he's an Angel." When everyone got silent and stared at Ace, he held up his hands. "Ain't mine. Ask Janice. She's the one who scheduled my neuterin' after D was born."

"Fuck," D muttered, then added, "On both accounts." He glanced up to where the women stood talking. "Who does she think he is? An' why does she care now?"

"Don't got shit. Not even a name. Coulda been anyone. 'Cept me," Ace added quickly.

"Grizz," Jag said.

"Nope," Ace answered.

"Rocky?" Hawk asked.

"She's thirty," Dex said.

"Well, that rules out Rocky an' Doc. Thank fuck," Jag said. "Nobody left old enough to be her pop. At least that's still breathin'."

"Right," Dex said.

Unfortunately, there was one person. Someone no one had mentioned. Only because he'd been making himself scarce for a while now and was flying low under the radar.

"One brother's old enough an' still breathin'," Dawg said. "Gotta work with that fucker every goddamn day." He glanced quickly to make sure Lily wasn't within earshot since Emma rode him about his cursing around their daughters.

All eyes turned to Brooke.

"Couldn't be. She's way too fuckin' hot to be Pierce's daughter," Jag said.

"Probably looks like her mama," Ace said.

"Which would make sense why Pierce would hit that," Dawg said.

"If Pierce shows up today he'll probably try to nail her, too, not knowin' she's blood," Crow said.

Dex sighed. "We don't know that she is."

"Don't know that she's not, either," Crow answered.

"He's old enough," Ace said, nodding.

"An' careless enough to have kids he don't know about," Diesel grumbled.

"Back in the day..." Ace's words drifted off. He shook his head. "Pierce was a busy boy."

Dawg grunted and scrubbed a hand down his beard. "Still harassin' women whenever they come into the gun shop. If he slowed down at all, I'd be surprised. Gotta smooth over ruffled feathers constantly. Even lost some sales due to him bein' too fuckin' handsy. Sometimes it takes everythin' I got not to punch 'im in the damn throat."

"Language," Emma hissed as she sidled up to her husband.

"Right, baby girl. Sorry." Dawg brushed her blonde hair off her forehead and pressed a kiss to it. "Lily good stayin' behind?"

"Yes, she loves Jewel."

"She ain't the only one," Crow said and whacked Diesel on the back.

D grunted. "We'll talk about this shit later. Get Z to schedule a meetin' tomorrow. No more talk right now. Too many ears 'round. Got me?"

A few "got yous" rose up. Then they went their separate ways to get ready for the run.

Dex could hardly unlock his jaw after gritting his teeth during the whole three hour long run. And it wasn't due to the cold weather. It was because he spent three fucking hours watching Brooke ride on the back of Crash's sled.

Yeah. Crash. *Fucker.*

Dex had told Brooke, "No," that she couldn't go along with him. Teach her a lesson that just riding his dick and yanking on his nipple rings did not guarantee her a spot on the back of his sled.

Fuck no, it didn't.

But she'd stood checking all the brothers out in the lot, her eyes searching for someone who may be her father, as everyone got into formation and mounted their sleds. And, *fuck him*, at the last minute, she hopped on Crash's sled.

Just like that.

When she wrapped her arms around Crash's waist, Dex just about leapt off his sled to rip her off him. But he didn't.

He was determined to act like he didn't give a shit. Even though everyone knew he did. So instead of letting everyone eyeball him and his miserable mood, he decided to ride last in the pack. Bring up the rear.

Problem was, he had to watch Brooke's long strawberry blonde hair flying free behind Crash as she plastered herself to his back, probably trying to stay warm.

In one of the parks where they pulled off for a break, Dex had approached her and informed her that she needed to get on his sled instead.

She disagreed. Very strongly, in fact.

And since all eyes were on them, he walked away, ignoring his brothers' smirks.

So now, after they returned to church, he sat on his sled, watching her dismount from the back of Crash's Harley with a huge smile on her face.

Fuck.

If she was trying to get him pissed off, it worked.

He didn't blame Crash. The woman was hot and the man knew Dex had no claim.

None at all.

His gaze ran over her from top to toe. Windblown hair, flushed cheeks, and a sparkle in her eye, all from the ride, as she stood talking to Crash by his sled.

A muscle ticked in his jaw as she leaned over, put a hand on Crash's shoulder and gave him a quick kiss on the cheek.

Then she headed in Dex's direction, opposite from where everyone else was headed, which was into church to get ready for the pig roast and to warm up.

Dex watched her hips *rock-n-roll* in her snug jeans as she strode toward him, her tits bouncing under her jacket with each determined step.

Her smile was long gone by the time she reached him.

When she did, she planted her hands on her hips and tilted her head slightly as she stared at him. "I thought you wanted a repeat of Friday night."

"Do you?"

"I did. But only if you took me along on your run."

He snorted. "Was on the fuckin' run."

"Right. Against your wishes."

He lifted a shoulder and let it drop heavily. "Got what you wanted."

"Not really."

Dex had a feeling those two words held a lot more meaning than what was on the surface.

"Are there going to be more people showing up for the pig roast?" she asked.

"Yeah. Hang-arounds. Prospects."

"Any other patched members?"

Dex shrugged again. "Don't know. Guess you're gonna stick around to find out."

"Is that going to bother you?"

Was it? And would it matter to her if it did? He doubted it. She was going to do whatever the fuck she wanted. "Gonna fuck Crash?"

Her lips twitched. "I wasn't planning on it."

"Sure?"

"Though he's a funny guy—and cute, too—he's not my thing."

He wasn't her thing. *Right.*

"Especially," she lifted her hand and waved it over her head, "with the man-bun thingy going on." She wrinkled her nose. She reached out and slipped her hand into his cut to tweak his nipple ring through the flannel shirt he had donned before getting on his sled earlier. The blood rushed through him and landed right in his dick. "He also doesn't have what you have."

"How do you know?"

"I asked him."

She did what?

Brooke gave him a big smile, her eyes crinkling at the corner. "I'm messing with you."

He released a breath he didn't realize he was holding. "Right," he muttered.

"Are you getting off?"

His eyebrows shot up his forehead.

Her lips twitched some more as she jerked her chin toward his sled. "Your bike," she added.

He snorted again and finally dismounted. As soon as he did, she stepped closer to grab his dick through his jeans. "You said you have a room upstairs?"

"Yeah," he breathed as her fingers gripped his hard-on through the denim.

"The ride got me wet," she whispered close to his ear.

He fought the shudder that wanted to run through him. "The ride or Crash?"

"The vibration of the bike. The memory of Friday night," she murmured.

"Just gonna use me?"

Brooke pulled back and smiled. "Yep."

Dex gave her a sharp nod and grabbed her hand. "Life's a bitch. Let's go." And with that, he tugged her into church and up to his room, ignoring all the eyeballs that tracked their path.

CHAPTER FIVE

Dex's head rolled back on his pillow as Brooke deep-throated him, one hand squeezing his balls to the point of pain, the other twisting one of his nipples.

He could hardly breath. He could hardly think. Everything on his body throbbed.

The scrape of her teeth over the head of his dick made his hips jerk up, shoving him even deeper into her mouth.

The woman hadn't gagged once. It made him wonder how she got so good at giving head. He pushed that thought away and reached out blindly to dig his fingers into her hair.

A sharp sting to his hand had him jerking his fingers back in surprise. The bitch had slapped him away!

He chuckled and smiled up at the ceiling. Fuck this woman.

Jesus.

Out of all the businesses the DAMC owned and ran, she had to walk into the one where he worked first.

Too bad she had only come into Shadow Valley for the reason she did.

But, hell, as long as she was in town and was willing, she could scratch, bite, smack him and twist his nipples until they were sore. Hell yeah, she could.

The sweet butts never fucked him with the intensity that Brooke did. And this was their second go-around for the night. A quickie before the pig roast and now this, afterward.

But this time it wasn't in his shithole room in church. Fuck no, it wasn't. It was in the room she rented at the Shadow Valley Motor Inn, which wasn't much nicer than his own room. However, at least the room had a bigger bed. And the sheets were somewhat clean.

Another bonus was them not tripping over the clothes he had all over his floor.

But that shit didn't matter right now. Right now, his dick was being sucked like there was no tomorrow.

Which meant he was about to blow his load.

Until he wasn't. With two fingers squeezing the root of his dick tight, she pulled away.

"Hey," he complained.

"I have other plans for that first," she told him as she shuffled to her knees and straddled his hips. Still holding his dick, she lined herself up and slowly sank down.

"Ah, fuck," he groaned as the wet, tight heat surrounded him.

She smiled down at him as she rode him slowly, taking her time, taking him deep. Grinding hard when she hit bottom.

"Touch me," she ordered.

He lifted his head and cocked an eyebrow at her. "Gonna smack my hand away again?"

"No. Just do it."

Every time she gave him an order, it made his balls tighter and his dick flex.

"Can I do you like you do me?" he asked. Because as much as he liked her giving it to him rough, he wanted to do the same to her.

"Do whatever. I'll correct you if you go too far."

I'll correct you if you go too far.

Holy fuck.

He snagged both of her nipples and rolled the tight tips

between his fingers. Her tits were some of the best he'd ever seen. Big and heavy but with perky nipples that made his mouth water.

He was dying to suck and bite them but she hadn't allowed that yet.

What the fuck...

She hadn't allowed that.

"My balls still there?"

She reached back and squeezed them until he jerked. "Yes."

"Thank fuck. Just checkin'."

She released a husky laugh. "There's nothing wrong with liking what you need."

"Think I need this?" he asked.

"Yes, I think you do."

"How 'bout you?"

"Yes, I definitely need it like this." Her hands covered his and her fingers encouraged him to pull and twist her nipples even harder as her pace picked up.

"Wanna be on top," slipped out of him.

This was the third time they were fucking and the third time she was on top. While he didn't mind it, he wanted to mix it up. Who knew how many more times she'd ride his dick before she blew back out of town.

He wanted to nail her hard to the mattress at least once.

"Gotta earn that spot," she drawled in her best deep biker voice.

He threw his head back and barked out a laugh. "How's that?"

"I'll let you know when you do."

"Hard to play the game when I don't know the rules."

"Keeps you on your toes," she reminded him.

"Yeah, long as it keeps you on my dick."

Her answer was her pussy clenching tightly around his dick as she began to ride him with abandon. She tossed her head back, her mouth opened and the most fucking amazing sounds came out of her, ones that made his own nipples harden. One of her hands dropped to where they were connected and she rubbed her clit. He didn't know where to watch first. Her face, her luscious fucking tits, which were bouncing and slapping like crazy, or her playing with her own clit.

It ended up being none of them as he squeezed his eyes shut, his balls pulling up high and tight. He was skating dangerously along that brink of no return.

Fuck. She needed to come before he did.

His eyes popped open. "Gonna come?"

She ignored him, sliding like a wild woman up and down on his dick. *Fuck.* He was going to lose it any second now.

She was not going to tolerate him leaving her behind. He could see her popping him in the mouth for shooting his load too soon.

"Babe..."

She dropped her head, her long hair framing her face as she stared down at him, her eyes unfocused, her breathing ragged.

"Babe..." he said again, hoping she'd answer before he had to beg. Because he was not going to beg...

No...

"Babe, gonna come?"

Oh fuck, please.

He felt a rush of wet warmth and the rest of her body went solid while her pussy went into wild spasms around him.

"Oh, thank fuck," he whispered, and squeezing his eyes closed once more, his hips rose off the bed as he came deep inside her.

Then she was on him, collapsed onto his damp chest as she ground her hips in circles, ringing every last drop out of his dick.

His breathing was no better than hers. Both were unable to talk until their heart rate slowed and so did their panting.

Finally, she said, "I don't know why you're so out of breath when I did all the work."

"Next time, gonna be on top."

She tilted her head until she stared up at him with those mesmerizing slate blue eyes. "We'll see."

He combed the damp hair off her face with his fingers. "Yeah, we will," he murmured.

She flicked one of his nipple rings with the tip of her tongue, "Yeah, we will," she repeated.

"You always like this?"

She lifted her head to meet his gaze. "Yes. Are you?"

"No."

She grinned. "You're not used to not being in control."

"Fuck no."

"I bet you bikers are used to bossing women around. Taking what you want, when you want it."

He considered her words for a second, but that's all it took. "Lemme get somethin' straight. We ain't rapists. Yeah, we like pussy. But we can get plenty of it without forcin' it on anyone."

"I didn't—"

He cut her off. "You were on that run. You were in church. You were fuckin' outside in the courtyard. You saw Diesel with Jewel. Hawk with Kiki. Z with Sophie. Jag with my sister. Slade with Diamond. Dawg an' Emma. Hell, Ace with Janice. They're all fuckin' bikers, all DAMC. They'd die for their fuckin' ol' ladies. Wouldn't hesitate a fuckin' second to step in front of a bullet for 'em. Just 'cause your mother got a raw fuckin' deal with someone—an' we don't even know who yet—don't mean we're all like that."

"Those so-called sweet butts aren't treated like property?"

"No one forces 'em to do shit." He hooked a leg around her and flipped her over until she was flat on her back and looking up at him. "Lemme tell you somethin' else... Hawk's woman was this," he held his thumb and index finger a cunt hair apart, "close to bein' raped. Had the shit beat outta her. Jazz was fuckin' raped by two men, beaten an' carved up. Jewel was taken against her will an' coulda easily been raped. We don't play that shit. You fuck with our women an' you're gonna get fucked in return."

"Who did it?"

Dex's nostril's flared as he sucked in a breath, trying to calm his anger. "'Nother club."

"What happened to that other club?" she asked softly.

"Some still around. Some not."

"Revenge," she said matter-of-factly.

"Isn't that what you're here for? Revenge?"

Her eyes slid to the side. "My mom died and that hit me hard. Cleaning out that attic... Finding that info, that diary. It ripped my heart out, Dex. I didn't know what I was here for, honestly, until it hit me Friday night. When those written words finally became clear. I wish I had known what had happened to her all those years ago before she was gone. I want to ask her questions, get some answers. But I can't. That opportunity is gone. There's only one person left on this Earth that knows the truth."

"She probably never wanted you to know. Didn't want to relive that shit if it happened the way you think."

"I think it did."

"Wanna read that diary."

"What? No."

"Yeah. Need to see it. Just the part that mentions the DAMC."

"Why?"

"You wanna find him. I might be able to read it an' pick up on info you'd never pick up."

She considered his words for a few seconds. "I'll think about it. If I do, no one else reads it."

"Can't promise you that. Thinkin' maybe Ace should. Someone around at that time." He stared down into her blue eyes. "Whataya goin' to do if we figure out who he is an' he's still breathin'?"

"I don't know."

"Revenge ain't always sweet, babe."

"I agree. But what if he's still out there? Possibly doing the same thing to others?"

"Could be. Got no proof to put 'im away. Probably some sort of time limit on that thing in your mom's case. Even if there ain't, it's your word against his. An' thirty years later, pigs ain't gonna take you seriously. The only way to deal with it, if it's true, is to do it on the D.L."

"Do what on the D.L.?"

Dex slid onto his back next to Brooke, tucked his arms behind his head and stared up at the ceiling. "Whatever needs done."

"What if he's still in your club?"

"Then we handle it."

"Who's we?"

"The club. Not you. We police our own, babe." He took a long inhale then continued, "Got another sister you didn't meet yet. Bella. Her ol' man—the first one, not the one she's got now—abused the fuck outta her. Tried to kill her. Stabbed her multiple times until he thought she was fuckin' dead."

Brooke sucked in a sharp breath and then made a noise.

"That ain't the half of it. Bella was pregnant by the fucker."

"She lost the baby."

He nodded. "Stabbed her in the gut on purpose."

She rolled onto her side, tight against him, and planted a hand on his chest. "Oh my God."

"Yeah," he grunted.

"And he was a member of your club?"

"Yeah."

"What happened to him?"

"Axel happened." He reached up and tucked a strand of her long, silky hair behind her ear. He regarded the naked woman next to him for a moment, then said, "Axel's 5-0. Was the first one on the scene. Though, I'm fuckin' glad he came along an' saved her life, not glad the pigs had Rebel arrested before we could find his ass."

"So, he's in prison?"

"No. One good thing came outta Rebel's being caught. He went to Greene."

"Greene," she repeated. "The prison you mentioned."

"Right."

"Where this Rocky and Doc are," Brooke stated.

"Yep."

"Should I guess what happened?"

"Nope. You already know. Doc's our grandpop. Not that it

woulda mattered. Doc woulda had Rebel taken out if he was our blood or not. Like I said, we take care of our own."

"Is she okay now?"

A smile crossed Dex's face as he thought of his sister. She was a strong woman. He'd always hoped if he ever settled down with an ol' lady, his would be as resilient and brave as Bella. "Yeah, she's great. Axel's her ol' man now."

"Wait. A cop?"

"Yeah."

"So, she's no longer a part of the club?"

"Oh no, she is."

"He doesn't mind?"

"He fuckin' minds. Don't got much say, though. Axel's also Z's brother."

"Z? Zak? Your club president?"

"Yeah."

Brooke propped her chin on Dex's chest. "Wow. That's... I don't even know what that is. How did that happen?"

"Bear an' Doc were the club's foundin' members. Vietnam buddies. Got out, then started the club together. That's what I meant when I said there were two trunks of the tree."

"A tree which is now twisted."

She remembered. She'd paid attention.

"Because of Bella and Axel?" she asked.

"Not just them. Jag an' my sister, Ivy. Diesel an' Jewel, too. Z an' Axel's pop is Mitch. Bear is... *was* Mitch's pop."

She shifted. "Who's this Mitch? Did I meet him yet?

"Nope. Mitch ain't a part of the club. Mitch is 5-0, too."

"Wow." She lifted her head. "Hey, how old is Mitch?"

"Old enough to be your pop, but ain't. Mitch grew up in the club but was never an Angel. Took a different path, draggin' Axel along with him. Z fought it."

"Did that create a rift in the family?"

"Fuck yeah," Dex breathed. "Big time."

"Does it cause problems with Axel and Bella?"

"Yeah. Sometimes. Bella's gotta ride that fine line between her loyalty to the club an' her loyalty to her ol' man."

"That has to be difficult."

"Yeah. Love my sister an' Axel's good for her. But Axel ain't good for the club."

"She won't walk away from the DAMC."

"No, it's in her blood. Like mine. Like Ivy's. It's even in Axel's."

"I guess he isn't welcome to things like the pig roast tonight."

"Sometimes he'll be with Bella. Though, things tend to be a bit tense when he's around. But he doesn't like her outta his sight too often."

"Why?"

Dex lifted his shoulders off the bed in a shrug. "Got enemies."

"Who does?"

"The DAMC."

"The club that hurt the women?"

"Yeah. The Shadow Warriors."

Brooke was quiet as her hand drifted over his chest and she flipped one of his nipple rings back and forth with the tip of her finger. "Who else haven't I met yet?"

Dex thought back on the run and the roast. Everyone had showed up at one point or another.

Everybody but Pierce.

However, he wasn't ready to tell her about Pierce. Not yet. When Zak got the lowdown on Brooke, the club president agreed that they needed a meeting to discuss it in more detail. To figure something out before jumping to conclusions. So, he scheduled an Executive Committee meeting for tomorrow afternoon. Now Dex just had to keep Brooke from doing too much digging on her own until then.

Since he had Mondays off from the pawn shop, if he could keep her occupied in bed until Monday afternoon, they'd be golden.

The brothers could figure out a plan and then go from there.

The problem was, Brooke didn't take orders from him. He doubted she took orders from anyone.

She wasn't quite arrogant like Pierce, but she had a strong personality. So, Dex could see Brooke being his blood.

Admittedly, that worried him. Pierce was already a stain on the DAMC. Adding a rape to his long list of problems would be the last damn straw.

Zak pounded his gavel on the wood table in the meeting room. The table that had the DAMC logo hand carved into its center by his late grandfather. That logo, that symbol of their brotherhood, was everything. It was the glue that held the club together. It meant family and loyalty.

It was not only carved into the table where the Executive Committee met, but there was a hand carved wooden sign above the private bar. A sign also hung over the back door into church with their motto: *Down & Dirty 'til Dead.*

And they not only wore their colors on their cuts but everyone had those rockers and symbols tattooed into the skin of their back. Every fucking one of them who sat around that table.

Z, Hawk, Diesel, Ace, Dex and Jag. The prez, the VP, the Sergeant at Arms, the Treasurer, the Secretary and the Road Captain.

The reason they were in that room this afternoon used to sit at the head of the table, as well. For ten whole fucking years while Z did his time in prison.

Pierce, being old school, hated the fact that Z had been trying to make the club legit. The man didn't like things changing. And Z had always been about change. Making things better for the club. Not just for the club, but for everyone.

However, old school meant murder and mayhem. And Z wanted the club to thrive, not be torn apart. Having members in prison or six feet under didn't do anyone any good.

Even so, Pierce couldn't wait to get his hands on the gavel once

Z got thrown into SCI Fayette. And everyone couldn't wait for Z to take it back once he got released. Everyone but Pierce.

"We're here for one thing today an' that's to discuss this shit with this woman." Z turned eyes to Dex.

This woman. "Brooke," Dex volunteered.

"Yeah, whatever. The woman who thinks some Angel raped her mom an' got her knocked up. Now she's here for what?" Z looked at Dex again.

"Find whoever that is."

"Yeah, no shit. But then what?"

"Maybe she wants to cut off his balls an' wear 'em 'round her neck," D grunted.

"Well, if it *is* Pierce, she's welcome to it. I'll help hold 'im the fuck down," Jag said.

Z raised his hand. "He's still a brother, so we gotta decide how we're handlin' this. We don't need her runnin' off to SVPD. Not that they'd do anythin', but we don't need the fuckin' headache."

"A-fuckin'-men," Ace muttered.

"Also, don't need a fuckin' rapist in our midst, either. So, if it turns out he did it, he needs to be dealt with swiftly," Hawk chimed in, his face serious. "That mighta happened thirty years ago, but who knows what other bullshit he's pulled since then."

Diesel grunted and all eyes turned to him.

"Got somethin' to say, son?" Ace asked his youngest.

"Nope," the club's enforcer grunted again.

"Don't need someone wearin' our colors doin' shit like that," Hawk said.

"If he did it in the first place. Know he harasses women, but bein' touchy-feely an' fuckin' rapin' a woman are different," Z said.

"Different to you, but you ain't a fuckin' woman," Jag grumbled. "If he'd been touch-feely with Ivy, he'd be buried next to Black Jack."

The thought of Pierce simply touching either of his sisters or, hell, even his cousins didn't sit well with Dex.

"He was a busy boy back in the day, can't imagine he slowed down much," Ace said.

"His ol' lady just left his ass not five months ago 'cause she caught him stickin' his dick in their house mouse."

"Ah, fuck. Didn't know that," Ace muttered.

"Can't believe Randi never left 'im sooner," Jag said, shaking his head. "Not sure what any woman sees in 'im."

"He can charm 'em when necessary. Seen it with my own two eyes plenty of times," Ace said.

Z smacked the gavel on the table. "All right, gotta get back to the bakery, so we need to get this wrapped up."

Hawk snorted. "For what? Not like you do shit at the bakery. Bella an' Sophie do all the work. Half the time you ain't even watchin' the kid."

Z frowned. "I watch Zeke."

"Yeah, suckin' on your ol' lady's tits. That's about it."

A chuckle rose up around the table.

Z cracked the gavel on the table top again. "Okay, let's decide what we're fuckin' doin'."

"First thing, gotta make sure Pierce *is* her daddy," Ace stated, sitting back in his chair and folding his arms over his chest.

"How we gonna do that?" Zak asked.

"DNA?" Jag suggested.

Z snorted. "Yeah, great. Easy answer to a difficult problem. They ain't gonna just open their mouths an' let us swab 'em without askin' a fuckload of questions."

"Think we need to do it on the D.L. Get their DNA on the sly. Figure out if he's even the culprit. If he is, then we need to continue this discussion. But until then, need to keep it under wraps. Got me?" D said.

"How can we snag their DNA without 'em knowin' it?" Jag asked.

All eyes turned to Dex, including Diesel's. "You're bonin' her. No problem gettin' some DNA."

Fuck. "Like spit?"

Diesel leaned forward and pinned him with a look. "Don't want you scrapin' her spit off your fuckin' dick. It'll fuck up the DNA. Just a few hairs. From a brush or somethin'."

Dex may be able to do that, if Brooke let him back into her room. The woman was unpredictable when it came to him asking her for anything. He already learned that in the short time since he met her. "An' what about Pierce?" he asked Diesel.

"Gonna get Dawg to grab some hair from him. Or somethin'. I'll figure it out."

"We need Axel involved since maybe he's got a way to get it tested?" Zak asked.

"Fuck no," D barked. "Don't want the pigs involved. Got it handled. Hunter should have a hookup."

"How long's this shit gonna take?" Dex asked D.

He shrugged his heavy shoulders. "Dunno. Also depends on how soon you get me that hair. Not pubes that were stuck between your teeth, either, brother. Got me?"

"She don't have any," Dex announced, even though that was completely untrue. But fuck his cousin and his smart-ass comment.

Ace chuckled, shaking his head and staring at the table. "Don't understand why women nowadays gotta shave all that shit off. Nothin' like a woman back in the day that had a bu—"

"All right! Meetin' adjourned," Hawk yelled, pushing to his feet. "Don't need to hear my father talkin' 'bout hairy snatches."

"Wasn't gonna talk 'bout your mother's," Ace said with a smirk.

"Jesus," Diesel muttered.

"Brooke ain't gonna be patient," Dex warned Diesel as his cousin rose from his seat.

Zak came around the table and whacked Dex on the back. "Keep her busy, then, brother." He gave him a big smile. "Took a good look at 'er. Shouldn't be no skin off your teeth."

"She can occupy 'er time playin' with your nips, cousin," Hawk chuckled and clapped Dex on the back, too.

CHAPTER SIX

Dex pounded on the motel room door. Since it was the third time he did it and he didn't hear a fucking thing in return, he was pretty damn sure Brooke wasn't in her room.

Just like he thought. She wasn't going to be patient.

And she certainly wasn't going to listen to him. He had told her to wait in her room, that he'd be back.

But, of course, with any perceived order coming out of his mouth she was going to do the opposite.

Because she could. And wanted to prove it.

"For fuck's sake," he grumbled and raked fingers through his hair. He dropped his head and stared at his boots for a minute as he tried to push the anger aside.

He pulled his cell phone out of his back pocket and sent out a mass text to all the brothers: *Any 1 C Brooke let me know.*

He closed his eyes and gritted his teeth at the answering texts.

She run off with ur balls?

Need 2 tie the leash tighter, brother.

MayB she found a man w bigger rings...

What-fucking-ever.

Dex stared at the text from Dawg: *Here.*

Oh shit. She was at the gun shop.

Dex quickly texted him back: *She lookin 4 Pierce or buyin a gun 2 kill him?*

Dunno. Get ur ass here.

"Fuck," he muttered and quickly strode to his sled, mounted, hit the starter and then headed to the outskirts of town to Shadow Valley Gun Shop and Range at top speed.

Within ten minutes, he was pulling into the lot. His gut twisted at what she might have discovered.

Dawg's sled was in the lot, but he didn't see Pierce's. Maybe that was a good sign.

He crab-walked his sled back into the spot next to Brooke's BMW. And after heeling down the kickstand, he turned his head to stare into the back of her car.

His dick twitched in his jeans at the memory of fucking her the first time.

Or her fucking him.

Either way, it was fucking hot.

He adjusted himself, then headed inside and out of the cold. When he stepped into the shop, once his eyes adjusted, they landed on Dawg.

The man was leaning back against the glass display case that held handguns and shaking his dark blond head. "She's a fuckin' pisser."

"Where is she?" Dex asked, rubbing his hands together to get them warmed up.

Dawg jerked his head toward the door that lead to the indoor shooting range. "In the back."

Dex's brows shot up. "She buy a gun?"

"Fuck no. Had one. Nice little Sig. Asked her if she needed any help with it an' she just about told me to fuck off. Though, she made it sound a bit nicer."

Dex glanced around the empty shop. "Where's Pierce?"

"Gone," Dawg grunted.

"Good. They see each other?" Dex asked.

"Nope."

"When's he gettin' back?"

"Dunno. Need to get 'er outta here before he does, though. 'Cause I can tell you, he ain't gonna pass up hittin' on that. An' if he does..." Dawg shook his head.

"It ain't gonna be good," Dex finished for him.

"No. An' seein' 'im will make 'er suspicious. An' like D told me, we need to keep it on the D.L. for now 'til we know if they're even related."

Dex plugged his hands on his hips and looked toward the closed door. He needed to convince Brooke to leave the shop with him. Though, if he demanded her to do it, she'd balk. If he even asked, she'd probably wonder why and then things could get sticky.

"Think you could grab some of her hair while she's here? Got the sample D wanted from Pierce. Figured if you get a few strands of hair, I can let D know what we got an' get that shit rollin'."

Dex eyeballed the larger, bearded man. "How'd you get Pierce's DNA?"

Dawg snorted. "Fuckin' cornered a woman yesterday, she slapped the shit outta him, gave him a bloody nose. Found some bloody tissues in the trash. D said that'd work. Put it in a baggie an' gonna run it over to the warehouse later. You get some DNA while you're here, I'll run that over, too."

Dex nodded, again staring at the door that lead to the range. "Anybody else back there shootin'?"

"Nope."

"Can you make sure nobody comes back for a bit?"

"Yep." He grinned. "Need about thirty seconds?"

"Thirty-five to be exact."

Dawg laughed. "If I didn't have Em an' the girls an' hadn't given up Heaven's Angels mighta asked if she needed a job. Got good tits, plus an ass that'd give any man a hard-on."

"Doubt her career goal is swingin' on a pole."

"What does she do?"

Dex opened his mouth. Then shut it. He had no fucking clue.

He didn't think she'd be sticking around, so asking her that kind of stuff never crossed his mind. *Damn.*

Dawg laughed again. "You don't even fuckin' know, brother. Hard to keep a woman in your bed if you don't show any interest in 'er fuckin' life."

"Not everyone's a whipped pussy at the center like you, Dawg."

Dawg grinned. "Don't give a shit what you call me. Got Em in my bed. Never been happier. 'Happy wife, happy life' is true as shit. Take it from me."

Dex had to admit Emma was a catch. Dawg was happy, though he was pretty sure the man would be happier if he didn't have to share management duties of running the gun shop with Pierce.

But that might change in the near future.

"Gonna just stand there, or go get some DNA?" Dawg said, laughing.

"Yeah," Dex grunted and headed toward the door to the range. He looked over his shoulder one last time. "Seriously, keep people out."

"From what I heard, you like an audience."

Dex shook his head and headed into the range.

Brooke stood with her feet apart as she squeezed off another round. She hit the paper silhouette dead center. Then again and again, until the clip was empty. She released the clip and made sure the chamber was clear before placing the gun in its case. She pulled her protective glasses off her face and removed the rubber plugs from her ears.

"Shoot 'im an' you'll get your ass locked the fuck up," came a deep voice from behind her.

Her heart skipped a beat, then began to race. She had no idea someone was there. She had not only been concentrating on her target, the earplugs had prevented her from hearing Dex come in.

She turned in the booth and saw him leaning back against the painted cement block wall, his arms crossed over his chest.

Her heart skipped once again, but this time it wasn't because she was startled.

Hell no, it wasn't.

He looked damn good. But he was trouble with a capital T. She didn't need to go down this path with him. Or any path. Take a detour? Maybe. But she had to remind herself that it was only for a few days.

Just until she figured out who her father was. As it was, she didn't want to waste a lot of time doing that. She needed to get back to her business, her house. Get her life back in order. Back to where it was before her mom died and she found that damn diary.

He pushed away from the wall and Brooke held her breath when he approached her, but he only leaned into the booth to hit the button on the wall. The target rode the track toward them until it was within arm's reach.

He slipped in next to her to study it. "That's damn good shootin'."

"You shoot?"

He traced his fingers over her gun laying in the open case. "Occasionally. I'm not that good."

"If you're going to carry, you should be that good."

He turned to face her. "Don't carry on the regular."

They were barely inches apart, his body heat mingling with hers, his breath sweeping across her lips when he talked.

"You mean you don't carry a gun." She reached around him and dug into the back pocket of his jeans, pulling out a folded knife. She held it up. "But you carry."

Dex plucked it from her fingers and tucked it back away. "Yeah. Stupid not to be prepared."

"For what?"

He lifted one shoulder. "Whatever's a threat."

She cocked her head. "These Shadow Warriors?"

He didn't answer her question, but instead asked, "How come you're so good?"

"I have to be."

"Why? You a cop?"

They've slept together for the past couple days and he even crashed in her motel room last night. But he never asked her anything personal about her life. She had asked most of the questions in her attempt to get information on her possible father.

"I'm a contract killer," she said with a straight face.

"What?"

She smiled. "Just messing with you. Again."

"Whataya do? Seriously."

"I'm an interior designer."

He simply stared at her.

He had to know what an interior designer was, right? "For commercial spaces. Like corporate offices and things..." she drifted off.

"Your boss give you time off for all this?"

She grinned. "Sure did."

"Got a generous boss."

She lifted her chin and met his dark gaze directly. "She sure is, since I'm her."

Surprise crossed his face. "Got your own business?"

"Yes."

"An' you can afford to take this time off to find your father?"

"I cleared my schedule, passed my current job over to one of my assistants. And, yes, I can afford it. I put enough away for a rainy day."

"Findin' the man who raped your mother's a rainy day?"

She winced. "No, my mother dying of ovarian cancer was a rainy fucking day."

It was his turn to wince. "Sorry, babe." He brushed a loose strand of hair from her ponytail out of her face.

She snagged his hand and held it still. "You know, most strong, independent women don't like being called things like 'babe.'"

"Yep."

"Yep," she repeated. "But that's not going to stop you."

He gave a single nod. "Right."

She rolled her lips inward and studied him. His hair was a ruffled mess, probably from being on his bike, his dark brown eyes matched his dark hair, his lips were full and definitely kiss-worthy, and he wore a thick wash-worn orange shirt under that leather vest of his. The cut he wore proudly, which clearly claimed he was a badass biker. He had a pair of sunglasses tucked into the collar of that long-sleeved tee. And she knew exactly what was under that shirt, too.

Her nipples pebbled at his hidden secret.

A black leather belt with a bulky brass buckle kept his worn jeans up over his lean hips, a chain looped from the front of his waist to his back pocket where his oversized wallet was tucked, and heavy black biker boots covered his feet. Heavy rings adorned his long fingers, ones she had to admit he could use with some skill, and a gold earring hung from one ear.

He also sported some facial hair today since he hadn't packed a bag with a razor when he slept in her bed all night at the motel.

Well, he didn't get much sleep.

Neither did she.

And the bags under her eyes were well worth the lack of sleep.

"Babe," he murmured.

She lifted her gaze to see his lips curved in a smile and the corners of his eyes crinkled in amusement.

Again with the *babe*. "We just had that discussion," she reminded him.

"No, you had that discussion." His lips twitched. "You done checkin' me out?"

"No."

His smile widened. That smile was not only breath-taking, but his brown eyes held a twinkle. "Wanna do me right here?"

"No." That was a complete lie. But there were much better places to do him other than an indoor gun range.

"Why not?"

"I have a perfectly good bed back in my room."

He reached out and dug his fingers into her hair, pulling it out of the ponytail she wore. "A wall would work." He tucked the black elastic hairband into the front pocket of his jeans.

She glanced around. "Yes, maybe. But people could come in. We already caused a crowd once, do you really want to do it again?" She might be into a lot of things, but public sex wasn't one of them.

"Dawg's got it covered."

Her eyes narrowed on the man who was tempting her to no end right now. "He has what covered?" Her pussy clenched at the thought of her pushing him against the wall and taking what she wanted.

Though his thoughts were probably opposite. He was probably picturing him taking *her* against the wall.

But they were in a public spot. Sort of.

Which could be exciting. Sort of.

"Ain't nobody comin' in for a bit," he assured her.

"You arranged that?"

"Yeah."

"And you thought I'd agree?"

He smirked and his eyes flashed. "Do you?"

She shoved him with her two palms, slamming his back against the wall with an *oof*. "We'll play this my way."

"As long as we're playin'..."

"Quiet," she ordered as she kicked off her shoes and began to unfasten her pants.

Dex's lips pinned together in obedience, but she couldn't miss the twitch at the corners.

He loved her bossing him around. That surprised the shit out of her.

It also got her blood flowing, as well as her juices. Her panties were already wet in anticipation.

She tossed her pants onto the small counter at the front of the booth and shimmied out of her panties, draping them next to her gun case. "Undo your belt."

He did as he was told, not saying a word, but his eyes said it all. They were heated and his gaze fell instantly to where she dragged her fingers next. Which was through her wet folds, gathering her slick arousal. She lifted her fingers to his lips. "Suck them clean."

When he parted his lips, she shoved two fingers into his mouth. With a groan, he sucked them, the tip of his tongue swirling around her digits.

She fought back a moan, too.

"Want your tits out," he said when she pulled her fingers from between his lips.

"Do you." She didn't pose it as a question, because it wasn't.

Instead of doing what he wanted, she popped the button on his jeans and roughly pulled the zipper down over his erection. He had gone commando once again this morning. She wasn't sure how comfortable that was for him, especially with his erection right now, nor did she care.

With a rough jerk, she slid his jeans down his thighs just far enough for his cock to be free. He reached down to grab it and she slapped his hand away. "I told you before that's mine. I didn't tell you to touch it."

"Fuck," he muttered as she dropped to her bare knees onto the cold, epoxied concrete floor.

She circled his cock with her fingers and took him into her mouth.

His hips twitched and jerked as she slid him in and out between her lips, getting him slick with her saliva, scraping her teeth over the entire length and across the crown.

He groaned, pushing his hips forward. "Fuck, babe," he moaned.

She released him just long enough to command him to, "Hush."

His body shook and she tipped her eyes up to see him with his head back against the wall, staring up at the ceiling and chuckling.

He wasn't going to be laughing for long. She sucked him with greater enthusiasm until his lips parted and his breath began to hitch. Then she sucked him even harder, snagging his balls tightly in her fist.

His hands were down at his sides and she couldn't miss his fingers twitching, most likely because he wanted to dig them into her hair and fuck her face.

Which she wouldn't let him do.

No. She would lead this dance.

She released his cock with a wet pop, then sank her teeth into the top of his thigh, making him jerk in surprise.

She rose to her feet, still not releasing his balls, and met his dark gaze. "Like being hobbled like that?" His jeans were still pushed halfway down his thighs prevented him from moving too much.

"If it means you're gonna ride my dick, then yeah."

"That's what it means," she confirmed. "How much time do we have?"

"Not much, so do what you're gonna do."

"Is that an order?"

He hesitated, then said, "Nope. A suggestion."

"Good answer," she purred. "You learn quickly."

"Ain't stupid."

She regarded him for a few seconds and finally released his sac. "No, you're not. I should make you drop to your knees and eat me."

Before she could stop him, he did just that. He was on his knees, his jeans still gathered around his thighs. He grabbed her hips and roughly pulled her forward, shoving his face into her pussy. The tip of his tongue flicked wildly over her clit.

He was good with his fingers but he was definitely better with his tongue. She separated her legs into a stance that was similar to her shooting position from earlier. And she let him do his thing, let him take over, just for a few moments.

She was enjoying his skills and it wouldn't take much for her to come with what he was doing. Reaching under his cut, she tweaked both of his nipple rings through his shirt and his tonguing got more intense until he gasped as she twisted his nipples as hard as she could. Then he was sucking her clit fiercely and scraping her sensitive nub with his own teeth.

She wanted to cry out but bit it back before she did. She didn't want to let him know how much he affected her. She wanted him to work hard for it.

The end result would give not only her more satisfaction but him as well.

Whether he knew it or not.

She threw her head back and the air rushed from her as an orgasm swept over and through her. Then he was up and away, lassoing her thighs with his arms, twisting around, shoving *her* against the wall, and with one thrust he was inside her.

He pulled her legs up and round his waist so he could pound her relentlessly. Each thrust pulled a grunt from him and a gasp from her.

She needed to be in control.

She needed to be in control.

But, *oh fuck*, this felt so fucking good. Not only letting him take over, but what he was doing. Showing her what *he* wanted, not her.

Taking what *he* wanted, not her.

He shoved his face into her neck, his warm breath beating against her own heated skin.

A thought swirled through her brain... She couldn't give him an inch because if she did, he'd want it every time.

And she wasn't ready for that.

No. She needed to stay on top. She needed to hold the power, take control of the situation.

Not him.

Not Dex.

She closed her eyes and allowed it anyway against her better judgement. Wrapping her arms around his shoulders, she encouraged him by digging her heels into the back of his thighs. Words were tumbling out of her mouth, into his ear, and she wasn't ready to let go yet.

Not yet.

For a moment she let him have it, that control she loved so much, that control she needed to keep her life in order and on track.

Her thighs gripped his hips tighter, her nails dug into the leather and clawed at patches on the back of his cut. Until she couldn't hold on any longer.

She fell. Fast. Hard. But he caught her.

He came at the same time, thrusting and grinding against her. Spilling himself deep inside her.

Filling her with Dex.

Dex. This biker. This man she never expected to meet.

The only one capable of letting her control slip.

Why him? Why now?

He stilled, but kept her pinned against the wall. His breathing harsh, his chest heaving.

His mouth against her ear. "Fuck, babe. Fuck."

Yes, that about summed it up.

She needed to give up on this hunt. This desire to find the man whose DNA she carried.

She needed to get the fuck out of Shadow Valley. Now.

Before she lost herself.

CHAPTER SEVEN

Dex stared at Jewel who sat behind Diesel's desk at the warehouse. The office chair sat far away from the desk to accommodate her belly. Which was huge. Dex winced. It looked way too uncomfortable for him.

He was glad he wasn't a fucking woman.

Every once in a while, she'd make a face and shift in her seat.

Hunter, who leaned against one of the walls, cleared his throat, pulling Dex's attention back to the former Special Forces operator who worked for D's In the Shadows Security.

"Got news," D grumbled, standing behind Jewel with his arms crossed over his huge chest. He was like a sentry behind his ol' lady, ready to take down anyone who came near her.

"Figured that's why you called me here. Not just for fuckin' tea."

"Got results," D said next, ignoring Dex's dig.

"If you're gonna talk in two-word fuckin' sentences, I'm gonna sit the fuck down because I'm gonna be here awhile."

D shot him a frown.

Dex turned to Hunter, who at least spoke in complete sentences. For the most part. "How'd you get results this quickly?

Only gave the hair thingy to Dawg yesterday while at the gun shop."

Jewel clicked her tongue. "Doing Pierce's daughter in his own business. Sort of ironic."

So, Dawg hadn't kept his mouth shut about his and Brooke's activities at the range yesterday. *Figures.* Dex's gaze dropped to Jewel. "Is that right?"

"Yeah," Diesel grunted.

"Ninety-nine point nine nine nine and so on percent right," Hunter stated. "And to answer your question, I pulled some strings. That's the only reason I got them so fast."

"Fuck," Dex bit out. So it was true, Brooke was Pierce's daughter. "That just complicates shit."

"Yeah, it does," Diesel grumbled. "Means what she's sayin' could be fuckin' true."

"Yeah," Dex breathed and rubbed one hand across his forehead while planting the other on his hip. "Need to have an Exec Committee meetin' to figure out the next step."

"How are you going to find out if Pierce really forced himself on Brooke's mother? Do you think he's just going to say yes when you ask him?" Jewel asked, then shifted in the chair with a groan.

D's brows lowered as he watched Jewel shuffle around. "What the fuck's wrong with you?"

She twisted her head to glower at her ol' man. With one hand on her distended belly, she shouted, "This kid. Jesus. He's huge. And killing me here. You think this is easy?"

D swatted a hand toward her, dismissing her frustration.

Dex rolled his lips inward to keep from laughing at the two of them. Jewel was perfect for his cousin, no doubt about it. She didn't take any shit from him, but they loved each other to death. Not that D would never admit it. Out loud, anyway.

Jewel turned back to Dex. She sighed while rubbing her stomach. "There's another issue."

"With the pregnancy?" Dex asked in surprise.

"No, with—"

Diesel cut her off. "Woman!"

Jewel rolled her eyes and waved a hand in the air. "Whatever. You tell him."

Dex glanced up at Diesel. "Tell me what?"

"Your cousin—"

"Woman!" D barked again, cutting his ol' lady off.

"Jesus," Jewel muttered.

Dex looked again at Diesel. "Which cousin?"

"Kelsea," Jewel answered before D could.

Dex frowned in confusion. "What about her?"

"Well—" Jewel started.

"Woman!"

Dex heard a loud snort from the direction of Hunter.

"Holy fuck, D, just tell him, then," Jewel huffed, her face turning red.

"Tell me what?"

"Kelsea is Pierce's daughter, too," Jewel spilled before D could stop her.

Dex's mouth dropped open for a second, then he snapped it shut. "What? How do you know?"

D muttered a curse before saying, "Annie told me. But since we were doin' DNA, had Jewel snag some of her hair, too. Figured it was a good time to be sure."

Dex blew out a breath. "Holy shit. Who knows this?"

"Me. Jewelee. Annie. Hunter. Now you."

Dex lifted a palm. "Wait. Kelsea doesn't know?"

D shook his head. "Fuck no."

"How long have you known?"

"Right after Z an' Sophie's weddin'."

"That was..." Dex's jaw dropped to the floor.

"Right."

"An' you kept it a secret?"

"Wasn't mine to tell," D answered. "Was Annie's."

"An' Pierce's," Dex added.

"No. He don't know. At least that's what Annie says."

"Our cousin an' Brooke are sisters," Dex murmured. That was a bit disturbing.

"Half-sisters," Jewel corrected him.

"Whatever. It's just fuckin' weird."

"You ain't related to her," D reminded him.

"Right. But still... it's just... weird."

"So stop fuckin' 'er. Send 'er on 'er way. That'd make things helluva lot easier."

Dex pursed his lips and placed his hand on his chest over one of his very sore nipples. After sex in the gun range yesterday, he'd stopped at church quick to shower and change clothes before meeting her back at the motel room.

Then the rest of the night she punished him for taking control at the range.

He'd loved every fucking second of it.

"Yeah, you ain't gonna stop fuckin' 'er, brother," D grumbled.

"You should see your face," Hunter added with a smirk.

Jewel laughed, then cried out, grabbing her stomach. "Ow!" She glared at D. "Never again!"

"Fuckin' fine with me. Didn't want this one," he muttered.

Jewel picked up a full water bottle off the desk and whipped it at him. He didn't even flinch when it thumped him in the chest and landed on the floor. At least the cap was on tight.

Hunter chuckled, dropped his head and shook it.

Jewel leaned over and gasped. Dex stepped closer to the desk in concern. The woman *was* carrying his future cousin after all.

Diesel grunted. "Probably just need to let one rip."

Jewel gave him a face. "Yeah, well, if that's all it is, then I just made a damn mess on your chair."

She used the desk to push herself to her feet and not only were her pants wet but Diesel's office chair was soaked.

"What's that? You piss yourself again?"

"Fucking D," she groaned, squeezing her eyes shut and gasping.

"Looks like her water broke, boss." Hunter clapped him on the back. "Congrats. Kid's coming."

"No," D said, his eyes a bit wider than normal.

"Yeah," Hunter insisted and laughed.

"Nope," D said, shaking his head.

"Yes!" Jewel screamed, grasping the desk hard. "Yes, D. This isn't fucking gas. It's your kid coming."

"Ain't the right time," he mumbled, turning pale.

Jewel's eyes went wide. "Says who? This kid says it is."

"Uh... you need to go to the hospital?" Dex asked, not sure what to do since D should be stepping in but the man was frozen in place.

"Of fucking course I need to go to the hospital!" she screamed. "Motherfucker!"

Dex grimaced at the pained expression on Jewel's face. "Diesel! Take care of your ol' lady!"

D only blinked.

"Don't you dare pass out!" Jewel screamed at him.

Dex pulled out his phone. "Oh, yeah. Pass out, D. I'm gettin' ready. Missed it the first time. This time I'm gettin' it all on video."

That seemed to snap D out of whatever shock he was in. He glared. "Fuck you, Dexter."

Dex laughed. "Get 'er to the hospital. I'll text everyone an' follow shortly."

Jewel leaned over and let out long, hair-raising wail, then bared her teeth. "Let's fucking go!"

With a tight jaw, Diesel picked her up in his arms and strode out of the office.

"He going to be all right to drive her?" Hunter asked as he stared out of the open doorway.

Dex shrugged. "Hope so." He quickly wrote a text and sent it out in mass to all the brothers. "I'll follow 'em."

"Yeah. Might be best."

Dex flipped his hand up over his shoulder in goodbye to an amused Hunter and hurried out of the room.

Dex paced the crowded maternity waiting room. He glanced at his phone for the hundredth time. He'd called Brooke twice and left messages both times. He'd also texted her once.

Fuck him, it was more like three times.

But that was all he was going to do. He wasn't going to beg her to get back to him.

He blew out a breath and scrubbed his hand over the stubble on his jaw. He was trying to be... *nice* and tell her why he wasn't showing up for their nightly fuckfest. Trying to let her know he wasn't just blowing her off for no good reason.

His gaze bounced around the room, then landed on Ace, who was pacing back and forth in front of the elevators. Dex's aunt, Janice, stood in one of the corners of the room with some of the other DAMC women. Dex's mom, Allie, and her sister and Kelsea's mom, Annie, were in that group, as well.

Dex studied Kelsea across the room. She was the only blonde, blue-eyed member of the Dougherty side of the family. The rest of them had dark hair and dark eyes. Well, except for Ivy, who was a green-eyed redhead. But that came from their father's side, from what his mother had said.

But blonde and blue-eyed didn't fit. However, no one ever knew who Kelsea's father was. His Aunt Annie just announced one day she was having a baby and that was that.

Whether there had been a discussion about who the daddy was with Ace and Allie along with Dex's grandmother, Lonnie, who fucking knew. He'd been too young at the time to understand or even care.

Plus, his own father had hit the bricks before Dex ever had a chance to know him. So, single mothers in his family were nothing new. Or even odd.

Ace had stepped in as a father-figure to all of them. He also stepped up as the head of the Dougherty family as soon as Doc had gone to prison for murder.

But now his uncle was becoming a grandfather for the first time. Dex made his way over to the club's treasurer.

"Gonna have to get used to this," Dex told him.

"Know it," Ace grumbled but kept pacing.

"Kiki an' Ivy gonna give you grandbabies soon, too."

"Know it," he mumbled.

"Janice is gonna be in hog heaven."

Ace stopped dead and concentrated on Dex. "Already was when Baby Z was born."

"True. But Zeke ain't blood."

"Just the same to us."

Dex nodded. "Right. Still family. But ain't the same."

Zak joined them, carrying Zeke on his hip. "Nervous, grandpa?"

Ace held out his arms and took the baby from the club prez. He made funny faces at Zeke, causing the kid to laugh. "Yep. Not for becomin' a grandpa. Got some practice in with this lil guy. But just wanna make sure Jewelee's okay. An' the baby's healthy."

"Jewelee's too stubborn to let birthin' a kid take her out," Z said.

"It's Diesel's kid," Ace reminded them.

Dex and Z laughed.

"True." Z shook his head. "Kid's gonna be a stubborn fucker."

"Is D in the room where she pops out the kid?" Dex asked.

Ace pursed his lips. "Dunno. Better be. If he ain't, Jewelee will never let 'im live it down."

"If she's sufferin', he's gotta suffer," Z said matter-of-factly.

Ace snorted. "Like you did with Sophie."

"Sophie ain't as hard-headed as Jewel." Z sobered and turned to Dex. "Speakin' of hard-headed, you've been keepin' Brooke busy?"

"Yeah, but was meetin' with D earlier when Jewel's water broke. Need to schedule a meetin' with the Exec Committee. He got results an' we need to talk about another issue."

"Can we do it now since we're gathered in one spot?" Zak

asked. "Who knows how long it'll be before D's son decides to make an appearance."

"He tell you he's havin' a boy?" Hawk asked as he stepped up between Ace and Z. "Didn't think they wanted to know the sex." Hawk dropped his head and lifted a hand. "Hold up. I mean Jewel didn't wanna know the sex. D still denies there's a little human in her fuckin' belly." He leaned forward and grabbed Zeke out of Ace's arm, lifting the kid high over his head. "Sorry, kid, didn't mean to fuckin' curse in front of you."

Zeke laughed as Hawk dropped him suddenly and flew him like an airplane in a circle with sound effects and everything.

"Nope, they don't know yet," Ace confirmed.

"So, about this meetin'," Dex started. "Don't we need D? He's a bit occupied right now."

"As Road Captain, Jag can vote in his place. *If* we need a vote," Z answered.

Dex nodded. "Think we're gonna need a vote."

"Fuck," Z muttered.

"Yeah. Though, ain't the half of it," Dex warned him. He turned and searched for Jag. "Yo! Jag!"

Jag was sitting in one of the waiting room chairs with Ivy on his lap. Ivy was talking to Bella, who was similarly curled up on Axel's lap in the next chair.

It hit him then how happy his sisters were. Ivy finally settling down with Jag, who worshipped the ground she walked on. Bella finally allowing herself to love Axel freely. And Z's brother worshipped everything about Dex's sister, too.

He was glad he didn't have to kick anyone's ass on behalf of his sisters. Though, Diesel had done a single knock-out punch on Axel when he'd caught the cop in Bella's bed one night.

Diesel tended to be more protective of Bella than Dex was. But then, they had all been raised on the same farm and were more like siblings than cousins.

Jag came over. "What's up, brother?"

"Gonna have a quick meetin'. If we need a vote, your vote will count since D's tied up," Hawk told him. Normally as Road Captain, Jag's vote didn't count unless another member of the Executive Committee was missing.

"This about Brooke?" Jag asked, his gaze sliding to Dex.

"Yeah," Dex grunted.

Jag glanced around at the crowded room. "We gonna do it right here?"

"Fuck no," Z answered. "Need somewhere away from everybody."

"Agreed," Hawk said. "'Specially if this is gonna go the way I think."

"Cafeteria?" Z suggested.

"Or outside," Ace spoke up.

"Wherever," Z grumbled. He lifted his head and yelled to Sophie, "Babe, come take my boy."

Sophie took her time coming over to grab Zeke. She wasn't one to jump when Z yelled jump. But then—Dex glanced around the room—none of the DAMC women were.

Shit, Brooke would fit right in with them. All of them were headstrong, strong, independent women. Even the ones without the DAMC blood running through their veins. Kiki, Sophie and even Emma.

It was just a fucking shame Brooke was Pierce's daughter. His eyes slid back to Kelsea and he frowned.

Pierce had ingrained himself deeper in this club than he even knew.

"Gotta have a quick meetin'," the club prez told his wife. "Headin' downstairs. Text me if the newest DAMC member comes into the world before we're back."

"I talked to one of the nurses. Seems it's going to be a longer labor than mine," Sophie said.

"She say if D's still upright?" Z asked with a smirk.

"The nurse is a he. And I didn't ask." She accepted her son from Hawk and gave Z a kiss on the cheek. "If you're talking club business in the middle of all this, I hope it isn't bad news."

Since she knew she wouldn't get an answer, she sighed and wandered away, blowing raspberries on her son's cheek.

"Let's go," Ace said. "Wanna get back up here ASAP."

"Agreed. Can't wait to meet my nephew," Hawk said.

Ten minutes later, they were gathered around a table in a dark corner of the cafeteria with disposable cups of shitty coffee in front of them.

"D should be here since he got the results. But no matter what, it ain't good," Dex started.

"Can already guess that Pierce fathered Brooke," Hawk muttered.

"Right. But like I said, that ain't all." All eyes turned toward Dex. "There's another little snag that we're gonna have to deal with if we strip the asshole of his colors."

"What's that?" Z asked.

Dex grimaced. "She doesn't know..."

"Who don't know what?" Ace asked, leaning forward, his shoulders tense, his eyes focused sharply on Dex.

"Kelsea."

Ace slammed his hand on the table causing the coffee cups to jump. "What 'bout her?"

Dex sucked in a breath and braced because he had a feeling at least Ace and maybe even Hawk might blow a gasket at the news about their cousin. "Kels is Pierce's daughter, too."

At first, complete silence met his announcement. Then Ace jumped to his feet and screamed out a, "Fucking motherfucker!" so loud that it could peel the paint off the walls. His face turned a mottled red.

With nostrils flaring, Hawk said, "Pop, sit the fuck down before you have a fuckin' heart attack."

Good thing it was late and the kitchen in the cafeteria was closed. They were the only ones in there except for a man in the corner nursing his own cup of coffee. Dex didn't blame him when he quickly got up and left after Ace's outburst.

"Jesus fuckin' Christ," Z muttered. "That's some bullshit right there. Did Pierce rape Annie?"

Ace, in the midst of sitting back down when Z asked that, shot back to his feet, his whole body shaking. "Gonna kill the fuckin' bastard. With my bare hands."

Hawk grabbed his father's arm and yanked it. "Sit down! Ain't killin' nobody right now. Got a grandbaby on the way. We're gonna deal with this."

"Don't know that answer," Dex admitted. "But it wouldn't make sense if he did. D might know more since he found out from Annie herself. He just confirmed it with a DNA test while Hunter was testin' Brooke an' Pierce's."

"Yeah, wouldn't make sense for her to continue to work part-time in the gun shop if he had. No one would wanna work next to their rapist," Hawk agreed.

"I'm gonna cut his fuckin' balls off an' fuckin' shove 'em down his throat," Ace muttered, finally settling back in his chair.

"Also makes sense why he was givin' Kelsea an' that Dark Knight the stink eye when they were dancin' at my weddin'," Z said.

Dex shook his head. "No. Here's the thing... D said neither of 'em know."

"What?" Jag asked, his brows almost stuck to his hairline. "How could Annie keep that from 'im?"

"If you got knocked up by Pierce would you tell 'im? An' then have 'im raisin' your kid? I fuckin' wouldn't," Dex answered.

Hawk grunted next to him.

"He didn't spend one fuckin' dime to help raise 'er," Ace grumbled. "Not one. Got off scot-free. Fucker."

"Annie must've had 'er reasons to keep it from 'im. From you, Ace. From all of us. Hell, even from her own fuckin' daughter," Jag said.

"Pierce bein' Kelsea's pop ain't enough to strip 'im of his colors," Hawk reminded them all.

"No, but rapin' a woman is," Dex said to Hawk. "Though, just don't know how to be sure 'bout that."

"Do we need to be sure?" Jag asked. "Or can we just boot his fuckin' ass like I wanted to a while ago?"

Hawk considered what Jag said. "Just on suspicion? Guess so. But the whole club's gotta vote on it. An' if what Brooke says is true, can tell you..." He drifted off, then lowered his voice. "It's gonna be more than just strippin' his colors, brother. Got zero tolerance for that shit. Zero."

Jag sat back in his chair with a satisfied look. "No fuckin' loss."

"Just don't know how Kels is gonna take findin' out her pop is Pierce one second an' then the next, he's banned from the club," Ace said.

"*Banned*," Hawk barked and laughed, shaking his head.

Ace continued, ignoring his oldest son, "Add on to that findin' out he mighta raped a woman. An' because of that, she got a sister."

Z shrugged. "Don't gotta tell 'er."

"Yeah, but Brooke's her blood sister," Dex reminded him. "Even if they only share half of Pierce's toxic blood, they're still sisters. Do we really want to keep sisters apart?"

"They don't even fuckin' know each other, Dex!" Ace yelled and slammed his hand on the table again. "All this goddamn drama an' bullshit. Don't need shit like this tearin' this club apart. Everythin' we all worked hard for. Pierce's like a fuckin' cancer. Need to cut 'im the fuck out. Keep it from both the girls. Have 'im disappear. Whatever. He just needs to get gone. Get our colors off his fuckin' back while we're at it."

Hawk blew out a loud breath, sat back and scrubbed a hand over his mohawk. "Fuckin' pop. Know you're fumin'. I'm pissed, too. But we gotta deal with this shit carefully. These women are strong," he glanced toward Dex. "They can handle more shit than you think."

Dex nodded his agreement. Brooke was definitely strong. He knew that just from the short time he'd spent with her.

"Fuckin' raised Kelsea like she was my own, Hawk." Ace slapped his hand a couple times on his chest. "Me. I fuckin' did it all. Supported her, her mother," he turned his eyes to Dex, "your mother an' you kids, too. I fuckin' did it. Not that motherfucker. Not your motherfuckin' father, either, Dex."

Hawk turned concerned eyes to his father. "Pop, gotta cool down. Don't need to end up in a hospital bed. The club helped financially. You gotta remember that. So in a way, Pierce did kinda support Kels. An' Annie didn't give 'im the chance to step up."

Ace frowned at his oldest son. "You defendin' him?"

Hawk raised his palms. "Fuck no. Just tryin' to keep you from bustin' a blood vessel. That fucker deserves everythin' he's gonna get.'

Ace huffed and sat back. He took a few slow breaths until his normal color began to return. "Gotta handle this somehow with these girls. Pierce is the easy part. Kelsea," Ace shook his head and looked at Dex. "That woman ain't my worry, but Kels is."

That woman. "Think Brooke should be our worry. He was wearin' our colors when he raped her mother."

"An' I ain't defendin' him, either, but you're takin' her word for it," Z said.

Dex's jaw got tight. "She says it's in her mother's diary that she found."

"It comes right out an' says it?" Jag said, leaning forward, his eyes dark.

Dex shook his head. "Dunno. Told her I wanna read it. She hasn't let me yet. Not even sure if she's got it with 'er." He turned his eyes to Ace. "Thinkin' you might need to read it, too, if we need some light shed on anything since you were around durin' that time."

Ace stared at him, his lips pressed flat. "Bad enough we're still dealin' with these fuckin' Warriors after all these decades, but now this, too."

"Can't get past the past," Jag muttered.

"D's handlin' the Warriors. Slow goin', but it's goin'," Hawk said, his voice low. "We clean up this shit, then the past can stay just where it belongs."

"Hopin' so," Ace mumbled.

"Right now, we got the future about to fuckin' join us upstairs. Need to get back up there for D an' Jewel," Z said, running fingers through his hair. "Zeke, D's son, your son, Hawk, and even maybe yours, Jag, if it's a boy. The future's upon us. We need to make sure our shit is cleaned up for all of 'em. Make sure this club lives on the way I imagined it would. Got me?"

"Didn't decide what we're doin' with the girls," Ace reminded Z.

The club prez rapped his knuckles on the table as he thought. After a few moments he said, "Crow ain't down here with us, but know exactly what that brother would say..."

Hawk nodded, finishing for him. "The girls are blood. They need to know it an' each other."

"Yeah," Dex said softly. "Guess I can tell Brooke. But not sure what she's gonna do or how she's gonna act."

"She'll probably wanna confront 'im," Jag said.

"Yeah, that's what I'm afraid of. She's fuckin' a pro shot with that Sig of hers."

Hawk snorted. "Well, if she takes 'im out then he's no longer our problem."

Dex frowned. "Yeah, an' she ends up in a concrete box for cold-blooded murder."

Hawk cocked a brow. "Do you care?"

Did he? Could he see her as more than a quick, but hot, lay for the past couple nights? Dex regarded his cousin for a long minute. *Fuck me.* "Yeah, I do."

Hawk's lips twitched and he whacked Dex on the back. "Welcome to the fuckin' club."

"Fuck." Dex shook his head. "Was the only one left on the committee with his balls intact."

"Brother, lost your balls when you got those rings in your nips," Hawk said.

"Ain't that the truth," Z agreed, then he quickly got back to business. "We'll figure out a chance for the girls to meet each other an' give Kels the news. Go from there. Once D's settled with the baby, we'll get the shit with Pierce handled. Yeah?"

An answering "Yeah" went up from the table.

Z looked at Ace. "Guess you're gonna have to handle Annie, as well. Prepare her for the shit that's about to fall."

"Fuck," Ace muttered.

"What don't kill us makes us stronger, right?" Jag asked.

"Right," Dex said.

"All right, time to get back upstairs. I'm ready to meet my grandson," Ace said.

"Down an' dirty..." Z began loudly.

"'Til dead!" came the answering shouts along with the fists being pounded on the table.

Then they all headed back upstairs to wait for the newest member of the next generation of the DAMC.

CHAPTER EIGHT

It ended up that there was no fucking need to rush upstairs to the waiting room. With stubborn parents like Diesel and Jewel, their kid was just as stubborn about finally coming into the world.

Everyone waited around for hours and hours. Some drinking coffee, some napping. But one thing was clear, *everyone* was getting impatient.

Dex had wanted to leave several times to head over to Brooke's motel. He still hadn't gotten an answering text or phone call.

And that was goddamn bullshit.

Dex looked around the room. Soon-to-be an aunt Diamond had her head on Slade's shoulder and his arm wrapped around her as they slept. Ivy was perched once again in Jag's lap, her eyes closed as well. Jag's were open, but barely, as he waited for his sister to give birth. Emma's daughter, Lily, was asleep draped over Dawg's broad chest, while his ol' lady was curled up in a chair next to him. Janice and Ace sat holding hands and talking to each other in a low voice, waiting for their first grandchild. Jewel's mother, Ruby, sat restlessly close by, flipping through a magazine. Hawk and Kiki were tucked into a corner by the elevators. Z sat on the floor, his back against the wall, Sophie between his legs, leaning back on his chest with Zeke asleep in her arms. Annie, Allie, and Kelsea, along with Grizz and Momma Bear played a quiet game of cards in another corner. Bella sat wrapped up with Crow since Axel had to leave hours earlier to work the midnight shift at SVPD. Crow's head was thrown back, his mouth wide open as he slept, his long, black braid draped over the back of the chair.

Dex turned his attention to another corner where Linc, Crash, Nash and Rig had gathered. He eyeballed Linc, who was texting someone on his cell phone. He wasn't certain if it was Jayde, who hadn't showed up. Dex was pretty sure Mitch would've frowned upon Jayde coming to the hospital and waiting around for the next generation of bikers to be born. And since Z's sister still lived at home, she tried not to create too many waves. She had already caused a big one when she went to work for the club's attorney, Kiki.

And though Jayde had a thing for Linc, it seemed as though the brother had been keeping his distance from her. Especially with her father Mitch being a cop, her brother Axel being one, too, and then their club prez being her oldest brother... Linc was just better off leaving her alone. The man had a good head on his shoulders so it didn't surprise Dex one bit that he was being sensible and not letting potential pussy get his ass in trouble.

The only fully-patched members missing from the waiting room were the two newest ones: Rooster, who probably had to work The Iron Horse until closing, and Moose, who was now managing Heaven's Angels Gentlemen's Club. And, of course, none of the prospects were there.

He wondered if Brooke had returned his calls or texts, would she have come to the hospital to wait it out with him. She could be cuddled up in his lap right now, drooling on his shoulder, like Diamond was doing to Slade.

Fuck. Brooke would probably make him curl up on *her* lap. She was one controlling woman.

He smiled to himself.

Every demand she had made on him so far when they fucked,

he had no problem following. When the time came that he got sick of it, he'd let her know. But right now...

Fuck. Right now was all they had, because who knew what the hell was going to happen once all the shit with Pierce went down and all the secrets were out in the open.

Brooke would want her pound of flesh and then she'd head back home. To wherever the hell that was.

Where the hell was that?

For fuck's sake, he'd never even asked.

Not that she'd volunteered that information, either. He now knew what she did, but not where she did it.

Dex shifted in the spot he'd claimed on the floor since there were no more available chairs. It felt as though every part of his body had fallen asleep. Brooke's bed in her motel room was so much more comfortable. Even if she was causing him pain by clawing him, biting him or ripping on his nipple rings.

She probably had a dominatrix dungeon in the basement of wherever she lived.

He should be worried about being tied up and beaten into submission by a woman, but for some reason that just made his dick twitch. He was fucked up. He never, ever thought he'd want a woman to dominate him before.

As he glanced around the crowded room again, he realized the last thing he needed was one of his brothers finding out. It was bad enough they now knew about the nipple rings.

Heavy footsteps slowly coming down the corridor from the direction of the maternity ward had him turning his head.

Diesel was lumbering down the hall, ripping off a yellow gown that barely fit him. His face looked serious, his expression not giving Dex a damn thing.

Dex climbed to his feet and shouted, "Yo! D's comin'," to wake everyone up.

One by one people's heads rose. Ace and Janice jumped to their feet and stepped forward, as did Ruby. Waiting. For something. Anything.

But no one said a word.

D simply stood there, not even blinking. Dex wondered if the man was in shock or something.

Janice had a tight grip on Ace, a worried look on her face as she stared at her youngest son.

Ruby had a hand to her mouth, almost as if expecting the worst.

And everyone else was as frozen as Diesel.

The ice was broken when Ace shouted out, "Well? What's his name?"

Diesel finally blinked, looked at his father then said, "Violet."

And before anyone could react, D dropped to his knees and buried his face in his hands.

No one moved. No one said a word. No one even breathed.

Janice rushed up to him, falling to her knees as well, and wrapping her arms around D as best as she could. "Son, what's wrong?" she cried, tears streaming down her cheeks.

"Nothin'. She's... perfect."

Dex sat on his bike and stared at the dark window of Brooke's motel room. He was fucking bone tired and he knew she'd still be asleep since it was only five in the morning.

He should be asleep, too. And the exhaustion should be from banging Brooke all night, not hanging out in a hospital.

But Violet DeeJay Dougherty had come into the world at nine pounds, three ounces and that miniature human had knocked the shit out of Diesel.

Hell, she'd surprised all of them.

No one, not *one* of them, ever expected Diesel to be capable of producing a daughter.

A baby girl.

Janice had lightened the mood in the room by whacking her

son upside the head for making them all worry by the way he reacted.

Dex still wasn't sure if D was okay with having a daughter. His cousin was a hard one to figure out.

Zeke. Violet. Hawk's unborn son. And then whatever Ivy and Jag ended up having. The fourth generation of the DAMC was in full swing. Hell, even Lily and possibly Caitlin, Dawg's teenage daughter, could be counted among them.

He was sure it wouldn't be long before Sophie was knocked up again since Baby Z was now over a year old. Plus, Di and Slade were probably getting a lot of practice on the mechanics of making a baby.

Whether Di wanted to be a mother or not, Dex wasn't sure.

And then there was Bella...

His sister had been robbed of that chance and any chance in the future. A loss to both her and Axel because they'd make awesome fucking parents. Whether they'd eventually adopt or not...

Dex mentally shrugged, sighed, heeled his kickstand down and, with a groan, dismounted his sled. He wasn't even sure Brooke would let him in, since she never responded to him at all.

Not even to the last text he'd sent an hour ago to let her know that Violet had been born.

He stood, about ready to collapse, in front of her motel room and lifted his fist to pound on the door. Instead, he dropped it, pressed his forehead to the wood door, leaned his weight into it and yelled out her name.

He closed his eyes as he waited for her to wake up and come open the door.

Jesus. He didn't think he could muster the energy to even fuck her.

He felt like he was sinking in quicksand. He needed to get horizontal soon.

"Babe," he yelled this time and forced himself to lift his hand to knock.

Nothing.

"Babe…" he said again. "Fuckin' let me in."

Still nothing.

He groaned. He slipped his cell from his back pocket and dialed her number. He held his breath to see if he could hear her cell ringing inside.

Nope. Her phone had to be off.

"Brooke, damn it," he yelled and pounded a little louder on the door.

Nothing again.

No light went on. No movement. Nothing.

Fuck.

He blinked. For fuck's sake, what if the Shadow Warriors snagged her while he was at the hospital twiddling his fucking thumbs?

He turned and realized something he should have seen from the get-go. Her Beemer was gone.

What the fuck?

Suddenly he was wide awake, his nerve ends crackling.

If those motherfucking Warriors took her…

He stalked over to the motel office and, even though the sign said closed, he rang the bell five thousand times until the owner got out of bed and came to the door in her curlers and housecoat, while wearing a pair of fuzzy slippers.

"What the fuck do you want? Sign says closed, idiot," she griped.

"I can fuckin' read. Need to know the last time you saw the woman in number four."

The motel maven blinked a few times as she looked past him, out the door and toward Brooke's room.

"The last time I saw her? When she fucking checked out!" With that, she slammed the door in his face.

Dex jerked his head back and took a steadying breath.

When she checked out?

"What time was that?" he shouted at the door. But the woman nor the door answered him.

He pulled his cell out again and texted furiously: *Call me ASAP.*

He needed to grab a couple hours of sleep before heading to the pawn shop. With a curse, he headed back to his sled.

Dex stood over his sister. Her head was down on her desk, her arms being used as pillows, and she was snoring lightly.

He felt the same way. The couple hours of sleep he tried to grab never came. He tossed and turned, wondering where the fuck Brooke took off to and why she wouldn't answer him.

Maybe he needed to get a hold of Hunter to see if he could track her down. But that meant he'd get shit for chasing a woman. Not only from his own brothers but from D's Shadows, too.

He'd leave that as the last resort.

Instead, he decided to see if Ivy could work her magic on the computer.

"Ivy!" he shouted, making her jump.

She lifted her head and frowned at him. "What? Can't you see I'm sleeping?"

"Don't let Ace catch you."

She grabbed a nearby bottle of water and took a swig. "He's not here. He's still at the hospital."

"Right. Just sayin'."

When he took a deep breath, her eyes narrowed on him. "What do you want?" she asked, suspicion lacing her voice.

"Need a favor."

"Of course you do."

"Ivy, need you to do somethin' for me, but it stays between us."

She sat up straighter, more awake than a few seconds ago. "What?"

"Just need you to find me some info."

"On who?"

He perched his hip on the edge of the desk. "Brooke."

Her brows shot up. "What kind of info and why?"

"Need her address."

"For what?"

"Seriously, sis. Just need her details."

Ivy wiggled the computer mouse and the screen lit up. She was a wiz with computers and the next best thing to getting one of D's guys to help him. "What's her last name?"

Dex's eyes slid to the side. "Uh..."

Ivy smacked him on the thigh. "Holy fuck, have you been knocking boots with her and you don't even know her last name?"

Ah, fuck. "No... know it. Just forgot."

Ivy snorted. "Liar." She tapped a finger against her bottom lip. "Okay, got her license plate?"

"It's PA. Not sure of the tag info, though."

"Jesus. We have her first name, and a state." She glanced up at him. "Phone number?"

"Yeah, got that."

"Well?"

He read the digits off his cell while Ivy typed them into the computer and then clicked the mouse a few times.

Ivy stared at the computer screen. "Monroe."

"Huh?"

"Her last name, dummy. Monroe. Brooke Marilyn Monroe." Ivy giggled. "That's cool. Almost as cool as Mick Jagger Jamison."

"Jag don't think it's cool," he reminded her.

"Yeah, well..."

"Write down her address."

"I need to do more digging for an actual address."

"Okay, well, hurry the fuck up then."

Ivy pushed the keyboard toward him. "Have at it if you think it's that easy."

"C'mon, sis."

Ivy stared at him for a moment. "What's going on with her?"

"Nothin'."

"Did she take off?"

Dex considered his sister for a moment, before breathing, "Yeah."

"So? You can't find pussy elsewhere?" Ivy raised a hand. "I'm talking other than the sweet butts or the strippers." When Dex didn't say anything for a moment, Ivy sat back in the chair and crossed her arms over her chest. "What's going on, Dex?"

"Nothin'. Just got somethin' to tell her."

Ivy pursed her lips and tilted her head. "Why does it have to be in person?"

Again, he didn't answer.

"You can't call her and tell her?"

"Not this."

Ivy leaned forward. "Fuck, who's her father?"

"Ivy..."

"Dex, fucking tell me. Who raped her mother?"

"Jesus," he muttered, dragging fingers through his hair. "Sis, we're gonna deal with it."

"You tell me or I'm not giving you shit."

"Ivy, gotta do this for me. Promise you'll know as soon as you can."

"This is complete bullshit, Dex, I'm telling you right now. Are any of us at risk?"

When his sister said "us" he was pretty sure she meant just the women. "No."

"Sure?"

Dex sucked in a breath. Pierce wouldn't dare touch one of the DAMC women, would he? But could he really tell his sister he was sure the asshole wouldn't?

"The sooner you give me Brooke's address, the sooner this can be dealt with, got me?"

"This is bullshit, Dex. You know it. You need to tell us who it is."

Right, and then be responsible for the women going all vigilante on Pierce's ass. Which would lead to Dex getting raked across the coals for talking club business with one of them. Even if it was his own sister and Jag's ol' lady.

"You'll know. When it's time."

Ivy gathered her long red hair up on the top of her head and blew out a breath. "I'm going to get you her info, but you have to promise me you'll tell me as soon as you can."

"Pretty sure Jag will tell you."

"Fucking Jag. He knows, doesn't he?"

Aw, shit.

"It was that meeting you had last night at the hospital," she said matter-of-factly.

"Don't give 'im shit, Ivy. Don't fuck up what you two have just to get some info you don't need right now."

"I'm not fucking up anything. We women have a right to know."

"You'll know!" he yelled. "Just give us a fuckin' minute to deal with it."

Ivy stared at him for a few long moments, then turned back to her computer. She typed furiously onto the keyboard and a couple minutes later she slammed her hand on the desk and sat back again. She turned green eyes to Dex. "Got it."

"Write it down for me, will ya?"

Ivy's lips were flat and her jaw tight as she scribbled down the address onto a sticky note. Then she slapped it into his palm.

"Get this dealt with," she said.

Dex stared down at the little slip of yellow paper in his hand. "Gonna, sis. Promise."

Ivy nodded.

"Can you hold down the fort? Call in some of the part-timers?" He lifted the note up. "Apparently, got a bit of a ride ahead of me."

"Fine," she huffed. "Do what you have to do."

He leaned over and placed a kiss on the top of her hair. "Love ya, sis. Wouldn't let anything happen to you or Jag Jr."

She snorted. "Jag Jr." Then she sighed, placing a hand over her still flat belly.

"You happy?"

Ivy raised soft eyes to him. "Yeah," she whispered. "Now it's your turn."

"Don't know 'bout that."

"I do."

CHAPTER NINE

Three times in one fucking day he found himself standing in front of a fucking door banging on it to get the fuck in. He was tired of this bullshit.

No sleep. No food. No nothing.

He was at the end of his fucking rope.

She needed to answer her damn door and she needed to do it soon. If she didn't...

If she didn't, he was taking matters into his own hands. And if she called 5-0 because a biker was breaking into her house, then so fucking be it.

"Open this fuckin' door," he yelled.

She was home. She had to be. He had spotted her BMW in the garage when he peered into the little window of the garage door.

He had driven over three hours down the freezing cold Turnpike to get to her place. He had stewed every minute of those three fucking hours and would camp out on her front stoop until she answered.

He knew she lived here. Besides the car parked in the garage that probably still had his DNA on the backseat, her last name was on the fucking mailbox in this typical upper middle-class neighborhood.

Suddenly the door jerked open and Brooke stood in the doorway in a white bikini, the bright color contrasting against her taut tan skin. Her hair was gathered messily on the top of her head and she had an open robe hanging off her slim shoulders.

But that gaping robe didn't hide how hard her nipples were. He could see their outline poking through the thin fabric of the bikini top. A top that barely covered her fucking tits.

Jesus fuckin' Christ, did she wear that in public?

Who wore a bikini in December anyway, for fuck's sake?

She was also wearing a... scowl.

"What are you doing here, Dex? I left for a reason. I didn't expect you to follow."

Dex looked past her into what he could see inside her home. It was a modern one-story house with open floor plan and high ceilings that looked professionally decorated.

Which made sense.

While not huge, it still screamed that the person who lived there didn't have to live on a tight budget. Or in a room above a clubhouse.

"Fuckin' didn't answer my texts or calls."

She plugged her hands on her hips and arched a brow. "And since when do I answer to you?"

His nostrils flared as he sucked in oxygen, trying to tamp down his temper. "Done with me, right?"

"What?"

"Done with me. Had your fun. Done fuckin' me. Done with your little fact-findin' mission. Just done. Right?"

Brooke opened her mouth, a look crossed her face he didn't recognize, then she said, "Right. Time to move on. Move past all of this."

"Move on," Dex repeated, his heart thumping heavily in his chest.

"Yes, I'm sure you've done it plenty of times. Thought better of doing something after you did it? Decided it all wasn't worth the aggravation?"

"Something," he grumbled. "You mean *someone?*"

Wasn't worth the aggravation. Was she talking about him? Or finding her father?

"Not just you. Finding my father." She waved one hand around in the air. "I'm done with this whole thing. It isn't going to do me any good to chase down the man who raped my mother. It's not going to change anything. He's not going to be punished and my mother no longer has to suffer with the memory. Which I'm sure she did every day for most of her life when she looked at..." Brooke stopped, her face paled and she gripped the door. "Me."

His gut twisted. "Babe," he breathed. "Doubt she blamed you."

She shook her head. "Go away, Dex. It was fun, but now it's over."

As she shut the door, Dex shoved his boot in its path, keeping her from closing it all the way.

"Don't shut me the fuck out," he growled.

"Why? Why do you even give a damn? The few times I've been around your club members, they just looked at me like I'm a problem they'd like to have disappear. I get that you want to protect your own. I don't belong in that category. That asshole does. It's natural to want to protect him."

"We ain't protectin' shit. We don't tolerate that kind of bullshit. If we did, it'd make us no better than an outlaw club. We ain't that. Fuckin' spent decades to build this club up an' we're not about to destroy what we built 'cause of one motherfuckin' asshole like Pierce."

Brooke blinked and her mouth dropped open.

Ah fuck.

He squeezed his eyes shut and gritted his teeth at his blunder.

"You know who it is?" she screamed in his face as she slammed both her palms into his chest, knocking him back a step. "You know! How long have you known? You slept in my fucking bed the last few nights and didn't say a word. You kept that information from me!"

"No." He needed to get inside. He needed for her to calm

down and listen to him. Problem was, he had no clue what the fuck he was going to say. No clue how to make this all better. For her. For him. For the club. For the past.

Her chest heaved as she yelled, "Yes!"

When she reached for the door again, he chest bumped her. She stumbled backwards deeper into the foyer. He stepped inside quickly and slammed the door shut, pausing just long enough to turn the deadbolt.

"Get out of my house!"

"No."

"See? That's the problem with you bikers. You don't know when you're not wanted. You don't know what no means. You just do whatever the fuck you want."

"Babe," he started, his anger rising almost to the point of hers.

"Don't you fucking call me that. I'm not a babe. I'm a goddamn woman who should be treated with respect. I'm not an object. A thing."

"Fuck," he muttered and when he reached out for her she scrambled back.

"Don't touch me."

"Babe... Brooke. Just let me talk to you."

"Talk? You could have talked all those hours when you were in my bed. You chose not to. You knew who my father was and didn't say shit!" Her screamed words echoed off the high foyer ceiling.

He took a step toward her. "No! Only had a suspicion. That's fuckin' it."

She took a step away from him. "But now you know? How?"

Ah fuck. Now he had to admit he took her hair without her permission. Had a fucking DNA test done without asking her first.

He was fucked.

None of this was worth the headache. Why the fuck did he ride over three hours to just east of Harrisburg to have to listen to her flipping out?

What fucking man asked for this bullshit?

"Babe," he said softly, trying not to flip his shit.

"Babe!" she shouted and threw her arms up. "Babe!"

"Fuckin' motherfucker," he muttered, closing his eyes. After a second he opened them to see her hands back on her hips. Which emphasized every one of her curves, the ones he could see from her wearing the bikini, to the ones barely covered by the white silky robe.

She was waiting for his answer.

"Got a pool?"

Her eyes widened. "What?"

He took another step forward. "You got a pool?"

"Are you kidding me right now?"

"No. Don't like this screechin' shit. Came here for a reason. And it wasn't this."

"You came here to tell me who my father was, right?"

"Yeah."

"Well, you told me. Now you can... *get gone*."

He straightened his shoulders and pulled himself to his full height. He took one more step toward her. Now they were only almost five feet apart. Close enough he could smell her. His nostrils flared as they filled with whatever lotion or perfume she wore. The same scent he ended up wearing every time he'd rolled out of her bed. "Ain't leavin'."

"There's nothing for you here, Dex. Like I said earlier, it was fun. That's it. I don't owe you shit. You don't owe me shit. I now know the first name of the man whose... *cum* created me. My sperm donor. And that's all he was and that's all he'll ever be." She lifted a palm. "Oh, wait. He'll be an Angel, right? Until the day he dies. Down and dirty 'til dead, isn't that right? Isn't that your club's motto? The one you have tattooed on your back, along with the patches that shows your blind 'loyalty' to each other? No matter what?"

"No. You're wrong, b— Brooke." He shook his head. "So fuckin' wrong."

"Yeah? How's that? What are you going to do with this Pierce?" She practically spat out the former club president's name.

"We're gonna handle it," he said with a calmness he was struggling to hold onto.

She closed her eyes, then barked out a laugh. "Right."

"Give you my word," he said softly, taking one more step towards her.

She opened her eyes and pinned them on him. "What's your word worth, Dex?"

When he didn't answer quickly enough, she closed the gap between them. As she raised her hands to him once more, he snagged her wrists, holding them tight.

She tugged them hard but he didn't release them.

"You know what your word is worth? Nothing. You're just a dirty, uneducated, misogynistic biker. That's all you are. That's all you all are. Nothing more."

A muscle in his jaw popped and he yanked on her arms, but she planted her feet on the tile floor and leaned back.

"Yeah? Had no problem cryin' out my name when my dirty, dumb dick was in your fuckin' pussy."

Her face turned red as she tried to pull herself free once more. He was not letting her go. No fucking way.

But he should. He should just walk away. Especially now that he knew the truth about how she felt about him.

He was a dirty, uneducated, misogynistic biker. Good enough to fuck for a couple nights, but that was it.

"Let me go," she hissed, yanking her arms again.

He did and she stumbled backwards, but by the time she caught her balance, he was rushing forward, his shoulder down, which caught her right in the gut as he threw her over his shoulder and rushed through the house.

"What the fuck! Let me go! What the fuck are you doing?" she screamed in his ear, pounding on his back, ripping at his hair.

He ignored it all, even when his eyes began to water from his stinging scalp.

Fuck this shit.

He just kept walking until he found what he was looking for.

With one arm still wrapped around her to keep her from falling, he jerked the glass sliding door open, using his boot to kick it wider. Then he saw his second destination, though it wasn't what he quite expected. He hurried over to the edge and tossed her into the air.

All he saw was a pinwheel of arms and legs and a cloud of blonde hair before he saw and heard the loud splash.

He stood against the side, his hands on his hips as she sputtered to the surface of the hot tub. Her wet robe clung to her like a second skin, her nipples hard as diamonds under her suit. She gasped, pushed the hair out of her face, then turned to face him.

He leaned over to unbuckle his boots, kicked them off, and slipped his cut off his shoulders.

"Don't fuckin' move," he growled at her as she pushed herself to the corner, wiping water out of her eyes. "Stay there."

"Fuck you," she said, but her temper had definitely cooled off. Just the effect he was striving for.

He grinned, tossed his cut on a nearby lounge chair and finished stripping himself of his clothes. And before she could get out, he climbed into the hot, turbulent water.

"Fuck you, Dex," she said again, her voice now mellow, drops of waters beading on her thick eyelashes and her face as she moved to the other side of the hot tub toward the step.

He caught her, wrapped one hand around the back of her head and pulled her to him, taking her mouth. With a groan she shoved her tongue into his, trying to take control once again.

He shoved her against the tub wall, peeling the robe off her. He yanked at the bow at the back of her neck and the one at the center of her back, letting her bikini top float away.

Her fingers dug roughly into his wet hair and her other hand found his rock-hard dick, which was sandwiched between their stomachs. He thrust into her palm as she squeezed him tight.

He broke the kiss, breathing hard, pressing his forehead to hers. "Just a filthy, stupid fuckin' biker. Sure you want this dick inside you?"

"No."

He pulled back a little to glance down into her slate blue eyes. "No, you don't want it? Or no, you ain't sure?"

"No, I want it," she breathed.

"Sure? 'Cause I'm pretty fuckin' dirty. An' dumb, too."

She closed her eyes and her hand on his dick paused mid-stroke. "I'm sorry. I was wrong. I shouldn't have said those things."

"Don't take your fuckin' anger out on me. I didn't do shit."

"I know."

"Don't wanna do you wrong, babe. Swear it."

"So do me right," Brooke murmured into his ear, tracing the tip of her tongue around the outer shell.

His large hands grasped her waist and set her ass on the edge of the tub, the water sluicing from her body. She was glad she had a six-foot privacy fence around her yard and sunroom since she was sure what they were about to do would shock the neighbors otherwise.

Funny, she had missed him being in her bed last night. This biker who she'd called dirty and uneducated in her frustration.

He was neither of those things. However, she didn't know him that well. In fact, hardly at all. They hadn't had any deep conversations during or after their sex sessions. She hadn't wanted to get to know him better and he hadn't pushed it. He'd been satisfied to just lay next to her quietly in the darkness of the motel room.

But now, for some reason, she regretted wasting that time.

"Get your bottoms off an' spread your thighs," he growled.

He was giving her orders. One night apart and he'd forgotten who was in charge.

It wasn't him.

"You take my bottoms off," she ordered, staring down at him as he stood there naked in the center of the hot tub. His cock was clearly visible under the surface of the rolling water, bobbing up and down with stream from the jets. His wet body, covered in colorful tattoos, glistened. The gold rings that pierced his nipples reflected the sunlight shining through the glass panels of the sunroom.

They made her mouth water.

He wasn't gentle, not at all, when he jerked her bottoms over her ass and down her legs, tossing them to the floor behind her. She bit back a gasp when he dug his fingers into her thighs and shoved them part, giving him enough room to get his head between them, the stubble of his beard scraping the tender skin of her inner thighs. Giving him enough room to suck her clit into his mouth. His teeth scraped across her sensitive nub making her hips jump.

And then those ringed fingers—those long, long fingers—found her core, pressing deep, finding that spot that made her drop her head back and her mouth gape open as the air rushed from her lungs. Lifting her hips, she groaned when he was not gentle at all. Hell no, he wasn't. He was rough and demanding with his mouth, his tongue, his fingers.

But she needed to keep her wits about her. Remember who she was. Not let him roll over her, drown her.

He reached up and snagged her nipple, gripping it roughly and pulling it as hard as she'd done to him so many times in the last few days. He twisted and pulled, causing a shock of lightning to race through her. She gripped his head and shoved it deeper into her pussy. He tried to pull away but she held him fast.

"Make me come," she demanded.

The two fingers he had inside her curled and stroked, and she did her best to fight her climax. She wanted him to work for it.

She didn't want it to be easy; she wanted it to be worth it.

She wanted to see if he was willing to put in the effort to please her, not just himself.

Though, she had to admit, he hadn't been a selfish lover at all back at the motel. Not once. In fact, she'd been the one who'd been selfish by taking whatever she could get from him for the short amount of time she was getting it.

And he had never complained once. Anything she threw at him, he had accepted.

It couldn't be that simple. This Dex. This man who had forcefully picked her up and carried her out here, reminding her that she couldn't always be in control.

Even if she wanted to be.

Sometimes she had to let go. Allow someone else to lead.

But again, she wondered: why him, why now? This point in her life when everything had begun to crumble. Her neat, organized life had come crashing down around her when she lost her mother. When she discovered her mother's secret.

And now everything still whirled wildly.

It spun to the point she had to get out of Shadow Valley. To get away from him, his club, even maybe run from the truth.

But he followed her and she hadn't expected that. Not at all.

He had no reason to. They had no connection. Nothing to bind them.

Simply sex.

Maybe... Maybe not so simple...

Before she could protest, he flipped her onto her belly and yanked her hips back toward him. His cock slid in between her crease, over her tight hole, then he drew the thick crown between her slick folds.

He did it again. And once more. He was waiting for something, but said nothing. *Shit.* He wanted her to...

She closed her eyes and covered her mouth with her hand to keep from crying out. To keep from begging him to fuck her. She wouldn't beg.

He should be the one begging.

For her permission.

She should be holding out.

But it was so difficult to do with this man.

Why did she want him to take over? Why did she want him to be the one to be in charge?

This was so unlike her.

She didn't like it like that.

She didn't.

Did she?

"Please..." slipped from between her lips before she could bite it back.

He nipped along her back and shoulder blades, up her spine to the back of her neck. His tongue traced a path along the side of her throat. He shoved her heavy, wet hair out of the way and sucked her earlobe into his mouth.

"Want my dick? Ask for it."

She had already broken her own rule by saying "please" once, what would it hurt to say it again?

"Please," she moaned, but refused to say anything more.

"Please what?" he growled in her ear, continuing to tease her with his cock, one hand squeezing her breast firmly, twisting her aching nipple until a sharp sensation shot to her core.

He was going to make her do it. Make her beg.

She couldn't. *She couldn't.* Because if she did...

Did she finally meet her match in this Dex?

Was he the one?

The one who would tolerate her domineering ways? The one who could give as good as she gave?

Impossible.

No.

Not him.

Not this biker. This man from a whole different world. One she wanted nothing to do with. She was only drawn to it for a specific reason for a short time.

She didn't expect to get mired down in it.

A simple trip to find her real father had turned and twisted into something else.

Something she least expected.

She tipped her hips higher. "Please..."

"Fuckin' tell me."

"...take me."

With one hard thrust he was deep inside her, his face buried in her neck, his teeth in her flesh. She wanted him to bite harder, like she did with him. She wanted him to give her no mercy.

She wanted to forget. And maybe he could make her do that.

But she wouldn't ask him for anything. Nothing at all.

However, she didn't have to.

He just knew.

He knew what she needed. So desperately craved.

With his mouth wide, his bite deepened, his tongue circled her damp skin, licking, flicking as he held her down and took her roughly. Air emptied from her lungs with each pounding thrust. The sunroom filled with the noise of their wet skin slapping together, his grunts, her groans as well as water splashing and spilling over the edge.

It wasn't enough. She need more from him. But she didn't know if he had it in him. This Dex.

Then his wet palm met her ass cheek with a sharp sting, causing her to gasp and jerk forward, though she had nowhere to go. She was pinned between the edge of the hot tub and his large body as he relentlessly slammed her harder with each thrust until he could go no deeper.

Her hips would hold bruises from the ferocity of his pounding her into the hard edge of the tub, her ass would bear a red mark from his hand, her neck would show indentations from his teeth, but it still wasn't enough.

He smacked her again, but this time she was ready, and the little air she had sucked in quickly hissed back out.

"Harder," she demanded through gritted teeth.

His breath beat hotly against her neck like a train trying to pick up speed.

Another stinging smack to her ass and another cry escaped her, then he released the breast he had a death grip on and curled his fingers around the front of her neck instead.

"Yes," she encouraged him. "*Yes.*"

The unexpected pressure squeezing her throat sent a shudder

through her and when he smacked her even harder this time, she came with an intensity she never experienced before. Her climax exploded through her, shattering her into a million pieces. She grabbed for them but couldn't catch them. Those pieces were so many, so far apart, she'd never find them all.

She'd never be put back together the same again.

He released the bite on her neck, and with a loud grunt, pushed deep and spilled himself inside her. The throbbing root of his cock made her twitch against her will, but she was too weak, too spent to even control that.

She collapsed like a rag doll over the side of the hot tub, his weight along her back, his chest heaving against her, and every once in a while, his hips would jerk just enough for her to know that he was still orgasming, even if his body had nothing left to give.

Then he stilled, his forehead pressed between her shoulder blades. As he sucked in air, his heart thumped so strongly she could feel it along her back.

She didn't demand that he move, remove his weight from her, because she didn't want him to.

She wanted him to remain inside her. Connected. She needed that heavy weight to remind her of what they'd just done. What just happened.

Though she had no clue what the fuck it all meant. Or where things would go from here.

CHAPTER TEN

Brooke padded barefoot across her bedroom, keeping a careful eye on the two mugs of coffee she carried. She didn't need to spill them on her white carpet. When she got to the end of the bed, she glanced up and what she saw drew a smile to her face.

Dex had a wrist handcuffed to each upper corner of the headboard. His legs were spread wide and thick black leather cuffs were buckled around each ankle with a strap connected under the bed to make sure he couldn't close his legs.

His nipples were swollen and red, his lips as well. His cock now lay flaccid along his hip.

They'd had a good night. An active night. And this morning was even better.

Surprisingly, he hadn't said no to any of her demands and he also had shown no fear to any of her suggestions. Things he'd never tried before.

Once again, she was pleased he was willing.

His eyes were dark as they roamed down her naked body. "Coulda let me go before makin' coffee."

"Could have," she said, then moved around the bed to place the mugs on the nightstand. "But I decided I like you like that."

"You decided," he repeated in a mutter.

She had broken out most of her toys last night because she had wanted to push his boundaries. No matter what she did, he'd refused to even murmur the safe word she assigned him. Not once.

Which worried her a little because for a moment she had forgotten herself and found it a challenge to see just how far she could go and how much he'd resist saying it.

But she finally remembered herself and backed off since she didn't want to ruin the experience for him.

Or her.

"Gonna help me drink my coffee or you gonna lemme go?"

With a sigh, she grabbed the cuff key from the dresser, but before releasing his wrists, she unbuckled the ankle cuffs and let them fall to the floor. Then she stared at him for a few moments, admiring his body, beautiful in its own way with the colorful tattoos, the dark scruff on his face and his intelligent brown eyes.

She had been so wrong. He was not a dumb biker. Maybe he didn't have a college degree. And he certainly wasn't a doctor, lawyer or financial wizard, but he wasn't stupid.

His speech habits left something to be desired, but she considered it similar to an accent, something that you picked up from your environment and the people who surrounded you. Though the rest of his "brothers" spoke the same way, she found it funny, for the most part, that the club women didn't. The men probably just didn't give a shit.

She didn't think Dex gave a rat's ass what anyone thought of him. Of how he looked, how he acted, or how he talked.

Even her.

He hadn't tried to impress her once.

No. She saw exactly who he was. He certainly didn't hide it.

There was nothing fake about him.

So many men in her past had done their best to impress her. And for what? To try to land in her bed? To have a relationship?

But after a while the gold plating would become worn and she'd see the real men beneath their shiny exteriors.

Eventually, they would look past her appearance and her

success to see her as she really was, as well. She was not a "yes" woman when it came to men. She didn't need to appease any of them. She didn't need their approval.

And sometimes that didn't sit well with them.

Sometimes? Hell, almost every time.

She was sure it would be the same with this one, too.

With some reluctance and disappointment, she unlocked the cuffs and pulled them from his wrists, tucking them away in a drawer. Then she moved back to the coffee and held out a steaming mug as he rubbed at his wrists.

He took the coffee from her and she grabbed the remaining mug to take a careful sip. After settling on the edge of the bed, she asked, "Did you mind them?"

"The cuffs?"

"Yes."

"No, long as it ain't the pigs slappin' them on me, I'm good."

She smiled, took another sip and studied him from over the lip of the mug. "You wore them well."

He grunted and swallowed a mouthful of coffee. He glanced down into his mug, surprise on his face. "Good shit."

"Yes, it is."

"Crow makes the coffee at church every mornin', thank fuck. Otherwise, it's toxic sludge."

She wiggled farther onto the bed, enough to sit cross-legged, facing him as he relaxed against the headboard. "How long have you lived above the club?"

"Since a prospect at eighteen."

That news surprised her. "You had to be a prospect?"

"Yeah," he grunted.

"Even though you were born, like you say, into the club?"

"Yeah. Everybody's gotta do their time."

"And your mother, Ace's sister, was born into the club as well." She was trying to picture this family tree—now twisted as he said—in her head.

"Yeah."

"What does Dex stand for?"

He lifted his dark eyes from his coffee. "Whataya mean?"

"You all have some sort of biker nickname, right? Dex has got to be short for something."

He snorted, then took another sip of the hot coffee. "Yeah. It's short for somethin'."

"What?"

His eyebrows furrowed and he placed his mug carefully on the nightstand. "Dexter."

"But it's a nickname, right? One they gave when you were a prospect? Like Rooster, Jester and Moose? Why Dexter? Did you used to wear some nerdy glasses or something? Is that why they gave you that name?"

He rubbed a hand over his forehead and stared at her. "My mom named me that."

Whoops.

"Went through some sorta fuckin' phase where she loved punk rock an' named me after Dexter Holland."

"Who's that?"

"Some singer in a band. The Offspring or some shit like that."

"Oh."

"Thought it was cool." Though, it was clear he didn't think it was cool by the expression on his face.

"Oh."

"She was wrong."

Her lips twitched and she hid it by taking another sip of coffee. "It's a good name."

"The fuck it is."

She lifted a hand. "But you could have changed it to some cool biker name. Like Diesel or Hawk."

"Those are their real names."

"Oh." She frowned. Who named their kid after fuel? She thought for a moment. "Crash and Rig?"

"Yeah, those are nicknames."

"See? Something like that."

"Right."

"Why didn't you?"

"'Cause prospects get shit names on purpose. An' since Dexter is a shit name, the brothers thought it'd be funny to make me keep it. That's why."

"But you could've changed it once you were patched in?"

He lifted a shoulder. "Guess so. But at that point it didn't fuckin' matter."

She leaned over and placed her mug next to his. "Well, I like it. I may have to start calling you Dexter. Like Dexter Morgan. He was cool."

"He was a serial killer."

She pursed her lips. "True." She lifted a finger. "But smart."

He snorted. "What'd be smart is if you fuckin' fed me so I got energy to fuck you good later."

"You think I cook?"

"Eggs are easy. Get cookin', woman."

She raised her brows. "You know I have a ball-gag, right? You saw it in my toy box last night?"

He grunted and grinned. "Can't eat your pussy with one of those in my mouth."

That aforementioned pussy clenched hard when Brooke pictured his head jammed between her thighs. "Hmm. Good point."

Dex rubbed his sore jaw and wiggled it. He wasn't doing that ball-gag shit again. He wasn't sure he had limits until last night when he discovered that he did.

He rolled over onto his side and studied the woman sleeping next to him. He traced a finger down the indentation of her spine, then back up, rubbing her long, soft hair between his fingers.

Fuck him. Two nights at her house. Two nights in her big bed. Two nights of her blowing his fucking mind.

She still had a mark on her neck from where he bit her hard the other day and he circled it gently with the tip of his finger.

His phone vibrated on the nightstand and he sighed, flipped to his back, then reluctantly reached for his cell.

He hit the power button and, once it lit up, he scrolled through the newest messages. He'd ignored most of them the past couple days and nights, but these he couldn't.

Diesel.

The new father didn't sound happy with Dex's disappearing act.

Need 2 deal with this shit.

Need ur ass back here.

Supposed 2 give her news not ur dick.

Get what we need n get gone.

"Fuck," he whispered. He had completely forgotten about the diary. If they were going to crucify Pierce, then they needed proof of what he did. It didn't have to be solid, but it had to be something.

Stripping the man of his colors was serious.

He texted the club's enforcer back. *U tell Kels?*

No. Need facts first.

Dex nodded to himself. He still couldn't believe that Pierce had not only fathered Dex's cousin, but the woman currently lying naked next to him.

He sent one last text: *Gettn diary n headn home.*

2day came the one-word order. He should ask D about the baby, but he knew his cousin wouldn't want to chit-chat. Even about his own kid.

He rolled onto his back once more and realized Brooke was not only awake, but watching him.

"Bad news?"

"No. Gotta get back soon." He watched her carefully to see if she'd show any disappointment in his announcement.

Nope. Apparently, he was the only one feeling disappointed.

"Right. I need to get back to work, too. I'm not getting much done by never putting on clothes and only getting out of bed long enough to shower and eat."

She leaned over and kissed his shoulder. Before she could move away, he curled his fingers around the back of her head and pressed her cheek to him, holding her close.

"Babe..." he murmured, unsure on what would happen once he left.

Would she just go on about her business and forget all about him?

He wanted to rub away the ache in his chest. A feeling he didn't recognize.

She placed a hand on his gut and snuggled closer with a sigh. Her skin was smooth and warm against him, her hair soft as it brushed against his cheek and chest.

He buried his nose into her hair and inhaled. He didn't think he'd ever forget that scent. It would always remind him of her. And their short time together.

One thing was for sure, he'd never look at sex the same again. Fuck no. She had opened his eyes to shit he never, ever thought he'd like.

But the problem was, he couldn't see himself doing it with anyone else.

He closed his eyes and blew out a breath at the thought of climbing on his sled and heading west once again. He needed to get home.

Because Harrisburg wasn't it.

He also needed to get that diary first. Needed to read what Brooke read. See the shit for himself.

Then the Committee needed to take action. Either move on from these accusations because Brooke interpreted something in her mother's words that just might not be true. Or they needed to remove the cancer from their club.

But one thing was for sure, he doubted Brooke was simply going to hand over her late mother's diary. And he had no fucking clue where it was. He doubted he could just ask and she'd willingly give it to him to take back to Shadow Valley.

However, she might let him read it since they had discussed that prior.

He combed his fingers through her hair. "The other day, you asked what my word's worth. Tellin' you now, my word to you is worth everythin'. Know we've been avoidin' the discussion about Pierce an' we need to talk about it before I leave. I promise we're gonna handle it... him."

"I hope you do."

"Plan on it. Just gotta trust me. Trust us to do the right thing." He hesitated. "Need you to do somethin' for me, though."

She turned her blue eyes up to him and his breath caught. He steeled himself against the strange feeling that went through him. The one he couldn't identify. Or maybe one he didn't want to.

"What's that?" she asked softly.

"Need to see your mom's diary."

She didn't say anything for the longest time, instead her gaze shifted to somewhere else in the room.

After a while, he said, "Need to read the part that's important. Not the whole thing."

"You don't believe me?"

"Babe, I believe you. Just need to be able to say what you read's the same shit I read. He ain't gonna be able to face his accuser, so just wanna be sure."

"What will you do with him if I show you her diary and you agree what I read really happened?"

She wasn't going to like his answer, but it needed to be said. "Babe, that's club business."

She lifted her head. "Dex, it's my business, too. If what my mother indicated is true..." She shook her head. "I'm the result of his actions. His actions which changed my mother's life. Which brought me into the world. His blood runs through my veins. And I know your club is all about loyalty and blood."

"It is."

"So maybe I should get a chance to face him. Make him look me in the eye and tell me the truth."

"Ain't gonna tell you the truth. Ain't gonna admit shit."

"Are you sure about that?"

No, he wasn't sure. And if it was him, Dex would want to face his mother's rapist, too. But the woman was wicked with a gun and he wouldn't put it past her to plug him right between the fucking eyes.

No matter what, he felt the need to protect Brooke and he couldn't tell her that. Fuck no. That would get her madder than a pissed-off hellcat.

"Get it. Gotta read it."

She cocked an eyebrow. "Is that an order?"

"Nope. A please an' thank you was on the beginnin' an' end of that question."

"There sure wasn't and that wasn't a question."

"Heard it. Need your ears cleaned out."

Brooke snorted. "Remember that ball-gag you had in your mouth last night?"

Dex tipped his eyes down to her, put his fingers against his jaw and wiggled it again. Yep, it was still achy. "Fuck yeah."

"Didn't like it, did you?"

"Fuckin' loved it."

She grinned and tweaked his nipple. "Liar."

With a sigh, she pushed away from him and rolled out of bed. He watched her the whole time because... hell, she was naked.

And her body was fucking hot.

And so was her pussy. And those tits.

Fuck.

How the hell was he rolling out of there today?

He lifted his head and groaned when she bent over to dig something out of a bottom dresser drawer, her ass and everything else pointing toward the bed.

His hand automatically went to his dick. But when she

straightened and turned he released it quickly, giving her an innocent smile.

"Were you touching yourself?"

"Nope."

She shook her head and threw whatever she had in her hand onto the mattress. He stared at the small book with the hard cover. It was clear what it was since "Diary" was embossed in gold lettering across the front.

Well, damn.

She moved around the bed and grabbed the robe hanging from the back of her bathroom door, sliding it over her shoulders and tugging her hair out from underneath it.

Heading toward the bedroom door, she tossed over her shoulder, "I'm going to make breakfast."

"Don't wanna be here when I read it?"

She shook her head, but didn't look at him. "I can't. Not again. Just put it back in the drawer when you're finished... please."

"Yeah," he grunted, waiting until she left before letting his fingers slide over the cover. As he heard Brooke head down the hallway, he picked up the diary and flipped through it.

He only wanted to read the part that pertained to Pierce, and he had no idea where in the diary it was.

As he flipped through, he realized the diary was empty. He closed the cover and began again, slower this time.

Cursive handwriting filled the first page, both front and back, the same for the second, the third, then the fourth... But that was it.

Four pages.

In the whole fucking diary.

He closed his eyes and sucked in a deep breath, paged back to the beginning and began to read...

CHAPTER ELEVEN

"Fuck," Dex muttered. He rubbed his hands over his face and wanted to scream. Instead, he rolled out of bed and went to retrieve the diary he'd thrown across the room.

Four fucking pages.

Four.

The fucker needed to die. Stripping the colors off his back wasn't nearly good enough.

At first glance, the words could have been interpreted as Brooke's mother had an affair. She blamed herself time and time again within those four pages.

But when you read between the lines, everything her mother wrote had a deeper meaning. And he read it twice to make sure he wasn't mistaken.

He wasn't.

Even though he was not mentioned by name, the DNA proved there was no fucking way it was anyone but Pierce. Hell, maybe her mother didn't even know his name.

Pierce was Brooke's father. That was proven.

And Pierce was Brooke's mother's rapist.

That was proven, also, by the last line on the fourth page, which was added months after the original entry.

My sweet, innocent baby girl should never be burdened by the actions of her father.

Picking up the diary, Dex stared at it. There were things mentioned in her passage that he recognized and Brooke wouldn't. And there were things mentioned, like a party, that Ace or Grizz might remember. Maybe if one of them read it...

Fuck, he was sure she wouldn't let him take the diary. But he needed the evidence so the membership could vote on removing Pierce from the DAMC.

Quickly. Permanently.

Those damning pages, along with the DNA results, were more than enough evidence. But he needed those pages. He glanced toward the open bedroom door and listened carefully to make sure Brooke was still busy in the kitchen.

He could hear her clanking something around. A pot, a pan, a dish.

He dropped his gaze to the diary and blew out a breath.

"Fuuuuuuuuck," he groaned. He opened the diary and ripped out the four pages. He quickly grabbed his cut which was tossed over the chair, folded the pages up and slipped them into a slit cut into the lining. Then he hurried back over to the dresser, pulled open the drawer and shoved the diary back under some folded clothes.

His heart was thumping ferociously. If... fuck, *when* she found out he stole those pages, she might never forgive him.

But it needed to be done.

His loyalty laid with the club first. Not Brooke.

With another glance toward the door, he reminded himself once again: the club came first, not Brooke...

A pounding came from what sounded like the front door. So loud it could be easily heard from where he was at the back of the house.

What the fuck? Had Diesel come looking for him?

Dex searched the floor for his jeans and found them in a pile with the rest of his clothes. Jerking them out from underneath his boots, he tugged them on as he heard Brooke mumbling to herself.

"You expectin' someone?" Dex yelled out.

"No. You?"

"Fuck no," Dex mumbled to himself, checking his back pocket for his knife. He jerked his head up when he heard her voice echo off the high ceiling in the foyer.

"Don't answer the door 'til I get there!" he shouted.

"Why? I—"

The woman never fucking listens...

The door slammed shut and his heart skipped a beat when he heard her call out to him.

"Dex?"

The obvious shake in her voice wasn't normal. This woman wasn't afraid of shit. He froze and the blood rushed through him as he looked around the room. He had no idea where she kept her Sig. He should've asked.

Fuck.

He held his breath for a second, listening.

But he heard nothing. In fact, it was way too quiet.

"Dex," she said again. Definitely not normal, but more controlled this time.

Taking a deep breath, he cautiously checked the hallway, which was clear, and rushed down it. As he turned the corner to head toward the front of the house, the business end of a handgun was jammed into his temple.

A deep male voice said, "Nice an' slow, fucker. Don't be reachin' for shit."

Fuckin' motherfucker.

As slow as he could, he pivoted his head just enough to see who held the gun.

"Hands to the back of your fuckin' head."

When he didn't move fast enough, the Shadow Warrior jammed the gun into his temple again. "Ain't no joke, motherfucker. Hands to the back of your head. Now."

He slowly raised his hands and did what he was instructed.

"Interlace your fuckin' fingers. Sure you know the drill," the gruff voice demanded.

Again, he did what he was told because he needed time to think, he needed a plan to get Brooke and him out of this fucking mess. And he needed to know if Brooke was okay first.

It would also help to know how many of these asshole Warriors were in her house. He didn't want to do anything stupid that would get them more in a jam or get Brooke killed.

He had to keep his patience and his temper, even though he wanted to squeeze the shit out of this Warrior's throat.

"Move."

"Need to see my woman," Dex said, trying to sound more confident than he was. Depending on how many Warriors were in the house, they may be screwed six ways to Sunday.

"Oh, you're gonna see her. Move!"

The Warrior jammed the gun deeper into his temple. As soon as Dex stepped out of the hallway into the living room, his eyes landed on Brooke.

He stopped short and the Warrior yelled at him, "Keep movin'!"

He ground his teeth and took a few steps closer toward another Warrior who held Brooke tightly against him. The biker had an arm wrapped tightly around her throat and another trapping her arms to her side in a bear hug. Her back was pinned to his chest.

But the most shocking thing of all was that Brooke's eyes weren't wide with fear. Fuck no, they weren't.

They were narrowed.

She. Was. Fucking. Pissed.

Dex had a feeling the Warriors would soon be wearing ball-gags, nipple clamps, cock cages and have a huge butt plug shoved up their asses, while she got out a bull-whip and shredded the skin on their back.

His balls shriveled a little at that image.

The Warrior shoved him forward, causing Dex to stumble and fall to his knees on her thick carpet.

"Keep your fuckin' hands behind your head, keep your fuckin' fingers interlaced an' cross your ankles."

Dex peered up at him. "Sure you ain't an undercover pig?"

The Warrior, who had salt and pepper stringy hair and a long bushy beard, answered, "Fuck no."

"Sure sound like it." He eyeballed the Warrior who held Brooke in front of him like a body shield and asked him, "Sure he ain't undercover?"

The Warrior standing over him jabbed him with the gun. "Shut the fuck up. Would put a bullet in your fuckin' brain right now if I didn't need you alive."

Well, thank fuck for that. He preferred to remain alive, too. "For what?"

"Wanna have you watch."

Oh fuck.

His eyes met Brooke's. She was glaring at the Warrior holding the gun on Dex. Just out and outright glaring at him as if she'd like to rip the windpipe right out of his throat.

His woman was a fucking badass.

However, when she opened her mouth, he realized she was a reckless one. "What are you going to do? Rape me? Is that going to make you feel like a man?"

The Warrior holding her grumbled, "Shut up, bitch."

"You need to have him," Brooke jerked her chin toward the Warrior standing next to Dex, "watch while you do it? You need to have other men watching you to get it up?"

"Shut the fuck up, bitch!"

She addressed the one holding Dex at gunpoint next. "Do you like to watch other men getting it on, biker boy?"

Her riling up the Warriors and pushing them like that was not going to help their situation.

The long-haired, greasy biker holding Brooke's neck squeezed his arm tighter. He appeared strung out on meth, which could make things so much worse. "Don't fuckin' talk to my prez like that."

Dex kind of agreed with that suggestion, however, he wasn't going to be the one to make it to Brooke.

Dex's gaze slid to the Warrior who held the gun on him. His patch *did* say "president."

Shit.

Was D's crew getting rid of so many Warriors, making their numbers low enough, that the president of their club was getting his own hands dirty?

"How the fuck d'you know I was here?" He'd moved his sled into her garage not long after he'd arrived. Not only because it was December but because he knew some of those asshole nomads hung around Harrisburg. Where Brooke lived wasn't that far from where they had snagged Slade. So, his sled couldn't have tipped them off.

"Don't know what you did to piss off your former prez but he's gotta hard-on for you."

Dex went solid at the MC president's words. "Whataya mean?"

"Musta done somethin' to piss him off. Why else would he give your ass up like this? An' your ol' lady's."

Dex's eyes met Brooke's again. She had no idea that her father and the former DAMC president were one and the same.

If she was mad now...

But what kind of bullshit was that? Why the fuck would Pierce give the rival MC a head's up on where he was?

Did he get wind about Brooke? Was he trying to prevent the truth from coming out?

Fuck. Pierce could take out Dex and Brooke but keep his hands clean by using the Warriors. It couldn't get easier than that.

If those fuckwads killed him and Brooke, the club wouldn't have any idea Pierce was behind it. They'd assume it was just the fucking Warriors being their typical dick selves.

They were more screwed than he originally thought.

"So here's the thing, *Dexter*. Gonna take turns havin' a lil fun with your snatch there while you watch. She's hot as fuck, 'specially in that robe she's wearin' an' nothin' else. Ain't that right, Crank?"

Crank. That was fitting for a fucking meth head.

Crank smiled and dropped the arm he had around Brooke's throat and shoved his hand inside her robe, grabbing her tit and shaking it.

Oh fuck. Even from where Dex knelt, he couldn't miss a fire light in her eyes and her nostrils flare.

She did not scream, she did not cry or shake, she did nothing but stand there and let it happen.

Dex could see the fury bubbling under the surface. Like a volcano ready to blow.

"Yeah, that's right," Crank agreed with his president.

Dex needed to do something. Kneeling on the living room floor wasn't doing shit to get them out of this. And, *fuck*, it certainly wasn't helping Brooke with her situation.

Her robe now gaped open, and both of her tits were exposed.

A muscle twitched in his jaw and he swore a vein popped out along his temple as the Warrior continued to manhandle her with his dirty fucking hands.

No doubt about it, these fuckers were going to die.

"For as long as you touch her, that's how long you're gonna suffer before you die, motherfucker," Dex growled.

"Goddamn, her tits are fuckin' nice," Crank said, chuckling as he pinched Brooke's nipple hard.

The only reaction Brooke showed was a slight grimace.

Dex was proud of how brave she was being.

"Gonna have to switch places, Crank. You ain't gettin' her first."

Crank frowned, apparently unhappy at the thought of coming in second place. "Wanna eat her snatch first, Sandman, bet it's trimmed up real nice an' pretty. Lemme see..."

When he jerked at the tie that held Brooke's robe loosely together, Brooke suddenly moved and it was so quick Dex froze, unsure of what the fuck she was doing.

With precise moves, Brooke kicked Crank in the shin, causing him to scream, twisted in the man's arms, kneed him in the nads, and as he fell to the ground, clutching his crushed jewels, she elbowed him in the back of the head, leaned over his crumpled body and yanked something out from under the back of his cut.

Spinning in place, she raised a gun and Dex dropped flat to the floor as she took her shot.

One. Two.

Blood splattered over Dex and the Warrior's gun dropped to the floor. Dex dove for it as Sandman collapsed next to him with a groan, gripping his right shoulder. Sliding the gun under his body out of Sandman's reach, Dex twisted on the floor until he could sit up. He grabbed the gun and pointed it at the man who was now in a pile on the ground, cursing, with blood flowing heavily from both shoulders.

Fuck, she was a good shot.

"Shoulda killed the fucker," he yelled at her, not taking his eyes off the downed Warrior.

"Really? You're going to tell me what I should've done? What the fuck did you do?"

Good point.

He slowly got to his feet, the gun still drawn on the Warrior's prez. "Don't you fuckin' move, ain't a good shot like her. Might miss an' just maim your ass."

"Don't kill him," Brooke said.

"He deserves to fuckin' die, babe."

"I agree. But do you want to go to prison for it?"

Fuck no, he didn't. "Ain't callin' the pigs."

"Oh, we're calling the cops. These fuckers broke into my house, wanted to cause me bodily harm. Wanted to do the same to you. This was self-defense, plain and simple. And as long as our hands are clean, we'll be fine."

"Says you. Ain't callin' the pigs." Plus, he had some questions to ask these fuckers before he decided what was going to be done.

Then Brooke was there, her robe gaping open and the tie gone. He made sure Sandman wasn't moving and then glanced over at Crank. Brooke had him trussed up with her robe tie.

Fuckin' goddamn. If they just hadn't been in a life-threatening situation, he'd be sporting a hard-on. This woman had balls on her bigger than most bikers.

Brooke kicked at Sandman with her bare foot. "He's bleeding on my carpet."

"Right." He eyeballed her. "Since this one's conscious, how 'bout gettin' some clothes on."

Brooke glanced down at herself. "Once he's secure."

Dex cocked a brow at her. "Whataya got to secure him?"

She smiled and lifted a finger. When she rushed back to her bedroom, he knew exactly what she was getting.

And when she came back out, she had pulled on a long T-shirt and panties, but her long legs were still exposed. *Jesus.*

"Really? Couldn't fuckin' put on sweat pants or somethin'?"

She ignored him and within minutes had Sandman cuffed behind his back, ignoring his bitching about his wounds. She had some blue nylon rope and tied his legs up once Dex flipped him onto his belly, then they went over and secured an unconscious Crank the same way.

"You don't want to call the cops, but now what do we do with them? We can't just let them walk away."

"Babe, ain't just walkin' away. Promise you that."

Dex moved over to the front picture window, moved the curtain aside and peered out. Two sleds. So, no one else was with them.

"You didn't hear their bikes pull up?"

Brooke shrugged. "I heard something but I thought it was a loud truck driving by."

"Gonna make a call. Might take a while to get this all cleaned up. But once I do, you're gonna have to keep an eye on 'em while I hide their bikes in the garage. Yeah?"

"Who are you calling?"

"D."

CHAPTER TWELVE

Brooke gripped the sink and dropped her head, blowing out a breath. After a moment she straightened, wiped her hand over the steamed-up mirror and took a good look at herself.

What the fuck happened to her life?

Her mother's cancer sparked a chain of events that there was no going back from. The suffering her mother endured had been horrible. One Brooke wouldn't wish on anyone. Then her death ripped Brooke's heart out and left nothing but a black, gaping hole behind.

What was worse, she was left to deal with her mother's estate alone. Her brother and sister both ended up living in California after college and while they had flown in for her mother's funeral, they both couldn't wait to head back. Again, leaving Brooke to deal with the aftermath on her own.

When she came across the stuff in the attic... Her life spiraled even more. Everything she thought her life was... wasn't.

To find out that the man who sired her had taken her mother without her consent. And her mother could have had an abortion and put the whole thing behind her as best as she could. But she didn't.

Instead, she had Brooke, loved her like she'd always been

wanted. Cherished her like her other children. Brooke never was treated any differently.

Even though the blood of a monster ran through her veins.

A monster.

Maybe that's why as she stood in the bathroom naked, her hair dripping wet, her skin freshly scrubbed, she felt absolutely nothing when it came to shooting that Warrior.

Nothing.

She really had wanted to kill him and she could have.

Luckily, common sense had stepped in. That and the fact that the Warrior held a gun to Dex's head. She needed the outlaw biker to drop the gun, not accidentally pull the trigger and kill Dex.

She closed her eyes as the man himself pushed open the bathroom door without even knocking.

Figures.

"You okay? Been in here a long time."

"I'm fine."

He pushed the door wide open allowing the damp heat to escape the room as he stepped inside. He still wore his jeans with blood stains because he had no other clothes with him. But he now had a long-sleeved thermal covering his numerous tattoos.

"Should you be leaving them alone?"

"Babe, you got 'em trussed up good. They ain't goin' anywhere. Ain't worried 'bout them, worried 'bout you."

He grabbed a towel off the rack and, moving behind her to wrap her in it, covered up her nakedness. Pulling her back against him, he stared into the mirror at the two of them together.

What she saw in that mirror was proof her life would never be the same again.

She closed her eyes for a second, then turned in his arms to look up into his dark eyes. "Dex."

"Yeah?"

"The former DAMC president that Sandman mentioned... That's Pierce, isn't it?'

Dex didn't say anything for a long moment. He just let it hang between them, so in the end he didn't have to answer.

She knew.

"Has he ever been in bed with that club before?"

"Dunno, babe. Gonna see if I can get more info from them before D arrives. If not before, then D can help get some info outta 'em."

"Why? Why would he want to take you out? Have me..." She let that thought drift off. Her rapist father sent bikers to rape his own daughter.

Whether that was his intent or not, it didn't matter. That's what would've happened if she hadn't gotten them out of that situation. Either way, Pierce sent a rival MC to deal with her and Dex.

"Thinkin' he found out 'bout you somehow. The accusations and why I headed out here. Not sure. Maybe tryin' to quiet you. Keep us from strippin' his colors. Dunno what's all in his fucked-up head."

"His blood runs through my veins."

Dex ignored her statement, instead saying, "Proud of you, babe. Most women woulda been wailin', screamin', cryin'. Not you. You kept your shit tight. Handled your business."

"Maybe it's because his blood does run through me." Maybe she was more like him than she'd like to admit. Maybe it was where her deep-seated need for control came from. She never knew why she was like that. Never knew where it came from since neither her mother or her father were like that.

Dex shook his head. "No. If he sicced the Warriors on us, got 'em to do his dirty work, then he ain't nothin' but a fuckin' coward. An' you're no fuckin' coward."

"But maybe he's just cold. Maybe I am, too. I don't feel anything."

Dex's body went solid against hers. "Whataya mean?"

"Shooting Sandman should upset me. It doesn't. I'd do it again in a second."

Smiling, Dex swept her damp hair off one shoulder. He pressed his lips to the side of her neck and kissed her. "That shit's sexy as all fuck."

She arched a brow at him. "Shooting a man is sexy?"

"You didn't see yourself. I swear you turned into some sort of chick like in the Terminator movies."

"Sarah Connor?"

"Yeah, babe. That was fuckin' hot."

The corners of her lips twitched. "You couldn't pick anyone more current?"

"Fuck no. She was badass." He pressed a kiss on her forehead. "Like you." He sighed. "Too bad we gotta wait for D to show up. Otherwise, I'd be showing you how much that turned me the fuck on."

He didn't need to show her. She felt it pushing against her belly. "There's something wrong with you."

"Yeah. Apparently, I like fucking kickass, dominant women."

"You just found that out?"

"Figured that out when you walked into a pawn shop in Shadow Valley."

"You didn't know what I was like then."

"All that mattered was that you were fingerin' that marble dick. Was a fuckin' goner after that."

Brooke tried to bite back the laugh that threatened to escape but she gave up and let it out.

Dex smiled down at her. "See, you ain't cold. Passionate. You like what you like."

Brooke cupped his cheek, rubbing her thumb over the beard on his face that was getting thicker by the day. "I like it when you let me tie you up and do naughty things to you."

Dex dropped his head until his lips were just above hers. She inhaled in his warm breath between her parted lips and he did the same. "I like it, too."

"We got two tied up bikers in my house, one bleeding like a stuck pig and you're hard."

"Yeah."

Yeah.

"Think we should stop his bleeding?"

"Fuck no. In the end, it won't matter if he bleeds out or not."

"So, he's going to die?"

She watched his face, but he kept it a blank mask. "D's gonna get it handled."

"Like the Pierce issue?"

"Promised you that we'd get him handled, too."

"I have a feeling you'll be handling him the same way."

"If those Warriors are tellin' the truth about Pierce tippin' 'em off to where we were? Fuck yeah."

"Dex..."

"Ain't talkin' 'bout that now."

Brooke arched a brow at him. "Oh yeah?"

He smiled. "Trust me on this." He closed the gap and gave her a kiss. Her brain told her she should keep it short. They had two dangerous men in the house, but she let herself melt against him, encouraging him to deepen it. His tongue tangled with hers and his arms tightened around her.

Surprisingly, she let him be in charge.

At least for those few stolen moments in the bathroom, where the rest of the world remained outside the door.

Brooke eyeballed the three large men who stepped inside. Suddenly, her house seemed so much smaller.

But, *holy hell*, they were worth looking at.

However, the one had a noticeable scar that ran diagonally down his face from above his temple across his nose. It stopped at the one side of his mouth, making it curl up at the corner just enough so he looked sinister.

The other two... well... Brooke noticed Dex frowning at her as he stood next to the men who definitely outsized him muscle-wise.

"Where's D?" he asked the one with the scar.

"He isn't leaving the baby," the man answered as he let his gaze run over Brooke. He didn't seem interested; it was more of an assessment. Maybe to see if she was a threat to him and his men. "Sent us instead."

Brooke stepped forward and held out her hand to the man who appeared to be in charge. "Brooke."

The man didn't hesitate and, with a firm grip, clasped her hand and shook it. "Mercy."

"Mercy?"

He didn't react to her question, instead clapping the man next to him on the shoulder. "This is Ryder." He pointed to the man on the other side of Ryder. "That's Brick."

"Interesting names," Brooke murmured, giving Dex a look that said, *See? You could've picked a cool name.*

Dex's lips flattened out.

"Where the fuckers at?" Mercy asked.

Dex jerked his chin toward the back of the house. "Dragged their asses out there. One was bleedin' pretty good."

"Yeah? From what?"

"Got a couple holes plugged in 'im."

Brooke noticed that Mercy's answering smile didn't quite reach his eyes. "Take us to them."

Dex led the three men through the house and into her sunroom, where she and Dex had dragged them. The two Warriors sat propped against the wall, and blood soaked the president's shirt under his cut. They'd moved them to where she had indoor/outdoor carpeting so she could hose it down after they were taken away.

The man named Brick moved forward, leaned over and jerked Sandman's leather vest open enough so he could see the entry wounds.

"Shit shootin', Dex."

Brooke stepped forward. "Wasn't him."

All three men froze and turned their attention to Brooke.

"Wasn't him?" Ryder asked.

"No wonder," Brick murmured, staring at her. "Next time double-tap center mass to stop the threat."

First of all, there wasn't going to be a "next time." Second, she didn't need a lesson from this guy. "I wasn't out to kill him. I hit him where I aimed. I just wanted him to drop the gun."

Brick rose to his feet, scratching his head, and Brooke didn't miss his thorough once-over of her. "Non-fatal shots to take down the target, disarm the threat. *Huh.*"

The biker was still conscious but was unable to talk due to the rags they had tied around their mouths. Even though he couldn't communicate, it still looked like the injured biker had a lot to say.

Brooke just didn't want to hear it.

Brick pointed to one of Sandman's shoulders. "You hit him there on purpose?"

"Yes."

"With what?"

"That one," Brooke tipped her head toward Crank, "had a .38 Special."

"How d'you get it?"

"I asked politely," she said.

Brick shook his head, his eyes holding amusement, and he turned to Dex. "Should've taken them out, brother. We could've just come in and cleaned up afterward."

"No." All eyes returned to Brooke. "I didn't want him killing them."

"Why?" Brick asked, surprised.

She didn't need to explain her reasons to these men she didn't know. "Because I didn't."

Maybe she shouldn't have phrased it the way she did since those same eyes turned back to Dex for an explanation. His mouth opened for a second, then he shut it.

Mercy snickered. "Fuck, dude. Got it bad if you're letting her give you orders."

Ryder snorted. "And listening to boot."

"You haven't seen her naked," Dex answered with a grin.

Once again all eyes turned to Brooke. She pursed her lips as she regarded Dex. She debated if she should address what he just said. But then, she understood that even though he was a biker, he liked it when she was in charge. He probably just didn't want that information getting out there. He was most likely trying to jam his balls back where they belonged by saying what he did.

She wouldn't take that away from him. She liked him just the way he was. And there was no reason to cut him down at the knees in front of three badass men to whom he needed to act just as badass in front of.

But, funny, they all expected a response from her. Like a tongue-lashing. Instead she said nothing and simply shrugged.

Mercy threw his head back and laughed, whacking Dex on the back, then got right back to business. "Brick and Ryder are gonna take the bikes. Make them magically disappear."

Dex gave Brooke a slight chin lift before turning his attention to the larger man. "Right. But got a few questions for these fuckers before you take 'em anywhere. Still need some answers. Figured it was best to wait 'til you guys got here. Make sure they're willin' to answer 'em."

Mercy stepped up to Sandman and kicked him in the leg. "His cut says he's prez."

"Yep," Dex answered.

"He should know all the fucking answers then." Mercy jerked his thumb toward Crank. "That one looks useless."

"Grabbed my woman, grabbed her fuckin' tits. Both of 'em were gonna rape 'er an' make me watch."

Brooke saw Mercy's eyes turn cold and his jaw tighten as he stared at the man who had grabbed her.

"These Warriors got a thing about hurting and raping women, don't they?" Ryder asked, a frown on his face as he also stared at Crank.

"Yeah, they got a thing about treating women like shit in general," Mercy answered. "Sounds like they need a lesson about respect."

"Too late for that lesson," Brick answered. He turned toward Brooke and gave her a big smile. "Wanna do me a favor and go retrieve any weapons you got off these fuckers?"

Brooke glanced at Dex and he gave her a small nod. With a sigh, she left the men alone.

Dex watched Brooke leave the sunroom, though he was pretty fucking sure she didn't want to. But she was letting him be in charge for now in front of D's crew. Thank fuck.

While he didn't mind her being bossy in private, doing it around other men, especially the three men in front of him was something else. And she recognized that fact.

But then, she was pretty fucking smart.

Mercy stepped up to Crank, grabbed a handful of his greasy hair and ripped his head up. "Think this one's got any answers at all?"

Crank's wide eyes turned to Dex and a muffled sound came from behind his gag. "Doubt it. Think he's just a tweaked out meth head. Warriors are probably havin' a hard time fillin' their ranks. Scrapin' the bottom of the fuckin' barrel."

"'Cause we keep weeding the fuckers out."

Dex nodded and pointed to Sandman, who was paying careful attention to what they were talking about and doing.

Mercy released Crank's hair and moved over to Sandman. "So, this one's got all the fucking answers."

"He fuckin' should," Dex agreed. "Since he's the so-called prez of that club of fuckwads."

Mercy grabbed Sandman's gag and ripped it down.

Sandman growled, "Fuck you," and spat at Mercy.

"Spitting ain't polite," Mercy said and ground the heel of his boot into one of his shoulder wounds, causing Sandman to groan. "Just a fucking scratch, you fucking pussy. She could've plugged you in the chest." Mercy squatted down beside him and smiled. "You let a woman best you. That's called karma, bitch."

The twisted smile that Mercy wore was enough to shrink any man's balls. Dex never wanted to be on the receiving end of it.

Mercy glanced up at Dex. "So, whatta we need to ask him?"

Dex stepped closer and looked down at the man. Sandman had to be in his fifties. If he was, then he'd probably been the Warriors' president for a while. Though, Dex didn't recognize him. They always had a feeling that this man laid low. He gave orders and let his minions do his dirty work.

"Why did Pierce give up our location?" Dex asked him.

Sandman bared his teeth. "Fuck you. Gonna kill me. No fuckin' reason to answer any of your goddamn questions." The man winced and groaned as Mercy smashed the heel of his palm into one of his seeping wounds, this time on the other side.

"Yeah, that's fuckin' right, you're gonna die. But how an' when will depend on how you answer these questions," Dex told him, figuring that was true. Mercy wasn't named Mercy for no reason. D's men were no joke. They probably knew torture techniques that Dex didn't ever want to know.

Or see.

Or experience for himself. That was for fucking sure.

"So, let's try this again..."

Before Dex could ask the question, Mercy held out an open palm and Ryder placed a large tactical knife in it. Similar to the one Dex carried.

Mercy weighed it carefully in his hand before turning it slowly as he studied it. Then in a sudden move, he placed the sharp point against one of the gunshot wounds and sank it deep.

"Could cut your fucking throat. But we need that right now for you to answer questions," Mercy growled. "So instead, I can carve those holes in your body a bit bigger."

He twisted the knife causing Sandman to hiss and shout out a curse.

"Why did Pierce rat me out?" Dex asked again.

Sandman gritted his teeth and said, "Don't fuckin' know. Didn't fuckin' care. Just knew I could get one of you by yourself. Take you out. You guys," he glanced up at Mercy, "have been takin' out my brothers. Time to get even."

Dex snorted. "You fuckers started this war. The DAMC didn't want nothin' to do with it. You assholes wanted Shadow Valley, a town where my grandfather had founded our club. Was you fuckers who couldn't keep movin' an' find somewhere else to grow roots. Nope. Had to keep fuckin' with us 'til good men had to die. You fuckers coulda stopped this war a helluva long time ago, asshole."

"Take me out an' someone'll step up in my place."

"Then we'll deal with him, too," Mercy murmured.

"Warriors will survive."

Mercy shook his head, slipping the knife from the wound. "Doubt that."

Dex shook his head. "Decades of this shit. Fuckin' decades."

Sandman's eyes narrowed as he pinned them on Dex. "We're gonna take your shit. Your businesses. Your bitches. Everything. We'll take everything you Angels know, everything you own an' everything you love. Even your fuckin' kids. Gonna take 'em all out an' then fuckin' give your bitches our dicks an' make them fat with our own kids. That'll be the ultimate revenge. All your DAMC bitches spittin' out Warrior babies." He laughed.

Mercy's spine snapped straight and his fingers tightened around the knife in his palm. "Done asking this fucker questions?"

"No." Dex turned back to Sandman. "Pierce used you to get to me an' his daughter." When the Warrior prez's eyes widened at that, Dex continued, "Yeah, that's his fuckin' daughter he set up." He had one burning question that needed answered. Even if Sandman didn't answer anything else, it was a question that he and all his brothers wanted an answer to, one they never thought they'd hear. "So my question is: Why'd you set Zak up all those years ago? He wanted an end to all the murder an' mayhem. Wanted better for our club. You fuckers could've settled elsewhere an' never had to cross our paths again. But you didn't. You fuckin' planted that shit in his place. Shit he did ten years for. An' for what? Nothin'.

Nothin' fuckin' changed." Why was he wasting his fucking breath? This fucker couldn't give a shit about what they did to Z. All those years wasted in prison for a crime he didn't commit.

"You fuckers think we did that. Blamed us. So, fuck you an' fuck your prez. Maybe you better look within your own fuckin' house. Who benefitted the most from your prez gettin' locked up?"

Dex took a step back, his heart thumping as that last question spun in circles in his mind.

Holy shit.

That was when Brooke stepped up next to him and held out two handguns to Brick, who took them quickly. She asked Dex, "What's he saying?"

"He's sayin' someone in the DAMC set Z up. Not the Warriors. Someone who didn't want the old ways to change when Z earned the gavel. Someone planted a chemical used to make meth in Z's place an' then called in a fuckin' tip to the pigs." His nostrils flared as he stared at Brooke.

"Someone. Pierce," she stated with a flat tone. "Zak did ten years in prison for something that bastard did?"

"Yeah," Dex grunted.

"Fuck," Ryder muttered, scrubbing a hand over his buzz cut. "The man's got no fucking soul."

"None what-so-fucking-ever," Brick agreed. "Never do your brothers in battle wrong."

Mercy pushed to his feet from his squat next to Sandman, but not before wiping off his bloody knife on the biker's cut. "The supreme art of war is to subdue the enemy without fighting," he quoted.

Dex tilted his head as he considered the scarred man before him. "You came up with that?"

Mercy let out a sharp laugh. "Fuck no. The great military strategist Sun Tzu. Fucking fitting, though, ain't it?"

Yeah, it was. For all these years, everyone thought the Warriors had set Z up. Everyone. And all that time, the enemy was in their midst. Pierce had done exactly like the quote. He stopped—or at least slowed—Zak's plans for the club without a fight.

Dex needed nothing else from the soon-to-be-dead fucker sitting on the ground. He needed nothing more to prove Pierce needed to be stripped of his colors.

But being stripped of his colors was the least of Pierce's worries.

When it came to dealing a final blow to Pierce, Dex was sure a line would form and there'd be some discussion who got to stand at the head of it. His gaze slid to Brooke.

His own daughter probably wouldn't hesitate for a second to snuff the fucker.

But like she looked out for Dex earlier—not only taking Sandman down with her shooting skills but by making sure he didn't get in a jam by killing the fucker—he had to protect her. Even if from herself.

He couldn't allow her to take her own father out, no matter what a piece of shit he was or not. He couldn't let her be burdened with that for the rest of her life. Something that could rest heavily on her soul. Diesel was the Sergeant at Arms, the club's enforcer. He'd let his cousin figure out how to deal with Pierce. Though, Dex already knew who most likely would do the job. He had a feeling the three men that worked for D currently standing in Brooke's house, along with the other three not here, might have a part in it. He just didn't know how it would all go down yet.

Those men were ruthless, but they helped keep the club clean, above board. Legal.

D did what he had to do to keep Z's dream alive for the DAMC.

Even though they weren't blood brothers, Diesel and Zak might as well have been. And once D heard that it was Pierce who set Z up? Dex could just imagine the big man's reaction.

Bringing a baby into the world wasn't going to soften D up. Not one fucking bit.

CHAPTER THIRTEEN

"Next time you're out in the Pittsburgh area, maybe you and me can go shooting," Brick suggested to Brooke as they stood in her garage. The two now unconscious Warriors had already been thrown into the back of a blacked-out SUV that looked like it had been swiped from the military.

"You're a good shot?" Brooke asked.

Brick only smiled but Mercy and Ryder laughed.

"Sometimes he can hit a target," Ryder said, clapping Brick on the back. He eyeballed the two Harleys. "Why does it have to be December and a three fucking hour trip back? I won't see my fucking balls 'til spring."

"You can't find your balls now," Brick told him.

"Found his balls. They were in your mouth," Mercy said to Brick.

Ryder grabbed his crotch. "Suck 'em, bitch." He glanced at the bikes again and shuddered. "Fuck. This ride's gonna suck."

"Sure fucking is," Brick agreed. "Not sure what you bikers see in riding your sleds in fucking winter. Nobody can be that dedicated."

Dex shrugged. "Ain't a pussy. Unless there's snow an' ice on the roads, my ass is on my sled. That's where it belongs, not in a damn cage."

Brick stepped closer to Brooke and lowered his voice. "When you want a real man... One that's almost as good a shot as you, and's got more brains to know better than to ride a bike in December, then look me up next time you're west of here. Yeah?"

Dex went solid, not only at Brick hitting on his woman, but because he moved to touch her cheek. Dex took a step forward to intervene, but as Brick reached out, Brooke stepped back out of range. He couldn't help but grin at that.

Brooke raked her gaze over Brick. "You're probably not as good as me," she stated with arms crossed over her chest.

That got D's crew laughing. Ryder and Brick mounted the Harleys, kicking them to life. Mercy gave Dex a two-finger salute and headed to the badass SUV he was driving.

"Thanks for takin' out the trash," Dex yelled as Mercy climbed into the driver's seat.

"My pleasure," Mercy yelled back over the roar of the sleds as they pulled out of the garage and down the road. Mercy followed right behind them.

If Dex had to be in a cage during winter, he wanted to drive whatever the fuck Mercy was driving. It was badass.

"What was funny? Are they misogynic assholes, too? They don't believe women can be better than men at anything?"

"Brick's a sniper. Or was," Dex said, raking a hand through his hair. "Fuck. Probably still is."

Brooke glanced in the direction the men went. "Oh."

Dex tucked a finger under her chin and turned her face toward him until her blue eyes met his. "Yeah. *Oh*. Ain't shootin' with 'im."

"Well, that's a given since I don't plan on being in the Pittsburgh area anytime soon."

"That ain't why. But, babe, you're headin' back to Shadow Valley with me."

"No," she shook her head, pulling away from him. "I'm not. I have a business to run, a house to clean up and evidence of a shooting to get rid of. I'm not going anywhere."

"Babe..."

"No, Dex. I'm not leaving."

It was time for him to step up and take charge, whether she liked it or not. He was not going to give even a little on this point. "Babe."

"Dex."

He didn't want to get into an argument about it. He needed to somehow convince her it was for her own good, but he needed do it in a way that didn't get her hackles raised. "Just for a few days at least. 'Til shit cools down." There was no way Dex was leaving her here alone. Not when Mercy just drove off with the Shadow Warrior's president. The man would never be seen again. However, that didn't mean the remaining Warriors wouldn't come looking for their leader.

If any of them had known Sandman and Crank's plans, it would lead them right to Brooke.

He couldn't leave her alone. Fuck no. He didn't care how good of a shot she was. He didn't give a shit if she had the most expensive alarm system in the fucking world. He was not leaving her behind.

And he didn't belong here in Harrisburg. He needed to get back home. Z needed to call an Executive Committee meeting and Dex damn well needed to provide not only the evidence of the diary, but tell them what a down and dirty snake Pierce was.

Standing in her garage, he studied the woman before him. The woman who had flipped some sort of switch inside him. Showed him his true self.

He never thought that would ever happen.

His whole life, growing up in the club, growing up around bikers, he knew he wanted to follow in his uncle and grandfather's footsteps. Hell, it was in his blood. Did he really have another choice?

Probably. Like Mitch and Axel, he could've just walked away.

But he never felt that need to separate himself from his DAMC family, from his real family. The DAMC was his tribe. But becoming a prospect, and later being patched in, was all expected. And it wasn't that he didn't want it. He did. So, he did it without hesitation.

But he was never like his "brothers." Not quite. He had a good fucking life but something always felt off. Like a small part of him was missing. But he never could figure out what the fuck it was or why.

He knew it wasn't that he wanted to go to college or have some fancy career. He didn't have any desire to be some rich fucker. To wear suits. Have a nine to five. He was happy with how he lived. He didn't mind working hard. Even if he had to work for Ace and, in turn, the club and not himself. He was fine with that.

But again, there was always a piece of him that was left unsatisfied. A craving for something he couldn't identify. An unscratchable itch.

No woman—hell, even multiple women in his bed at the same time—ever satisfied him completely. He could bust a nut until he was drained dry, but once he rolled off whoever was beneath him, he felt empty, but in a different way.

He'd gone through pussy like water. *Fuck*, more like watered-down beer.

But the woman standing before him wasn't beer. Wasn't even Jack Daniels. Fuck no. She was like a bottle of Johnny Walker Blue. And that quality sip of whiskey was worth every fucking cent.

She stirred something in him that he couldn't get elsewhere. And he didn't want to even try, because he knew it was impossible.

This woman *got* him. She understood what he needed. How she fucking did it, he didn't have a fucking clue.

She was what he needed. The satisfying scratch to that unfulfilled itch.

Because of that, there was no fucking way he was leaving her behind. No way he was leaving her vulnerable to the Warriors.

For if they had raped her earlier this morning...

If they had injured her in any way...

If they came back and tried it again... Even if it wasn't for Pierce this time, but for revenge on taking out their prez...

His nostrils flared and his chest tightened.

No. Just fucking no. She was just going to have to let him be in charge right now. Let him make the decisions that were best for her.

He just didn't know how to go about it without pissing in her Cheerios.

"Babe," he began, stepping up to her in the cold garage, cupping her cheek and running his thumb over her soft skin.

She shook her head, breaking the contact, her eyes unreadable. "Please don't declare some sort of affection for me right now."

His head jerked back and he dropped his hand like it had been burned.

"I see it on your face, Dex. I see you struggling with something. I just... I just can't right now. Not now."

Dex heard her unspoken words in his head: *maybe not ever*.

She waved her hand toward the direction Mercy and his men went. "This shit is not my life. It's yours."

He dropped his head and stared at his boots for a moment, trying to slow his racing heart, his racing thoughts.

After a moment, he lifted his head to face her head-on. "Babe, I didn't bring you into this life, you did. The minute you stepped into Shadow Valley. Actually, the fuckin' second you decided to find your father. An' when you walked into the pawn shop, *you* walked into *my* life."

Her brows furrowed as she stared at him. "I had no idea about any of this. About what that diary would lead me to. I didn't even realize what my mother's words really meant until after I was in Shadow Valley. I had read it, yes, but I refused to really see through the words to their true meaning. I wish I never found that fucking diary."

Dex closed his eyes at the hurt in her voice and curled his fingers into his palms. If she hadn't found that diary, read those cryptic words, he never would have met her. He'd still be feeling unsatisfied, still be searching for what he had no idea he was looking for. Something he'd never find in random snatch.

That needed to end. Here and now.

"Brooke," he began again.

"No, Dex. I can't do this with you. I have a very successful business here. I own a house *here*. In Harrisburg. Our lives couldn't be more different. Just because we connected," she waved a hand around, "sexually doesn't mean we should be together."

No way in hell was this all about the sex. "Didn't fuckin' say—"

She stopped him with a raised palm. "You don't need to say it. I see it written across your face. Even in the small amount of time we've spent together, I've learned to read you."

That's because he allowed her that. He never would have permitted that with anyone but her. He was himself around her. Open. Not worried about judgment.

He never in his fucking life felt that around anyone else. Even his family. His brothers.

That was one reason why he'd always kept his nipple rings a secret and had even forced the sweet butts to keep their traps shut about it.

Brooke continued, "I understand why you're feeling the way you do. I do. I..." Her words drifted off and she turned to avoid meeting his gaze.

Dex lost his breath as he watched her shoulders curve, almost as if in defeat. This strong fucking woman. The strongest one he ever met next to Bella. And all the DAMC women were as strong as fuck. But to see her shoulders round and her head drop into her hands twisted his gut.

Not once had she broken down with the threat of rape, the threat of death, the threat of two fucking Warriors with guns in her home. But this? This defeated her somehow?

This connection between them?

Dex considered this only the beginning. They were only

finding each other now. If he left and headed home while she stayed here...

That connection could be broken. And what scared him the most was that it could be severed permanently. Once he was out of her life, away from her, she could shut that damn door and lock it.

Because who in their right mind wanted to deal with the shit the DAMC was dealing with?

D's crew might take their president out, cut the head off the snake but the Warriors still had the rest of the body, even if it was getting thin. And then there was Pierce.

A man who raped her mother. A man whose blood ran through her veins. The man who unknowingly fathered Kelsea. The man who framed Z for selfish reasons. The man who sent Dex's sister, Ivy, into a situation that could have ended in disaster.

And who knows what other shit Pierce had done throughout the many years he was an Angel. These were only the things that were coming to light. Dex wondered what still remained in the dark.

"Need to get back, Brooke, but can't leave you here," he said softly. "Need to go deal with Pierce."

At her father's name, her head shot up and he could see her visibly take a deep breath.

He waited for her to say she wasn't going. That he could fuck off. That she was capable of taking care of herself.

He was floored when she didn't.

Instead, she turned her head and glanced over her shoulder at him as she pressed the button for the automatic garage door. "I'll go. For a few days. That's all. Then I'm coming back here."

Relief washed over him. That at least gave him some time.

Not just time to keep her safe, but time to figure out what he wanted with her and how he was going to get it. Maybe it'd give him time to convince her to give him a fucking shot.

She opened the door that separated the garage from the house. "It'll give me an opportunity to face Pierce."

Ah fuck.

She had let herself feel something for the man who laid beneath her. Something she'd never felt before. Brooke wasn't sure if she liked that feeling because she was never one to be emotionally clingy.

And if she was going to be, she wasn't sure if Dex was the right man to cling to. Though, at the moment, she was riding his cock in a room at the Shadow Valley Motor Inn, so she wasn't quite "clinging."

His fingers dug into the flesh of her hips as she rose and fell at a slow pace. She was purposely drawing out both her release as well as his. Why? Because their time was coming to an end soon. She had only agreed to come back to his hometown to face Pierce. To look that man in the eyes and see if he held any regret for changing her mother's life in only one night. That was all it took to change everything for her mother. Hell, not even one night. Probably not even ten minutes.

So here she was, savoring her own minutes with a man she *wanted* to be with. Maybe not forever, but for at least this moment.

A man who was much more complex on the inside than what his outside showed the rest of the world. Beneath his biker exterior, there were more levels to Dex than most people could see.

She had peeled away a few of those layers from him during those days they spend together the last time she was in Shadow Valley. In those two nights at her home in Harrisburg, she had also uncovered a few more. Away from everything he knew, he had opened up, whether he realized it or not. He could drop the badass biker persona and show Brooke who Dexter Dougherty really was.

She didn't quite like the fact that he had to hide the real Dex away. But real or not, he looked right sitting on the bike he rode in the bitter-cold weather for three hours on their trip back to town. She had followed him in her car with her heat blasting, as if in some way that would help keep him warm.

"Babe," he murmured.

She opened her eyes, not even realizing she had closed them, and met his dark gaze.

"Where d'you go?"

"Nowhere. I'm here," she whispered. Her pace had come to almost a complete halt. She began again.

"You okay?" he asked, apparently not believing her.

"Yes," she answered. "I'm fine."

He still didn't believe her. Like she told him in her garage, she had somehow learned to read him. She'd never had that connection with a man before.

Or maybe she just never wanted to.

But why him? What was it about this man that made her feel differently?

Maybe it was because he wasn't anything like the typical man she'd dated in the past. Not that Dex and her were dating. The only label that could be put on what they were doing was... screwing.

That was it.

She paused, planting her palms on his chest and leaning forward until her mouth hovered over his. "We're screwing."

His lips twitched. "Yeah."

She hadn't tied him up this time. Sadly, her rope and both sets of cuffs had disappeared with those Warriors. And she didn't pack any of her toys because she wasn't planning on staying long.

Just long enough to confront Pierce. To spend a few more fleeting moments with Dex. Even if they ended up being vanilla moments.

However, she wasn't picking up her life and moving it here to Shadow Valley to have some fantasy fairytale happily-ever-after with this biker. He wasn't picking up his, either, to move closer to her.

Things like that didn't happen in real life. Books? Movies? Songs? Yes.

But not in real life.

Real life was *way* more complicated than that.

As she pressed her lips softly to his, he inhaled her breath and then gave it back. She accepted it, closing her eyes, appreciating something she wasn't used to.

It wasn't normal for her. Probably not for him, either.

Tenderness.

Right now, she had no urge to bite his lip, scratch his flesh, leave her marks over his skin.

No. She felt no need for that right now.

Right now, it was just him and her. Their breath intermingling, their tongues touching, their lips melding. She couldn't ignore how he filled her. How deep he was inside her. Not just his cock. But him.

Dex.

Brooke pushed up and away to stare down at him, her heart beating furiously in her chest. She tried to swallow the little bit of panic that bubbled up. Just as she tried to beat down the warm feeling that swirled around her, pulling her deeper. Drowning her.

She had left Shadow Valley the first time because she was afraid of losing herself.

But maybe that wasn't it at all.

Maybe...

Just maybe...

She was afraid of finding herself instead.

CHAPTER FOURTEEN

Dex surged up, twisted his body and rolled Brooke beneath him. Obviously, he figured out something was going on with her.

He pressed his forehead to hers. "Stay with me, babe, right here. In this room. In this bed. Don't go anywhere but here."

"Dex," she whispered, not sure what to say.

He lifted his head and shook it. "No, look at me."

She raised her eyes to meet his dark ones as he swept her hair out of her face.

"Right here, babe. Stay right with me."

His deep, gruff voice sent a shudder through her.

He began to move, to take over, to show her how right things were between them. Whether she was on top or he was.

Either way seemed to be fine with him. It hit her then that she always didn't have to be strong. Not always.

When she didn't want to be, he could step in and be strong for her. Support her. She could lean on him when and if she needed to.

She knew right then that he wanted that, too. Craved that.

He moved in and out of her like a gentle wave, not crashing against the shoreline, but a slow surge like a rising tide. He took her mouth, exploring every inch of it, drawing a moan from her, which he captured and kept. When he finally broke their kiss, he traced the tip of his tongue along where her pulse beat furiously along her throat.

He kissed the hollow of her neck and across her collarbone. Down her chest and over to her nipple, sucking it gently, then doing the same to the other. Her fingers slipped through his hair, finding purchase, holding him close, encouraging him to continue.

Normally, the few times he'd been on top, she'd gotten wild, scratching and biting, clawing her way back to being in control. This time she didn't have that desire. She let him guide the two of them slowly to the brink. To the very edge of that surf.

Her cries were soft, not demanding.

For once she wasn't telling him what she wanted. She allowed him to figure it out on his own.

And he knew what she wanted. What she needed. At least in that very moment between the two of them. She needed to let go and he was helping her do just that.

He trailed his hands down her arms and intertwined their fingers together. He lifted their clasped hands and pushed them into the mattress alongside her head, in the midst of her hair that was spread out around her. Then he kissed her once again.

With their bodies, their lips, and their fingers connected, he kept it slow. And she liked it. She wanted it to last. To never end.

"Babe," he murmured against her lips.

She stopped him by taking his mouth, encouraging their tongues to tangle, discouraging any more words.

Surprisingly, he let her do it.

The roll of his hips reminded her of a rocking ship in a calm sea. While his pace remained steady, their breathing did not. Small whimpers escaped the back of her throat, her hips rose to meet each one of his strokes.

They took turns giving and taking. And soon neither was on top anymore, they were equal. Simply enjoying each other. Taking each other to the crest of one wave. Then they rode the next one. And the next.

Until, finally, they fell asleep in each other's arms.

Dex stared up at the motel room's water-stained ceiling. He really needed to get his own fucking place. He was going to start looking right away and stop waiting for D to realize that the apartment above the pawn shop would no longer work for a family of three.

He tipped his gaze down to the woman who was sprawled across his chest. Well, he wasn't going to start looking right away because he wasn't moving from this bed until she did. He combed through her hair, enjoying how the silky strands felt over his skin and over his pierced nipples. When she gave him head, he loved when that soft hair tickled his balls and his thighs.

Yeah.

He thought about what happened last night. The sudden switch in her. He had no idea why it happened and he wasn't sure how he felt about it when it did.

She had given herself to him. Not with words. Hell no. Nothing had been said. But something changed. He recognized and encouraged it. Whether that was fucking selfish on his part...

He shrugged mentally. Last night was a turning point. He was not letting this woman go.

He didn't know what she'd think of that. Though, once he admitted it to her, he was pretty damn sure she wouldn't hesitate to let him know her feelings.

He had no idea how they would make it work, but he was determined to try.

The problem was, he doubted she'd just walk away from what seemed to be a successful business or simply give up her house, especially for him. Would she be willing to give up everything she'd built for a biker like him?

Even if she was, the house would be the easy part. They could find something in Shadow Valley since new neighborhoods were popping up everywhere outside of town. Even something temporary until they could find what she wanted. And whatever she wanted was fucking fine with him since he only needed a roof over his head and her in his bed.

But the business part…

He knew it took time and effort to build a business since the DAMC owned quite a few. And in the last year, he watched Slade and Diamond build a new one from scratch. It involved a lot of hands-on work, as well as planning. And a lot of scratch, as well.

A lot of fucking money was being funneled from the club's fat coffers. Now that Shadow Valley Fitness's doors were open, Di and Slade were busier than ever. In fact, they rarely ever saw those two. If the couple wasn't sleeping, Dex had a feeling they were fucking like rabbits or working like dogs.

So, he knew that moving a business wouldn't be easy. She'd be starting from scratch. She would have to build up new clientele in and around Pittsburgh. Re-establish her name, her brand. Maybe some of the women could help her. But he wasn't even sure she'd agree in the first place.

Dex brushed the tips of his fingers over Brooke's shoulders.

She wasn't a woman who would sit back and just be an ol' lady.

He snorted.

Her gray-blue eyes blinked open and she stretched but remained glued to him. He bit back a satisfied grin.

"What time is it?"

"Early," he answered.

He wanted to talk about last night. But if he suggested it, she'd probably balk at the idea. So instead, he just needed to be patient and wait for her to reveal whatever changed when she was ready.

Though, being patient about it may be a problem.

"What happens now?"

He assumed she meant with Pierce and not with them.

"Got a meetin' this mornin'. Gonna tell the Executive Committee what we found out, then justice will be dealt."

"Justice," she repeated softly.

"Yeah."

"I want to be there."

"For the meetin'?"

"For the justice."

"Not sure that's a good idea."

"Well, I want to be there anyway. I have a right to be."

"Not so sure 'bout that, either."

"Dex."

He shifted, but not enough to dislodge her from his chest. He liked her right where she was. "Look, Brooke, lemme set somethin' straight with you. This club..." He inhaled to brace himself. "The DAMC don't let the women call the shots. An' I know how much you like to do that shit, but it ain't gonna fly with the rest of the brothers. Can tell you that right now. Goin' in there an' makin' demands ain't gonna work. Don't care how good of a shot you are. Don't care how strong of a woman. It ain't gonna fly."

"The women have no power," she stated flatly.

"The truth?"

"Yes, I want to hear the truth."

His answer might surprise her. "The truth is... the women got more power than they know. Than any of the brothers will admit. But not just any women. The ol' ladies. We all pretend like they don't, but they do. Know why?"

"Why?"

"Because they got their ol' man's ear when things are dark an' quiet. When they're layin' in bed together. When things aren't fuckin' hectic. The ol' ladies hear shit when they shouldn't. Can put a seed in their ol' man's ear when one needs to be planted."

"How do you know when you've never had an ol' lady?" She lifted her head. "Or have you?"

"Nope. Never had one. Never wanted one." He left off the "'til now" part. "But I know by some of the shit Ivy lets slip when she shouldn't. By shit they all say when they think we ain't listenin'. We can shout to the fuckin' roof tops that club business ain't women's business, but the ol' ladies got their hands firmly on their ol' man's nuts. And they know how to squeeze them *juuuuust* right."

Brooke rolled her face into his chest to smother her laugh.

He frowned. "Think that's funny?"

She twisted her neck to face him again, but she didn't hide her amused smile. "Yes. I think it's hilarious. You men... you bikers... You all look and act tough. Like badasses. Leather, denim, chains, knives. *Guns*. But—"

Dex quickly pressed a finger to her lips to stop her. "But nothin'. We're exactly what you see."

"Bullshit."

"Ain't bullshit, babe. Are who we are." He brushed the pad of his thumb over her bottom lip. "But we all got a side of us which we show our women an' now our kids."

"Do you think now that Diesel's child is born, he's going to be a loving, sweet father to his baby girl?"

Dex had to think about that for a moment. "Dunno how D's gonna be. I know that little girl's gonna have a father who will lay down his life for 'er. No matter what. He'll protect her to the end. Who knows how lovin' he'll be. Can't say how lovin' he is to Jewelee in private. Can guess, though. Jewel ain't one who'd sit back an' let their relationship be one-sided. Don't mean D's gonna show that side to everyone else. An' he certainly ain't gonna let her call any shots in front of the others."

"So, all you guys have a side you keep hidden?"

Dex lifted his shoulders. "Probably."

"And your secret is?"

"Should know what it is by now."

She flicked a fingernail over one of his nipple rings. "So, I know what your secret is. What you keep from everyone else. Why is that?"

"Truth is, babe, didn't quite fuckin' know it myself 'til you came around."

She lifted her head, stared at him for a long moment, then

shifted until all her weight was on him, until she covered him with her whole body.

And that weight on him felt fucking good. Satisfying. So fucking right. "Babe..."

"Yes?"

"You know Pittsburgh ain't far away from Shadow Valley, right?"

Her brows knitted together. "Yes. So?"

"An' the 'burgh's a lot bigger than that city you live outside of."

Her eyebrows knitted together. "I know it is. So?"

"Just sayin'."

"I didn't realize I needed a geography lesson."

"Speaking of geography. What d'you think of Shadow Valley?"

"Right now I don't like it."

Well, that wasn't a good fucking start. "Why?"

"Because of who lives here."

"You mean Pierce?"

"Yes."

That made sense somewhat, but he wondered how she'd feel about it once Pierce was taken care of. "Gonna get that handled. You'd like it better once he's gone?"

"I'll give you that answer once that happens."

"Gonna hold you to that."

She sighed. "What time is the meeting?"

Dex's gaze slid to the old digital clock on the nightstand. "Not for another couple hours, yet."

"So, we have time?"

He smiled. "Yeah, got time. Whataya have in mind?"

"You need a few reminders," she stated firmly.

"Do I?"

She pressed her mouth to his ear and breathed, "Yes, you do."

"An' you're gonna give 'em to me?"

"No one better to give them to you other than me."

He snorted. "Then what the fuck you waitin' for?"

She snagged his earlobe firmly between her teeth and tugged. And that shit wasn't gentle at all.

He smiled.

His Brooke was back.

Dex did a double-take when he walked into the meeting room. Diesel sat at the far end of the table where the prez normally sat with a tiny Violet tucked into the crook of his arm.

She looked like a miniature doll next to his huge muscles. She also looked innocently unaware of being surrounded by pure brute and solid tattoos as she slept.

"What the fuck?" Dex asked as he grabbed a seat a couple of chairs down from him.

D shot him a glare. "Gotta keep it down," he grumbled, checking on his daughter to make sure her eyes were still shut.

"Where the hell is Jewel?" And why did D have his less-than-a-week old baby in his arms?

"Probably in The Iron Horse downing a bottle of whiskey," Ace said in a loud whisper as he walked into the room. He approached D and held out his hands, offering to take his grandbaby.

Diesel just shook his head. It didn't seem like he wanted his father to take his child.

Z came in next, stopped short, closed his gaping jaw and sat to D's left. "Where's my gavel?"

"Ain't hittin' that thing on the table an' wakin' 'er up."

Z snorted loudly and D shot him a glare. Z's brows rose and he lifted his palms in surrender. "Okay."

Hawk wandered in next, stutter-stepped when his gaze landed on his younger brother. He was the next to approach him, his hands out offering to take Violet.

D shook his head again. "No."

Dex asked, "Have either of you got to hold 'er yet?"

"Fuck no," Ace grumbled quietly.

"Nope," Hawk said with a frown, pulling out the chair next to D carefully so the legs wouldn't squeal against the floor. "Gonna have to steal 'er away when her private security detail ain't holdin' her. Which seems to be all the time."

"She gonna be in here the whole time?" Z asked. "'Cause we got business to talk 'bout."

"Yeah, an' you know club biz ain't women's biz," Dex stated softly with a smirk. "Even if she's only five days old."

D grunted in answer.

"Is Jewel takin' her before we start?" Ace asked his youngest son.

"Nope. I'm watchin' her."

Ace blew out a breath and leaned back in his chair, scrubbing a hand down his salt-and-pepper beard. "Can't watch her every second of the day. She needs her momma."

"Jewelee gets Vi when she's hungry."

"The way you're actin', woulda thought she came outta your vagina, D," Jag said.

Hawk's lips twitched. "Jesus Christ. Never thought I'd see the day..."

Jewel poked her head into the open doorway. "Baby, can I have her now?"

"No. Shut the fuckin' door."

Dex met Z's eyes. "We're seriously gonna have a fuckin' meetin' with an infant in our enforcer's arms. What the fuck has happened to this fuckin' club?"

Z dropped his gaze to the table and his whole body quaked silently as he shook his head.

"Might as well go grab Baby Z, too, an' they can have a fuckin' play date while we talk business," Jag griped.

Ace made a noise and Dex looked over at him. He was laughing, too.

"Might as well get rid of the fuckin' pool table an' set up playpens an' shit. Bottles of titty milk instead of Jack. Get Nash to start playin' nursery rhymes. Fuck," Dex grabbed his balls. "We're turnin' into a bunch of bitches."

"Shut up, Dex. Call the meetin' to fuckin' order, then," D muttered, fussing with the purple blanket that was wrapped around Violet.

From the little Dex could see of her, she had an almost full head of dark hair, which shouldn't surprise anyone between Jewel and D. But he wondered what her eye color was. Blue like Jewel's or brown like D's. It was probably too early to tell yet.

He was right when he told Brooke the tree was now twisted. With Violet's birth, the founding members' genes had been officially combined. Ivy and Jag's kid would combine the Doc/Bear lines as well.

He wondered if Doc or Bear ever considered that they'd eventually be related by blood. It had been a while since he'd visited Doc at Greene, maybe he should do that and ask him. He had a feeling his grandfather would be tickled pink... or purple.

Then suddenly a stink rose up that made Dex's eyes water. "What the fuck?"

Hawk shot to his feet and moved down the table. Z's gaze dropped to Violet and then up to D.

"Now what?" Jag asked. "Gonna change her right her in the middle of the meetin' table? But, fuck, that shit's just nasty. Jesus Christ."

D rose to his feet, walked to the door, opened it and yelled, "Jewelee, come get your kid." The baby's wail as well as the eye-watering stink trailed out the door with him.

Jag snorted. "Figures."

"Tell her to bring some air freshener or somethin'," Hawk yelled out, his complexion a bit green.

"Gotta get used to that, son," Ace said, laughing. "Gonna soon have a shittin' machine in your house, too."

"An' that's why I got Kiki."

"Kiki ain't gonna let you not change diapers," Ace said.

Hawk shot a look at Z. "Z don't change 'em."

Z smiled and shrugged. "Do it wrong a few times, a couple disasters later, an' they'll never ask again."

D came back in the room and shut the door behind him.

"No air freshener? Ain't no windows in here," Hawk muttered.

"Let's get this shit over with," D said, settling his bulk back into a chair with a grunt.

"Meetin' called to order," Z announced and pounded his fist on the table.

CHAPTER FIFTEEN

Brooke sat on a stool at the private bar in church, staring at the closed door of the meeting room. They'd been in there longer than she expected. How long could it take for Dex to lay out the evidence and for them to decide what to do with Pierce?

She sighed and glanced over at Jewel who was sitting on what looked like a brand-new couch along one of the walls. There was a hand-written sign pinned above it that read, "No skanks allowed."

She laughed and moved over to sit down next to her, watching her nurse Violet. "Is it creepy that I'm sitting next to you while you nurse?"

Jewel grinned. "No. It doesn't bother me. Now if Grizz," she lifted her chin to a weathered, gray-haired man who was sitting at the end of the bar, nursing a beer, "decided to plunk himself down beside me and stare, then I might get a little creeped out."

"How's your husband with the baby?"

Jewel turned her blue eyes to Brooke. "Ol' man. When we got together I was told," she dropped her voice and grunted, "*No rings, no weddin's, no babies.* I fucked up the last part."

"You don't mind that he doesn't want to marry you?"

Jewel carefully lifted one shoulder, not enough to disturb the nursing baby. "Nope. A piece of paper isn't going to make him a good husband or father."

"Is he?"

"What?"

"A good father."

Jewel tilted her head, then stared down at the baby. She ran a hand over Violet's dark, downy soft hair. With a gentle smile she whispered, "Yeah, surprisingly he is. So far."

"So far?"

"Well, so far she only sleeps, eats and shits. But I have to say he watches Violet sleep almost all night. He's gotten no sleep since she's been born because he's constantly checking to make sure she's still breathing. I swear almost every fifteen minutes. And if it wasn't dangerous, he'd probably want her to sleep in bed with us. Between you and me," Jewel adjusted Violet in her arms, "I think he can't believe he created something so beautiful and not a beast like him."

Brooke wondered about that "beast" comment. "Well, you helped, too."

Jewel smiled down at Violet as her little bow shaped mouth sucking intensely. "Yeah," she breathed.

A loud roar could be heard through the closed door, making them both freeze.

Suddenly looking pale, Jewel whispered, "Oh shit. The beast."

A shiver slid through Brooke. The door to the meeting room was flung open with a bang and a very pissed off, red-faced enormous man lumbered through it at a fast clip.

Diesel stomped to the middle of the room like he was King Kong and Brooke waited for him to beat his fists on his chest, but instead he pointed a big finger at Jewel. "Take her home. Stay there. Ryder will be there waitin'. Got me?"

"D..." She quickly tucked her breast away and placed Violet against her shoulder, patting the baby on the back as she rose to her feet.

"No lip, woman! Go."

"But—"

"Get gone." He turned to Brooke and snarled, "You, too." Before Brooke could answer, he turned and roared, "Find the fucker. Get 'im here now. NOW! Get everyone here. No excuses. Gonna vote."

"Jesus, D, you have to calm down," Jewel stated as she gathered the diaper bag and the baby's things.

Brooke noticed a man with darker skin and long, straight black hair running down the steps. As he hit the bottom, his eyes landed on Jewel and the baby. He moved quickly over to them to help her.

"I'll take her home," he stated to D who looked like a highly annoyed bull ready to rush a bull fighter waving a red cape.

"No. Need you here. Doin' a vote," Hawk muttered at the same time texting on his phone. He looked up and said, "Text Nash, Rig and Crash. Tell 'em to get here now. I just texted Linc, Moose an' Dawg."

"What's this about?" the other man asked.

"Time to strip someone of his colors," Hawk muttered.

"Fuck," the darker man muttered, then his onyx-colored eyes landed on Brooke in surprise. But before he could move closer, his gaze bounced to someone behind her.

She knew exactly who when Dex's hand landed on her shoulder. She turned to face him. "Guess that went over smoothly."

"Fuck, thought he was going to flip the fucking table. That table's gotta weigh five hundred pounds. It's all hand carved wood."

"He didn't take the news well. Apparently," she murmured as she watched Diesel cautiously.

"Fuck no."

Brooke glanced around the large room. "Where's Zak?"

Dex just shook his head.

"Is he okay, at least?"

"If you just found out you got stabbed in the back... No, that was worse than a fuckin' stabbin'. Ten fuckin' years in prison, babe. *Ten.*" Dex blew out a breath and shook his head. "Ten fuckin' years of his life gone because of Pierce."

"My mom had to look at her reminder for thirty years."

His brown eyes landed on her. "Babe, said this before... doubt she blamed you. Loved you. Z lived in concrete cell away from everyone he ever cared about."

She slipped a palm under his cut and planted it on his chest. "I know. There's no comparison. Sorry."

As she watched the caramel-colored skinned man with the gorgeously high cheekbones escort Jewel out of the back door, she asked, "Is he a club member? I met him the morning of the club run, right?" He wore a DAMC cut, but still...

"Crow? Yeah."

Crow. That's right. "He's Native American."

"Half. Yeah."

As the door shut behind them, Brooke glanced up at Dex. "Isn't that a little odd?"

"What?"

Brooke shook her head. "Nothing. Never mind." She was glad to see their biker club was accepting of people of different ethnicities, but it seriously surprised her. When she had done quick research online about motorcycle clubs, it seemed that the white bikers stuck with their own, as did the Black bikers, the Latinos, and so on. She hadn't noticed any mixing of races.

She was pleased to see that information was wrong.

Or maybe the DAMC was just different. More accepting. Who knew. That wasn't an issue to discuss at this time.

There was something currently more pressing.

"I can only assume this vote is about Pierce," she murmured as she glanced around the large common area. Diesel, Hawk, and Jag were talking with the older man, who had his head hanging and was shaking it, his fists clenched on the bar.

"Yeah."

"Then I guess I'll settle in and wait." As she moved toward the couch where Jewel had been nursing Violet, he reached out and grabbed her wrist, halting her on the spot.

"Babe... You gotta go."

She stared down at his hand around her wrist, making him quickly release her. “What do you mean? I’m not going anywhere.”

“Yeah, babe. Can’t be here during our meetin’.”

“Why not?”

Dex visibly braced. “Talked about this. ’Cause you’re a woman.”

She closed her eyes and shook her head. “Wow,” she whispered.

“Way it is. Ain’t gonna change.”

The back door opened and Crow, along with three other bikers walked in.

“Tell you what, go up to my room. Soon as the meetin’s over I’ll come get you, yeah?”

“I want to face him, Dex.”

“Know it. Not sure what’s gonna happen. Z is...” Dex inhaled sharply. “D... Ace... I mean, never thought... this shit...” He ground the heels of his palms into his eye sockets.

She grabbed his cut and gave it a little shake. “I know. It has to be difficult. It’s devastating to find out one of your own could be this... horrific. It’s shaken your club to the core.”

“Yeah, babe. That’s puttin’ it mildly. So, need you to not gimme any shit an’ head upstairs since I know you won’t go back to the motel willingly.”

She studied him. The pain from the betrayal was evident in his eyes. Glancing around the room as more bikers gathered, she could see the anger and betrayal felt by all of them.

The room crackled with it.

She nodded. “Fine. I’ll wait for you in your room.”

“Gotta promise me you’re gonna stay there no matter what you hear.”

Her eyes widened. “Dex...”

“Promise me that an’ I’ll promise to fill you in afterward. Later.” He reached into his pocket and pulled something out.

She stared at the set of keys he held. His Harley key and a couple others, but the one he held up between his fingers was his room key.

She couldn’t believe she was going to give up this easily and do as he suggested without a fight. But he didn't need extra stress on top of what was already a tense situation.

And she didn't need to challenge him in front of his club brothers. That would get them both nowhere except irritated.

She slid her palm over his warm chest, over his nipple, traced the piercing through this shirt with the tip of her finger, then cupped his cheek. "Fine. We'll talk afterward."

She didn't miss him visibly relax at her answer and he leaned over, whispering, "Thanks, babe," against her lips before kissing her quickly, and pressing his keys into her hand.

With a slight nod and a sigh, she turned and trudged up the steps to his room.

Diesel stood in front of the bar next to Hawk. Z would normally be calling a church meeting to order but Dex could see Z standing behind the bar struggling to keep his shit together.

He wasn't the only one struggling. D was an over-stretched wire ready to snap. Ace stood close to Z, probably to make sure he didn't leap over the bar, strangle Pierce to death and then end up back in that concrete box for the rest of his life. Those ten years had been enough.

Actually, more than enough.

As VP, Hawk took over, but he was even having a tough time masking the fury on his face.

Before Pierce had arrived, clueless on what the fuck was going on, D had instructed Moose and Linc to stand at the back of the room, guarding the door. Not to keep anyone out. Fuck no. To keep Pierce in. Once he heard why this emergency meeting was called, he might just bolt.

Dex would, if he was him.

But he wasn't and he'd never be. Pierce had no sense of not only loyalty but decency.

As Dex stood toward the back of the crowd, his gaze bounced over his brothers. He could never fuck any of them over. His loyalty remained true. This room was full of family.

And you just didn't fuck over family. Blood or not.

Dex caught a glimpse of Crow who stood against a wall, his knee cocked, his foot planted firmly on the wall, his arms crossed over his chest. And his dark eyes were pinned on Pierce.

Something was up with him. When D explained to some of the members what the meeting was about before Pierce arrived, Crow had gotten quiet. More than usual. He'd actually gone behind the bar to down two double shots of Jack before wiping his hand across his mouth and heading to the other side of the room, his jaw tight, his eyes hard.

The man had been seething ever since. But it was more than the fact that Pierce had fucked over Z. No, Crow's expression had turned to granite when D mentioned the diary pages and the evidence about Brooke's mother being raped.

Something about that discovery had cut Crow deep.

Dex just didn't know what. Though the act of rape should bother each and every one of them—and it did— this was something more.

"This ain't gonna be a meetin' like you all expected," Hawk yelled out, standing on a metal milk crate so he could be heard easily. "There's a member among us who's done some heinous shit."

A grumble went through the room.

"Fuckin' foul, heinous shit. Not only to outsiders but to his own brothers."

A collective roar and boot stomping filled the room.

"So, yeah, this ain't a regular church meetin'."

Diesel stepped forward. "Fuck no. Got you all here for a fuckin' vote to strip one of us of 'is colors."

The room stilled. Stripping someone of their colors was serious shit. A few brothers looked around nervously, trying to figure out who it was and hoping like hell it wasn't them. Which made Dex raise his brows.

Nash yelled out, "Who?"

Hawk, Diesel and Z's gaze landed on Pierce, who was perched on the edge of one of the pool tables. His feet dropped to the floor and he stood.

Dex studied the man who had sent Warriors to rape and kill his own fucking daughter. And to kill one of his own club brothers.

He shook his head. To call him a monster wasn't even good enough.

Dawg moved around the pool table to stand behind Pierce. "Figurin' it's this piece of shit," he yelled out.

A mumble went up.

"What the fuck? You talkin' about me?" Pierce asked Hawk.

Hawk gave him a sharp nod. "Bring 'im the fuck up here, Dawg."

Dawg grabbed Pierce's arm, but Pierce jerked out of his grip. "Can fuckin' walk. Haven't done shit. If you're gonna accuse me of somethin', I better get an opportunity to fuckin' respond."

Neither Hawk nor Diesel answered him. Dawg stalked behind Pierce as the former prez made his way through the group to stand in front of the bar, his back to the room.

"Don't even know where to begin," Hawk muttered, brushing fingers over his short mohawk.

Jag stepped closer and yelled out, "How 'bout the fact that he sent Ivy into Dirty Dick's an' the Dark Knights territory without any of us fuckin' knowin' it. Coulda went sideways for 'er real fast. Good thing the Knights' enforcer didn't let that happen."

A grumble rose up.

"The bitch wanted to go," Pierce said. "Didn't approach 'er, she fuckin' came to me."

"As prez, you shoulda told her no, fucker," Jag muttered, running an agitated hand over his jeans. "Or brought it to a vote. No excuses."

Dex had a feeling Jag was just itching to plant a fist in Pierce's face. He'd been wanting to do it for a long while.

Slade moved next to Jag. "How 'bout the fact that he touched

Diamond when she was just fuckin' fifteen."

Jag's head spun toward Slade. "What?"

Slade nodded. "Cornered her. Touched her. Shoulda lost his fuckin' balls after that."

Dawg grabbed Jag before he could rush up to Pierce. "Fuckin' touched my sister when she was a fuckin' kid?"

Pierce stood silently with his jaw tight.

Jag turned to Slade. "Why didn't you say nothin'?"

"She didn't want anyone to know. But since we're airin' shit out, figured it needed to come to light. She's gonna fuckin' kill me. Just sayin'. Ain't gonna get pussy for a long time."

"Gonna deny it?" Jag screamed at Pierce. "Gonna say my sister lied?"

The room got deadly quiet. All eyes were pinned on Pierce.

"Begged me to pop her fuckin' cherry."

Everyone in that room went completely solid. Like stone.

"Wait... what?"

Oh fuck. Slade's surprise meant he hadn't been told it went that far. Slade only thought she'd been touched. That was clear by the fury that crossed his face.

"You touched her like that?" Slade leaped forward, his fists clenched, and Crow was there, holding him back.

"Brother," Crow murmured. "His time's comin'. A fuckin' fifteen-year-old." He shook his dark head and blew out a noisy breath.

Dex turned his attention back to Pierce, who definitely looked a bit paler than normal. He raked shaky fingers through his short salt-and-pepper hair.

"Anybody else wanna come forward?" Hawk asked, then mumbled, "What the fuck with all this shit. Otherwise, I'm gonna get to the main reason we're votin' today."

"There's worse shit than rapin' a fifteen-year-old?" Slade shouted, his face almost purple as he tried to pull away from Crow. Crow planted his feet and hung on as best as he could.

"Didn't fuckin rape her!" Pierce yelled out. "She fuckin'

wanted—"

Before he could finish, Grizz came from nowhere and popped Pierce right in the mouth. Dex wouldn't be surprised if everyone's jaw dropped right then and there.

"Shut the fuck up." The old man shook his hand out and wandered back to his stool to take a long chug of beer.

Hawk turned surprised eyes from Grizz back to the crowd. "Okay, then. Di ain't here to settle that an' ain't gonna make her confirm it right now. So... here's the thing. Know of another woman he raped."

Curses and random shouts moved through the room.

"What?"

"What the fuck!"

"Piece of shit!"

Hawk held up the folded pages from Brooke's mother's diary. "Got proof here that he did it to someone else."

With the back of his hand pressed to his bloody mouth, Pierce turned his head quickly and glanced at what Hawk was holding. "What's that shit?"

"Proof that you raped Brooke's mother," Hawk answered.

"Who the fuck is Brooke?"

"Don't fuckin' act like you don't fuckin' know. She's your fuckin' daughter, asshole." Dex stepped up to the bar, and turned to face everyone. He pointed at Pierce. "This fucker set Brooke an' me up. Sent Warriors to Brooke's house to take out his own fuckin' daughter. Get rid of Brooke an' me before I got the proof to nail his fuckin' ass." His eyes swung to Slade. "Had no idea, brother. Didn't need that diary if Diamond had stepped forward." He raised his palm when Slade opened his mouth to speak. "Can understand why she didn't, though. Ain't faultin' her." He looked around the room. "So the man ain't only a rapist, but a fuckin' snake lyin' in bed with the Warriors. Usin' them to do his dirty work. Fuckers almost raped Brooke. Would've taken the two of us out. But, luckily..."

Now was not the time to tell everyone what a badass his

woman was. That it was her that saved their ass, not him. Yeah, probably best to keep that to himself. He was sure it would get out soon enough.

"You sayin' you're accusing me of rapin' some woman because of some shit written down? That ain't shit. I don't' even know who the fuck she is."

"Was," Dex murmured. "Brooke's mother's dead now. An' you mighta got away with it if she hadn't written that shit down. But she did. An' your own daughter found it."

"Don't got no daughter," Pierce sneered.

"Yeah, you do. Two, matter of fact," Dex said, pulling the DNA results from the back pocket of his jeans.

Pierce stared at the papers in Dex's hand, his eyes wide. "What's that?"

"DNA proof."

"Of what?"

"That you fathered not only Brooke, but Kelsea."

The former DAMC prez went from pale to sheet white. "What?"

Hawk growled, "For fuck's sake, don't tell me you touched Kels, too?"

"Didn't fuckin' touch no one."

"Liar!" came the high-pitched scream as Brooke ran through the room, then leapt toward Pierce. He stumbled back as all her weight hit him, her hair and fists flying.

"Oh fuck!" Dex shouted, rushing forward to get hands on Brooke. D was there, peeling her off Pierce as she wailed on him, kicking and hitting. Before D could pull her off, Pierce's fist connected with her face and her head whipped back.

Diesel picked Brooke up like she weighed nothing, swung her around and shoved her at Dex, who caught her but stumbled back in an attempt to keep his balance. When he finally had two feet firmly on the ground, he held onto Brooke tightly as her chest heaved and she made a sound that raised the hair on his neck. She held her hand to her face.

D stood over Pierce as the man rose to his feet, staring at Brooke. "Don't know who the fuck you are." That was a fucking lie. Somehow the man had found out who she was and why she had shown up in Shadow Valley over a week ago, otherwise he wouldn't have sent the Warriors to "deal" with her.

"You fucking knew my mother thirty years ago!"

"Thirty years ago? I fucked a lot of bitches over the years." His eyes narrowed as his gaze raked over her. "Oh yeah. Look just like her. Hot little piece of ass. Liked to play hard to get. Say no. Pretend she didn't want it even though I knew she did. Her moans were fuckin' sweet. Her fightin' me even sweeter." He grabbed his dick. "She made me come real fuckin' hard."

Dex never saw Diesel move so fast. His hand shot out in a flash and gripped Pierce's throat, raising the fucker to his toes.

D stared at him, his nostrils flared, his chest rising and falling quickly, then he shook his head and tossed Pierce to the side.

Pierced stumbled but caught himself, putting a hand to his throat. "You wanna fight me over snatch?" He raised his arms out. "Come get me, then, brother."

Egging D on for a fight was asking for a death sentence. Pierce was being reckless and he knew when he said that shit to Brooke that he'd evoke some sort of response.

D grunted. If smoke could come out of a man's nose, the room would be full of it. "Ain't your fuckin' brother. None of us are your brothers anymore."

"Been a part of this club for over thirty-five years. Longer than most of you been born. Think you can just toss my ass out?"

"You told the Warriors where we were," Dex shouted. "Ratted us the fuck out, Pierce. Didn't care that they were gonna rape an' kill your own blood."

Pierce spit on the ground. "Ain't my blood no matter what that paper says."

Z stepped around the bar and in front of Pierce. "Let's talk 'bout rats." Zak took a deep breath and shook his head. "Spent ten fuckin' years..." He got right into Pierce's face, his finger a cunt hair away from the man's nose as he screamed, "TEN FUCKIN' YEARS in a fuckin' hole because of you, motherfucker. Ten fuckin' years of my fuckin' life. If I didn't have a fuckin' wife an' son, I'd put a bullet between your fuckin' eyes."

"What's Z talkin' about?" Dawg asked.

Zak turned to face them all, pointing at Pierce, who finally wore a look of shock and some fear as shit hit home. If his asshole wasn't puckered before, Dex was pretty sure it was now. The man finally realized he wasn't getting out of this with just some lame-ass excuses.

"This is the fucker that set me up all those years ago. Not the fuckin' Warriors. Had me locked away so his ass could sit at the head of the table."

Dex was expecting Z to turn around at any second and punch the fuck out of Pierce. But before he had a chance, Slade jerked free from Crow's grip and slammed his palms into Pierce's chest, screaming, "This is for Diamond." Then with one strategic punch knocked Pierce out cold.

The former president of the DAMC crumpled to the ground.

Brooke jerked against Dex so hard that she broke free and rushed over to Pierce, lifted her booted foot and stomped him right in the nuts with her heel.

A collective groan went up as everyone winced and their hands covered their own junk instinctively.

Even D winced and turned a little green at that.

Dex was pinning his own thighs together and blew out a breath. "Damn," he whispered.

D looked at Dex and jerked his chin toward Brooke, who still stood over an unconscious Pierce, her hands curled into fists as she glared down at him.

Dex moved up behind her, wrapped his arms around her waist and pulled her back against him gently. "Babe," he whispered against her ear. "Need to go back up to my room, got me? Gotta do it now, yeah?"

She didn't answer for the longest time and he began to wonder if she heard him. She just continued to stare at the man who was in a crumpled, unconscious heap on the floor.

"Babe... Brooke. Go upstairs. Be up there shortly."

Suddenly, her spine snapped straight and she nodded. "We have to talk."

Dex closed his eyes for a second. That didn't sound good. "Yeah," he said softly.

He reluctantly released her and without even a look at him, she made her way back through the rest of the men and up the stairs.

After she was out of sight, he turned back to the front of the room.

"Let's vote!" Crash yelled out.

"Should he be awake when we do it?" Hawk asked.

Grizz came over and poured his full pint of beer over Pierce's head. Pierce groaned, sputtered and shook his head, his eyes unfocused. "What the fuck..."

"He's conscious. Let's vote," Hawk announced. "All in favor of strippin' this piece of shit of his colors?"

A roar of "ayes" rose up.

"Ayes fuckin' have it. He's done." Hawk spit on Pierce.

One by one, all the brothers stepped up, spit on Pierce and turned their backs to him as they returned to their spot in the large room.

Crow was the last one to approach. "Assume you don't need me to cover the colors on his back."

Diesel growled. "Fuck no. Strippin' his colors is gonna go way deeper than the skin on his fuckin' back."

Crow nodded, then spit on Pierce, even though the man now had one hand covering his face along with one on his balls.

Dex was surprised that Pierce didn't say shit the whole time. He didn't beg for any leniency.

Nothing.

He knew what his future held.

Justice was about to be served on a cold fucking platter.

CHAPTER SIXTEEN

W*e have to talk.*

Every step up the stairs was a dreaded one. He tightly gripped the bag of ice within his fingers. He just left one shit show and he wasn't looking forward to walking into another.

With gritted teeth, he wondered what was going to be waiting for him behind his bedroom door. Listening carefully, he moved down the hallway and then stopped in front of his room. Footsteps. Constant, rhythmic footsteps.

She was pacing impatiently.

Fuck.

He braced himself as he opened the door and stepped inside. His room was one of the larger ones, luckily, but that still didn't give her a lot of room to pace.

"Been pacin' the whole time?"

She stopped short and turned her troubled blue eyes to him. The look she gave him got him in the gut. "What the hell else was I supposed to do? I was sent to your room like a fucking child."

"Babe," he sighed, closing the door behind him and locking it. He snagged the keys she had thrown on his dresser and shoved them deep into his pocket. He held up the ice. "Brought you ice."

"For what?"

"The shiner that asshole gave you."

Her hand raised to her eye automatically, then she rushed into his tiny bathroom, flicked on the light and inspected her black eye closely in the spotty mirror. "Son of a bitch."

"Figured it was gonna turn, so brought ice," he said as he squeezed in behind her, mentally cursing how small his bathroom was. He needed to move the fuck out of church. It was time.

He lifted the ice up and offered it to her. She snagged it out of his hands and pressed it to her eye with a hiss.

They stood quietly for a moment. He wanted to wrap his arms around her, pull her back against him, calm the anger he knew simmered beneath the surface, but he wasn't sure if she'd let him.

"What are they going to do to him?"

"Strip him of his colors," Dex answered. Though those words sounded simple, they had a much deeper meaning. However, he wasn't going to lay out to Brooke what everyone knew would be done to Pierce.

Everyone knew, but didn't want to *know*, either. Not actually saying the words was safer for everyone in case questions popped up down the road.

She pinned her gaze to his in the mirror's reflection. "Dex, what are they going to do to him?"

After a hesitation, he said softly, "Babe, like I said, strip him of his colors."

She turned and leaned back against the sink, holding his gaze. "That's not enough. Diamond..." She breathed the last and that also got him right in the gut.

Fucking Diamond. No one had a clue that had happened. No one. She had kept that from everyone, including Slade, her brother, Jag, and most likely Bella, too.

After D and Hawk escorted Pierce out of church, with Z following behind at a slower but determined pace, Crow and Dawg had drilled Slade for more details. Apparently, Diamond admitted to her ol' man one night that Pierce had cornered and touched her, but that was all she told him.

It was possible she didn't remember it all. Maybe she had blocked it from her memory. Because, for fuck's sake, he doubted Pierce would admit to everyone that he took a fifteen-year old's virginity if it hadn't happened.

And they all doubted that Diamond would've given it up willingly to Pierce. She also wasn't the type of woman to sit back and let someone abuse her like that.

But then, she had only been fifteen at the time.

Diamond was always one to avoid coming to church and club parties, using the excuse she didn't like being around the "skanks." But maybe that was only part of it.

How Slade would handle that devastating discovery with Diamond remained to be seen. That would be between the two of them. Though, Crow was more than agitated at the whole thing. His constant murmur of "baby doll" under his breath was a bit strange.

"Babe... Trust me." He grabbed Brooke's chin and met her gaze directly, making sure she was clear on what he was saying but also what he wasn't saying as well. "It's gonna be enough. He's gonna get his due. Ain't gonna hurt anyone ever again."

T*rust me.*

That was just it. She wasn't sure she could trust him now. It was funny, because somehow and in some way, she had begun to trust Dexter Dougherty during the time they've spent together. Hell, she allowed him into her home. She allowed this biker to start slipping into her heart.

And now?

She pushed away from him and out of the bathroom to give them more space, so she didn't have to be so close to him. She couldn't bear to be that close. Not right now.

Brooke spun on her heels to stare at the man who followed her out of the bathroom. She should be angry at him. Pissed. But she had a difficult time holding onto even a thread of that anger. Even with everything that went on downstairs. Everything she heard while listening at the top of the steps when she promised to wait in his room. Everything she heard after she came back up, saying she'd once again wait in his room, but didn't.

She only had gone into his room once the meeting had broken up and Pierce had been removed from their clubhouse. When she knew Dex would come upstairs looking for her.

The man who she'd been sleeping with, who she was beginning to feel something for, who she trusted, had betrayed that very trust.

She should be really pissed because he *had* betrayed her. He had gone behind her back and took things she didn't give permission for him to have. "You took those diary pages against my wishes."

She needed to be pissed because it might push out the hurt his actions caused.

He dropped his head, ran a hand through his already disheveled dark hair and blew out a long breath as he stared at the floor. "Yeah," he said so quietly she almost wasn't sure if she heard him.

"Yeah?" she repeated, trying to encourage her own anger, fury. Anything but the deep ache in the pit of her stomach. "You took something that was mine, Dex, without my permission."

"Yeah."

"Can you even look at me?"

He raised his head and met her gaze. "I took 'em. Had a good reason, though, babe."

"You mean what you thought was a good reason. I told you that you could read them, but no one else. No one else, Dex. Your word should have been enough proof for them." She swallowed down the lump that rose in her throat. "You didn't need to show it to everyone. You didn't need to let them read my mother's private words. The demons she spilled on paper in an attempt to wash them from her soul. That wasn't for their eyes, Dex. It wasn't. You knew I didn't want anyone reading them." Her breath hitched but she pushed onward. "You took them anyway. And you didn't say a fucking word."

She felt it then. A flicker of anger. But with that hollow feeling in her heart, in her chest, a flicker wasn't enough.

He inhaled a deep breath but said nothing. Which was smart on his part, because she wasn't done yet. Not nearly done.

She needed to rid herself of that ache. That bone-deep disappointment in a man who came into her life when she least expected it, then flipped it and pinned it to the mat like a professional wrestler. "How'd you get my DNA?"

His eyes widened slightly, but he quickly hid it by rubbing a hand over them. "Fuck," he muttered.

She tried to keep that clawing disappointment from her voice. "Think I wasn't going to find that out? Your first mistake was assuming I'd go upstairs and wait. That was never going to fucking happen. What happened downstairs affected me also, Dex. I had every right to know what was going on, what would happen to the man who raped my mother." Her voice cracked. "To the man whose demented genes created me."

"Babe."

She lifted a palm and shook her head. "No, Dex. Don't *babe* me. I'm not your babe. I'm no one's babe. Not now. Not ever." She stepped up to him until they were toe to toe. "I'm going to ask you again and I want an answer. I want the truth. How did you get my DNA and when?"

"It was just some hair."

"Hair," she repeated. "How did you get my hair? Did you pull it from my head when I slept by your side? Did you take it from my brush when I wasn't looking? Like the diary pages?" She couldn't control her voice shooting up a few octaves. She hated losing control but right now, she needed that indignation to embrace her, protect her. Fill that hollow.

"How?"

"One of your hairbands."

"When?" Her breath hissed from her as she thought about

when he had access to them since she rarely wore her hair up. "When you pulled it from my hair at the gun range?"

He didn't say anything, just avoided her eyes.

"Dex, answer me. At the gun range?"

"Yeah."

"When you fucked me? Is that why you did it? To distract me from what you were doing? Are you that fucking sneaky?"

She spun around and stepped away from him. Her chest was tight, her stomach in knots. She was so disappointed. Everyone around her had disappointed her. Her mother for keeping that secret. Her brother and sister for not caring enough to help with her mother's illness and estate. The man she thought was her real father, for going along with her mother's lie. And now, Dex. "You violated my trust."

"Know it. Had to be done. Didn't have a choice, babe."

Babe!

Just throw a *babe* on the end of a sentence and that made everything A-Okay in his book.

"I'm going back to the motel tonight. Alone. And then I'm going back home tomorrow morning. Alone. Do you hear that, Dex? *Alone*."

He reached out but she stepped out of his reach. "Babe, you can't. It's too risky."

"*You* don't get to tell me what to do, Dex. You don't. You don't have that right."

His head dropped back and he stared at the ceiling for a few seconds before his body heaved when he barked out a loud, "Fuck!"

When he dropped his eyes to her, a sharp pain shot through her. He was hurting, too.

Everything that went down tonight, it did affect her. But it affected him as well. It affected every one of the members of his club family. Every single one.

Not one of those bikers didn't hurt from what they heard tonight. Not fucking one was left unscathed.

But they would get over it. Move on. Like she needed to do.

She needed to put all this behind her. And she couldn't do it by continuing to spend time with the man before her.

She needed to get out of Shadow Valley, get away from the DAMC and get her life back on track.

And she needed to get away from Dex that second, because she didn't want to do anything but hide under the covers and cry. She wasn't going to do that in front of anyone. Not even him.

So, she needed to get back to her motel room, close the door, turn off the lights and just allow herself to purge her tears, her sadness, her disappointment.

Then she needed to pick herself back up and head home to Harrisburg and forget Shadow Valley even existed. Forget Pierce. Forget the DAMC.

And, once again, she knew that would be impossible if Dex remained in her life.

She grabbed her jacket she had thrown on a chair, made sure she had her car's key fob, then moved to the door.

She stopped and stared at it for a moment. However, that gave Dex just enough time to move up behind her. He planted his palms against the door on either side of her, caging her in. "Babe," he murmured into her ear. "Brooke..."

His warm breath made her hair flutter against her ear and neck, causing her to fight back a shiver.

She had this crazy desire to turn around. To kiss him, to shove him onto his bed, make him submit to her and fuck him until she forgot everything that was said downstairs. Everything that happened with the Warriors back at her house. Everything she read in her mother's diary. And for even a moment, forget the suffering her mother went through, not only thirty years ago at the hand of the man she faced earlier, but her suffering during her long battle with cancer.

She should allow herself to simply enjoy the man who was pressed to her back right now. The one not saying much of anything, just waiting to see what she would do. Probably hoping that she'd stay and do the same thing she desired.

But she didn't do any of that.

Instead, with tears burning in her eyes, she shoved the lock bolt open and twisted the lock on the knob. "I need time to think, Dex. Some time to process. Just give me that, please."

She yanked opened the door, and he let her shut it behind her. As she moved down the quiet hallway, she heard him scream "fuck" behind the door.

She forced her feet to keep moving forward and not stop until she got to her car.

CHAPTER SEVENTEEN

Dex crab-walked his bike backward into the spot next to Brooke's Beemer. He shut it down and yanked his bandana from the lower half of his face and pulled the goggles he wore during cold weather off his head. He shrugged off his heavy leather motorcycle jacket and threw it over his arm, then he turned to stare at the door of Brooke's motel room.

A sliver of light peeked from between the two curtains that had been drawn together.

She was awake.

He had given her an hour before he followed. But that hour had been rough as fuck. He stopped himself multiple times from charging out of his room and chasing her the fuck down because there was no fucking way he was leaving her alone tonight.

Even though she was one of the strongest women he'd ever met, he'd seen what tonight did to her.

Hell, he'd seen what tonight did to everyone in that meeting. Especially Zak.

He could only imagine how tonight was going to affect not only Diamond's life, now that the truth was out, but how it might devastate Kelsea's when she finds out who her father is. Or was.

And heard some of the recently uncovered things her "father" had done in the thirty-five plus years he was an Angel.

Dex stepped up to her door and raised his hand to pound on it when it was flung open.

His breath caught as she stood in the doorway, wearing nothing but a clingy, silky robe. The light from the room caused a glow behind her that made her look surreal.

Fuck.

Fuck.

Fuck.

She was so fucking beautiful. So sexy. So confident.

He knew right then, right there, she was everything he needed in his life.

Everything.

She was the first woman to ever *get* him and he wasn't letting that go. He knew that was rare and that he'd never find it again.

"What the fuck are you doing here? I told you I wanted to be alone."

Her searing words, her anger hit him dead center in the chest. He was prepared for it, though. "Heard you."

"So when I slam this door in your face you'll know why."

"Ain't slammin' it. I'm comin' in."

She stared at him for a second. "No. You're not."

"Comin' in, babe."

"My name is Brooke."

"Yeah, babe, know what your fuckin' name is."

"Then learn to use it."

A muscle popped in his jaw as he ground his teeth. She thought she was the dominant in their relationship and, yeah, he allowed her to be because he liked it in the bedroom. But there came a point where that shit wasn't going to fly with him.

Like now.

"Want me to use your name, Brooke? Is that what you fuckin' want, Brooke? Need me to use it to remind you who you are, Brooke? I can do that." He pushed past her into the room, grabbed the door, ripped it from her hand and slammed it shut. He twisted the deadbolt and turned to face her. "But, Brooke, you ain't kickin' me out of this room. I'm fuckin' stayin'. Got me?"

She shook her head, her eyes narrowed dangerously. "No, you're not."

"The fuck I'm not." He flung his arms wide. "I'm standin' in your room. I'm stayin'. Ain't kickin' me out of your fuckin' life, *Brooke*. Not lettin' that happen. Know shit's twisted right now. Know shit's upside down for you. But it ain't just you. It's all of us. We're all damaged in some fuckin' way."

She pressed a hand to her forehead and something crossed over her face. The strong Brooke that he knew and loved was crumbling before his eyes.

Fuck.

Did he actually love her or was that his dick thinking out loud?

"My mother suffered twice, Dex. Twice. Once from that bastard's hands and then she suffered again when she was fighting cancer. I watched helplessly when she withered away to nothing. I couldn't do anything to help her besides be there for her. I did that, but it never felt like it was enough. I wanted to take that pain from her and I couldn't. And then to find what I did... to figure out that she'd suffered badly in another way... I know I'm not the cause of it, but I was the result, Dex. And I had no idea. For thirty fucking years, I had no clue. I had no idea what my mother saw every time she looked at me. What if she saw that monster? What if I was the cause of her reliving that nightmare over and over?"

Her whole body hiccuped and she covered her mouth with a shaky hand. She spun away from him and rushed to the other side of the room.

She was heading into the bathroom. She was going to go in there, lock the door and shut him out.

Fuck that.

He rushed after her, wrapped an arm around her waist and yanked her backward until she slammed into him. "You're not fuckin' hidin' from this. You're not hidin' from me. Fuck that shit."

She inhaled a shaky breath and then yelled, "I just want to be left alone."

"No."

She struggled against his hold, digging her nails into his arms. "Let me go and leave me alone, Dex. I don't need a reminder of where I came from, who I came from and that's nothing but what you are. A damn reminder."

Dex went solid against her. He tried not to take her words personally, because she was hurting and just lashing out, but it was hard not to.

She clawed at his arms, but luckily, he wore a long-sleeved tee that protected his skin from her desperate attempts of escape. "Let me go!"

"No," he growled in her ear as she struggled against him.

"I can't do this with you. Not now."

"You're doin' this. You're gonna let it all go an' I'm gonna be here when you do it. Gotta get that toxic shit outta your system. It's the only way to move the fuck on. Got me?"

She let out a scream that pierced his ear drums. He grunted when she elbowed his gut and kicked his shin in an attempt to escape his hold.

"You fucking bikers! You have to force yourself on women! You don't care about the damage you cause!"

"Ain't the same thing, babe. Not forcin' you to do anything but face the shit that's eatin' away at you deep down inside."

"You don't know what's eating at me. You don't know shit."

"Bullshit. I know 'cause I see you sufferin'. See it. Feel it, too, Brooke. Jesus fuckin' Christ. You ain't the only one sufferin' so stop bein' a selfish bitch."

Dex knew by calling her that, by poking at her deep-seated pain, she was going to snap. But it needed to happen for her to release that building pressure. To rid it from her system. And if he needed to take the brunt of her anger, then he was willing to do so.

She froze in his arms. "*I'm* a selfish bitch?"

His life flashed before his eyes, but he said it anyway, "Yeah."

"*I'm* the one being selfish?"

He was playing with fire. "Yeah, you are."

"Fuck you, asshole. Fuck all of you. I can't wait to get the fuck out of this goddamn town. I'm never setting foot in it again." The tone of her voice had turned high, almost a shriek, enough to make him wince, but he wasn't backing off. Not yet.

"That ain't gonna happen," he murmured.

"Says who?"

"Says me."

"Then you're talking out of your ass. Because I want nothing to do with you, your club, or Shadow Valley. I found out the shit I needed to and I'm... I'm done."

"Ain't done. Not with me. Not with the Valley. Not with my club, Brooke. Ain't done. You don't want anything to do with the DAMC, but it's too fuckin' late. Got a sister who's DAMC. Even though your father was a piece of fuckin' dog shit, you're now family. We accept you as family no matter what, babe. You belong to me; you belong to this club."

"I belong to you?" she asked in a harsh whisper. "*I* belong to *you*?" She jerked against him. "I must have missed that memo. You can't treat me like property. I don't belong to anyone! Especially you!"

He pressed his cheek to the side of her face and tightened his arms even more. "Babe, you do. You just don't see it yet."

"I don't belong to you." This time it wasn't a scream, it was a whimper.

Her body went lax against him but he was still afraid to loosen his hold. It could be a trick since she was smart and cunning.

But when her knees buckled, he held her up, supporting her weight. Her head fell forward and her body heaved.

Jesus fuckin' Christ.

Sweeping her off her feet into his arms, he took two long strides to the bed and placed her down gently. Brooke covered her face as her body wracked with silent sobs. When she curled up into a ball, his stomach felt hollow, like it had been scooped out with a large spoon.

He quickly shed his cut and took off his boots before sliding next to her, gathering her into his arms and once again squeezing her tight.

His fucking heart squeezed because it was painful to hear her finally let it all out. The tears, the frustration, that bitterness she was clinging to. She probably wasn't even aware of all that toxic shit she was hanging onto. But now that everything had come to a head tonight and there was nowhere else to focus, it was finally coming to the surface.

"Everything I thought was my life was a lie," came muffled from behind her hands.

"Don't let that asshole steal your real life away from you." He gently pulled her hands away from her face and even though he was glad she was purging herself of all the shit buried deep down, seeing her red-rimmed eyes and her tears rolling down her face twisted his gut. "Loved your dad?"

She blinked up at him in confusion.

"Your real dad, not your sperm donor. You loved 'im?"

"Yes."

"Your mom?"

"Of course," she answered without hesitation.

"They give you a good life?"

She sniffled. "Yes."

He tapped her temple gently. "Your parents loved you, too. Made you who you are. A strong woman." Raking his fingers through her hair, he pulled away the strands that clung to her damp cheeks. "That's all that fuckin' matters, babe. Don't let Pierce's evil shit win by destroyin' you. He's a nobody now. He'll no longer exist."

She closed her eyes and didn't say anything for the longest time. "Judge and jury."

"What?"

Her blue eyes popped open. “You’re all judge and jury. Then you dispense your own justice.”

“When necessary. That bother you?”

“Was there any other choice if I wanted him to meet justice?”

“No. ‘Cause 5-0 ain’t gonna do shit. ‘Specially with no solid proof. Even that diary.”

She got quiet again for a moment, then turned troubled eyes to him. “If my mom would’ve come forward. Said *something. Did* something other than just scribbling it down in a diary... Diamond...”

“Maybe. Maybe not. Don’t know that. Don’t blame your mother. Sure she did her best.”

“I loved her, Dex.”

“Know it, babe.”

“It was so rough for her in the end. I felt so helpless.”

“But you were there for her. By her side. That’s all you could do.”

“Yes, but it wasn’t enough. It wasn’t.” A whole fresh batch of tears began to stream down her face.

He rolled to his back, wrapped his arms around her head, holding her close and pressing his lips to her temple.

Like Brooke had felt with her mother, he felt the same with her right now. Helpless. However, he could do the same thing he told her: be there for her, remain by her side until she was all cried out.

He nuzzled his nose into her blonde hair and inhaled the scent of her shampoo. It was hard to believe it was only this morning that they had woken up in this very bed and had some awesome sex. Things went all fucking downhill from there.

But it was over. Pierce was handled. The Warriors were handled.

And he hoped she’d eventually forgive him for stealing her DNA and her mother’s diary pages without her knowledge.

He also hoped she’d realize how much she belonged with him.

He held her for hours, even after her tears dried up. During that time, he refused to let her go, not even for a second.

Because letting her go wasn't an option. But he needed her to feel the same way.

Brooke's eyes blinked open and she turned her head toward the sound of her phone vibrating on the nightstand. She did a quick mental check.

She was still in her motel room, still completely dressed and still pinned against Dex.

His breathing was steady as it blew across her cheek. After carefully peeling herself out of his embrace, she grabbed her phone, but it had gone to voicemail before she could answer it.

Three missed calls. All unknown. She frowned. Who was calling her at...

The time displayed on her phone said 3:34 AM.

What the hell...

She couldn't believe she slept through three calls. She turned and glanced down at Dex sleeping. No, she could. She had cried herself to sleep in his arms last night. And being in his arms, she had felt safe and... something else... Enough to sleep soundly.

Something else.

What did she feel for the man who had forced his way into her room? Hell, forced his way into her life.

The man who had the balls big enough to follow her home to Harrisburg. Follow her to her motel room after she'd told him to leave her alone. And not just once either.

He had balls big enough to allow her to let her be herself in the bedroom when it came to sex but never lost those balls afterward, outside the bedroom.

She wondered if he'd shown that secret side of himself to anyone besides her.

If he wasn't a biker, didn't live in Shadow Valley, didn't have a connection with the DAMC, then he *might* have been perfect for her.

But he wasn't.

So, she needed to ignore that feeling... that *something else*.

At this point, she saw no reason to get entangled in something that would never last.

She pressed the voicemail icon on her cellphone and lifted it to her ear.

"Ms. Monroe," the deep recorded voice said. "This is Trooper Jenkins, a fire marshal for the Pennsylvania State Police. I need you to call me back as soon as you can. Your house has been involved in an alleged arson and we want to make sure you're safe. Please contact me on my cell as soon as you get this message at—"

The phone tumbled from Brooke's fingers and landed on the bed. The deep voice in the message rattled off some numbers and some other stuff, but she didn't know what. Her heart stopped as she stared at the phone that caused a glow in the room that suddenly seemed glaring.

Dex sat up abruptly and, leaning over her, grabbed the phone. He hit the replay button and put it to his ear.

"Fuckin' motherfuckers," he barked as he pulled the phone away, and hit another button. After a few seconds, he said, "Yeah, it is. This is her phone. She's safe. What's goin' on?" After a few more moments, he muttered, "Be there in about three hours." A pause. "Shadow Valley. South of the 'burgh." Another pause. "Yeah. Right. Got you." He disconnected the phone, threw it back onto the bed, then gripped her face within his large, warm hands.

She could only blink at him. She couldn't focus because her thoughts kept whirling around in her head like a cyclone. She couldn't get them to stop no matter how hard she tried. "Dex," she whispered.

"Yeah, babe. Get your shoes on, gather your shit, pack up your Beemer. Gotta drop off my sled at church, then takin' your cage to Harrisburg. Got me?"

"But—"

"No fuckin' buts. Get it done. Now. Gotta go."

"But..."

He didn't release her face, but shook her gently. "Listen. No buts. Get movin'."

She felt herself nod, but it didn't feel like herself. It was like someone else was nodding for her.

What the hell was happening?

She tried to concentrate on the man all up in her face. "What are we doing?"

"Headin' back to Harrisburg. Gotta deal with this shit an' the pigs. They need to talk to you."

"My house..."

"Yeah, babe. Don't know the extent. Gotta get rollin' now. Got me?"

She nodded again, pushed out of the bed, automatically straightening the rumpled clothes on her body. She gathered her belongings without thinking, without feeling. Without anything. The only thing that kept her going was Dex's firm commands.

Nothing remained of her inside. Nothing.

She was completely fucking empty.

Dex pulled her BMW over to the curb as close as the firefighters would allow. Which wasn't close because they had their rigs blocking the street and along with a few parked pigmobiles.

Before they could even get out of the car, a cop approached them asking who they were. When he explained who Brooke was, he got a long eyeballing from the man in a black and gray uniform. Dex bit his insult back because he needed to keep his shit together and the Trooper that called Brooke needed to talk to her.

He also didn't need to be arrested for disorderly conduct and let Brooke deal with this whole new shit show by herself.

The pig pointed toward another man in a suit that stood scribbling shit down in a notebook. The blond guy looked up, saw them approaching and met them halfway.

He held out his hand to Brooke as he introduced himself and then ignored Dex once he noticed the colors on Dex's back.

What-fucking-ever.

Would it have been smart to leave his cut in Brooke's cage? Probably. But fuck everybody who was judging him right now. He wasn't hiding who he was. They could suck his fucking dick.

Dex turned his eyes from Brooke talking to the Trooper to what remained of her home.

What remained was nothing but ashes, glowing embers, her stone fireplace and some random blackened skeletal remains of her house. Smoke still rose up as the firemen poked and prodded, looking for hot spots and hosing some areas down.

He took a few steps forward, drawn to the devastation and sick to his stomach at what the Warriors had done.

Because no one else had done this besides that scum sucking MC. That wasn't even in question. It was because of this, he knew Brooke hadn't been safe at home. This was why he insisted she come back with him to Shadow Valley. He knew that the Warriors would seek retribution for their president going missing.

And her house was his last known location.

As he moved forward as if in a trance, staring at what remained, a fireman reached out and grabbed his arm. He looked up and the man jerked his chin back to where Brooke and the Trooper talked. "Your woman just collapsed."

Dex spun and saw the Trooper squatting down next to Brooke who had fallen to her knees, her head in her hands, her body curled over itself.

"What the fuck?" he yelled, rushing back to her. He pushed the Trooper out of the way, dropped to his knees, and grabbed Brooke, pulling her into his arms. "What the fuck happened?" he asked the cop standing over them.

"More bad news," he murmured, concern in his dark eyes as he stared at Brooke.

"What?" What else could there be? How much more could this woman take?

"This fire is being deemed an arson at this point. But I just found out another arson took place. Though, not in my area."

"Yeah and?"

"Whoever hit her house, hit her business, too. This was personal. Not random."

No fucking shit. But he wasn't saying that.

The Trooper met Dex's gaze, his eyes hard. "Do you know who could've done this?"

Dex's nostrils flared but he kept his face hard, unreadable. "Nope."

Trooper Jenkins' mouth flattened out. "Right." His spine snapped straight and he faced Dex head-on. "Dealt with people like you before. Like I said, it's definitely not random. Someone's targeting her." He tilted his head. "Or you." He tapped his pen against his notebook as he jerked his chin toward the patches on the front of his cut. "Or your club."

Dex stood, pulling Brooke up with him, pressing her face into his chest and holding her tight. "Don't know who that'd be."

The Trooper nodded, not hiding the fact that he didn't believe Dex. "Right." With a sigh, he pulled a couple business cards from his pocket and held them out to Dex. "If, for some reason, you suspect anyone who might have done it, here's my card. Hang onto one. Give the other to her insurance company."

Dex said nothing but pulled the cards from his fingers and tucked them into his back pocket.

Jenkins stared at Brooke for a moment, then said, "Sorry this happened to her. No one deserves this. Maybe she needs to pick different people to associate with."

Dex ignored his dig and dropped his attention to Brooke as the Trooper strode away. "Babe," he whispered, stroking her hair.

"It's all gone." Her words were smothered into his shirt.

"Yeah."

"Everything I've known. Everything I built. Everything that was... me. I have nothing left."

"Not true, babe."

She pulled away slightly and looked up at him, her blue eyes wide. "What? What do I have left? They took everything from me. Everything, Dex."

"Babe, got me. Got all of us."

Her mouth dropped open. "Us? You mean your club? The very thing that caused my life to spiral into the depths of hell?"

Dex locked his jaw from saying something he would regret later. He needed to keep his head on straight. He didn't need to make this any worse for her. Because, yeah, he got what she meant. He understood why she'd blame the club.

Pierce created her and, because of that, was the catalyst of all the shit that resulted from that moment. The man had been an Angel, had been embedded deeply into the DAMC for longer than either of them had been born. He'd been the club's president for a decade.

So, yeah, he got it. He could understand why she wanted nothing to do with the DAMC.

But that didn't mean he'd accept that.

"I have nowhere to live," she said softly, the deep sadness in her words like a twisted knife in his chest. "My business is gone."

"Know you're probably gonna hate what I'm about to say to you, but... gotta take this as a new beginnin'. A fresh start."

"I can't just walk away from my business, my clients. Hell, even my employees."

"You'll figure it out. Got insurance, right?"

She nodded, staring toward what remained of her former house as the smoke rose up into the early morning sky.

"The Trooper said that a Molotov cocktail was used to firebomb my offices and showroom." She released a bitter laugh. "A fucking *Molotov cocktail*! What the hell?"

Dex mumbled, "Like they tried to do with Sophie's bakery."

She turned surprised eyes to him. "They burned her bakery down?"

He shook his head. "No. Tried. Sophie was livin' above the bakery. She was lucky that attempt failed."

"But what did she do to them?"

"Fuckin' nothin'. Besides being involved with Z."

"So, if I hadn't been involved with their president's disappearance, if I hadn't been Pierce's daughter and if, for some reason, I'd just been with you, this still might have happened to me?"

If, for some reason, I'd just been with you.

That sentence drove home what he knew. That certain circumstances had brought them together. If seeking the truth hadn't brought Brooke to Shadow Valley, they never would've crossed paths, and even if they had, other than for a reason they had, she never would have looked twice at him. Not once, probably, either.

"Just being with you could've brought on their wrath?" she asked when he didn't answer.

"Can't answer that, babe. Don't know. Don't know what goes on in their fucked up minds. Can't say that you bein' with me wouldn't have drawn their attention. They kidnapped Kiki, an' only because she was seein' Hawk. Was at his place at the wrong time. She wasn't DAMC, but they didn't know that. You bein' with me could be a risk." He scrubbed a hand over his stubbled chin. "Don't wanna tell you that so you're scared to be with me, but gotta be honest with you. This shit's been goin' on forever. Don't know if it'll ever end." He shook his head and stared at his boots. "Just don't know, Brooke."

"But I'm not with you," she whispered. "We were just thrown together... We..." She took a deep breath. "I'm here. You're there."

"You got nothin' here anymore."

"My employees..."

"They'll find their own way."

"A business."

"You can rebuild. Don't hafta be here."

"What are you saying?"

"Don't need to say it out loud, babe. You know what I'm sayin'."

Her brows furrowed as she stared at him. "No. I need to hear it. I need you to spell out what you want. Because I'm not sure that what you want is the same thing I want."

He grabbed her hand and began to tug her toward the burned-out remains of her house. One of the firemen yelled as he yanked her close. Close enough to feel the heat of the smoldering ashes.

He dug into his cut, into that slit cut inside his vest, and pulled out the pages from her mother's diary, holding them out to her. She stared at them blankly, her brows still furrowed.

"That shit's the past." Swinging his arm out over the devastation before them, he continued, "This house is the past. Your business is the past. This has given you a chance to start fresh. Take those pages, babe. Burn them. Cleanse yourself of that poison. Yeah?"

She turned blue eyes up from her mother's handwritten words to him. "And you think you're my future."

"Yeah, babe, I do. Know it's gonna be a difficult road to get back on your feet. Know it. Gonna be there every second for you, gonna be there to help you every step of the fuckin' way. Help you as much as I can. Don't know shit about decoratin' or anything, but whatever you need, whatever I can help you with, I'll do it. An' not just me. The whole fuckin' club, *my* family. *Your* family. We'll be there for you. Babe, you are now DAMC."

"Because you think I belong to you." It wasn't a question, but a soft statement.

One that she was going to deny. Tell him that she didn't, she never would. She was a strong, independent woman and she didn't need anybody. Dex. The DAMC. Her sister. Nobody.

She was gearing up to tell him to go fuck off. To laugh in his face because she didn't need a man like him in her life. He was so not her caliber and for him to think so would be laughable.

That was what she was about to say to him and, when she did, it was going to fucking kill him. So, he needed to convince her otherwise, before she shut him out. Before she closed herself off to the possibility of a future with him. A future back in Shadow Valley. Not a future where they lived hours apart, where he could be easily forgotten as she went about building a new life. Without him.

He dropped to his knees. Right there on the wet ground, in the mud created from dirt and ash and water from the fire hoses. Right there at her feet. He grabbed both of her hands and pressed his forehead to them for a moment, gathering his breath, gathering his courage to fight any disappointment she'd rain on him.

When he finally looked up, met her eyes, which were shiny, shocked, even scared, he began, not caring who watched them, not caring who heard. "Babe, beggin' you. Just give me a chance. Give us a chance. Know we're not from the same world. Hell, from the same universe. But it works. I promise, it works. Look at Kiki an' Hawk. Hell, he was fuckin' in county jail an' she was his lawyer. Can't get any more different than that. Look at Z, the prez of a MC who did ten years in prison an' Sophie, a sweet baker who probably never had a parkin' ticket. Look at Axel, a fuckin' cop, an' Bella, a born biker chick. An' then there's Emma. A kindergarten teacher." He shook his head and snorted. "Dawg was runnin' a strip club when a kindergarten teacher walked the fuck into his life. Can't get much more different than that. An' it works for 'em, swear it. Those men would die for 'em. Every single one of 'em. An' babe..."

She closed her eyes.

He squeezed her hands. "I'd die for you."

Her fingers flexed within his. "Don't say that," she whispered.

"It's true. Never thought it would happen to me. Never thought I'd find the right woman that'd make me feel that way. But fuck," he blew out a breath, "you fuckin' walked into that pawn shop an' gave me wood that wouldn't quit. Knew it right there an' then, I needed to know you."

"You just wanted to fuck me."

"Yeah, that too. But believe me, a lot of good-lookin' women walk into that pawn shop. Not one of 'em... not one, babe, had ever affected me like you did. I get now what Z, Hawk an' Dawg say about how when they found their women it hit 'em hard. The second I saw you it hit me just as fuckin' hard. So," he released her hands and pushed to his feet, cupping her cheeks, not allowing her to avoid his gaze. He needed her to see him. See how much she meant to him. Because this could be his only shot. "Beggin' you, babe, just gimme a chance to prove I'm everything you need. Promise I'll do my damnedest for you every fuckin' day. An' if one day you decide I ain't good enough, that I didn't do my fuckin' best for you an' you wanna walk away, then ain't gonna stop you."

She sucked in a breath and her eyes went wide. She jerked her face out of his hands and said, "Dexter Dougherty, you'd let me just walk away from you?"

His heart stuttered, then began to beat furiously. "Only want what's best for you, babe."

"You think you might not be it?"

"Fuck that. Know I am."

"Then I'll ask you again... You'd let me just walk away from you?"

His lips twitched. "Truth, babe? No. Would never let you walk away. Would do everythin' in my power to keep you by my side. Keep you where you belong."

"Dex," she whispered. "We haven't even known each other that long."

"Yeah, babe. We've known each other our whole lives," he patted his chest, "in here. Was only just recent we found each other. Realized you're what I've been missin' all my fuckin' life. Hopin' it's the same for you."

She shook her head. "You're something else."

"Ain't gonna deny it."

She turned and looked over at the remains of her home. "So much stuff has happened. *So much*."

"Yeah. Know it."

She held out her hand and he knew exactly what she wanted. He placed the folded, torn-out pages from her mother's diary into her palm. She closed her fist around them, then took a step toward some remaining embers. After looking one last time at the crumpled papers in her hand, she dropped them onto the glowing hot coals. The pages instantly ignited and burned quickly until there was nothing but a swirl of paper ash. Some of those remnants actually floated up into the December air.

Dex stepped up to her and grabbed her hand, giving it a squeeze. She didn't pull away, but instead tightened her fingers on his.

"Can't change the past," he murmured. "But can put it behind you."

"You're right, you can't change the past." She tugged on his hand and looked up at him. "But you can shape the future."

He jerked her toward him and into his arms. He pressed his mouth into her hair. "Sorry, babe. Sorry all this shit had to happen to you. Sorry you had to deal with so much loss."

"The house. My business. Those are things I can rebuild. Start fresh, like you said. Losing my mother... That was, still is, the hardest. She was the only reason I stayed in this area. Now everything's gone that held me here. I realize I can go anywhere I want now."

He said nothing and just waited.

And waited.

And fucking waited.

"Yeah," he finally said, hoping that would spur her to continue.

"Yeah," she echoed him on a breath.

"Babe."

"Yes?"

"That all you gonna say?"

"No."

He waited again as they stood at the edge of her burned-out home. He was trying his damnedest to be patient, but that was wearing thin. It was now mid-December and even though the air was a little warmer around the house because of the fire, it wasn't that warm, and he only wore his long-sleeved tee and his cut. His nipples had pebbled painfully and his piercings ached from the brisk weather. He rubbed a palm over one of them and that caught her eye.

"Kelsea."

He frowned. "What about her?"

"I want to meet her."

"Yeah. Not sure she knows yet."

"She's my sister. I want to be there for her. Get to know her."

"Yeah, babe. Got it."

"That will be part of the whole 'shaping the future.' I assume I'm her older sister."

"Yeah, you are."

"Maybe she can help me with restarting my business."

"Yeah, that'd be good. She don't do shit but party an' get her ass in trouble. But, babe... She lives in the Valley."

"I know. Pittsburgh's only like twenty minutes from Shadow Valley, right?"

"On a good day."

"Well then, we'll make every day a good day."

He locked his knees so he wouldn't fall at her feet once again. He couldn't believe things were going his way, but they were and he wasn't going to fuck it up.

"Do you think your uncle would mind you sticking around Harrisburg for a week or so while I get my stuff sorted? I'll need to meet with the insurance companies and my employees, figure out what I need to do since I now have nothing. Not even clothes or paperwork. Or anything. I mean it's like being totally reborn."

That it was. "Don't think Ace will fuckin' mind me stayin' here to help you get your shit sorted."

"While we're getting that shit sorted, maybe we can figure out where we're going to live. I'm not staying in your room at church with you."

"Can't anyway."

"Why?"

"We discussed this shit."

She snorted. "Oh, that's right, because I'm a woman." Her gaze bounced back over the remains of her house. "Then we might have to find somewhere temporary until I can get a check from the insurance company."

"Got it covered."

She arched an eyebrow at him. "What?"

"Wanna house? Want one just like this? Got it covered. Club will cover it 'til your check comes through. Got some green stashed away, too. That's one bonus of livin' for free at church, can bank a bunch of money."

"How much money?"

"Probably enough for a healthy down payment dependin' how big a house you want."

Her mouth dropped open. "An' you lived in that hovel?"

"Yeah. Just slept, showered an' jerked off in there. Didn't need much." He met her blue eyes and he pulled her into his arms. "Babe."

"Yes?"

"You comin' to Shadow Valley for me or Kelsea?"

"Well, I have to say you." She reached into his cut and tweaked his nipple. "I have so many more things I want to do to you yet."

He smiled at her words. "But your toys are gone."

"Yes, but they're replaceable."

"Glad you were in the Valley with me, babe, when the Warriors struck. Because one thing I fuckin' know is, you ain't replaceable. Got me?"

She pressed her forehead into his chest and wrapped her arms under his cut and around his waist. "Yes, Dex, I got you."

"Got your back, babe. All this shit's just a bump in the road. What don't kill you makes you stronger. Though, not sure how much stronger you can get. You're one fuckin' amazin' woman, Brooke. Can't believe you're in my arms right now. Can't believe you're comin' home with me."

"Don't sell yourself short," she whispered. "You're not so bad yourself."

He dropped his head and took her mouth, kissing her long and hard. Claiming her, letting her know that, yeah, she belonged to him, but he belonged to her, too.

"Let's go find a motel."

"So I can get my affairs in order and call the insurance company?"

"Yeah, that, too."

They wandered back to her cage, but he stopped suddenly, drawing her to a halt.

She looked at him with a question on her face.

"Just gotta say... *Thank fuck* you walked into the pawn shop that day."

Her lips twitched. "And *thank fuck* you undressed me with your eyes. Just like you're doing right now."

"Nope. Ain't doin' that. Got told by some bossy chick that it's sexual harassment."

"Yes, well, there's a punishment for that."

He smiled and tugged her faster toward the car. "Can't fuckin' wait."

EPILOGUE

Brooke sat at a table under an enormous tent and her gaze bounced over the crowd. Nash's band, Dirty Deeds, was set up along one side, playing some classic rock songs. At least their volume wasn't deafening today like it normally was at some of the parties and pig roasts the club had at church. The "guests" could talk with each other easily and not have to yell back and forth.

Kiki, in a simple, but stunning ivory dress, was wearing a huge smile and dancing with her father. Well, the glowing woman should be smiling. She married the man she loved beyond life today. And she was getting closer to having her first child with him. Her huge baby bump kept bouncing against her father awkwardly, but it seemed as though neither father nor daughter minded.

Hawk wasn't dancing, of course. Instead he was sticking close to Kiki's mother and his own parents, Janice and Ace, even though his eyes followed the woman who had his first name tattooed onto the back of her neck and now his last name tacked onto her own with a hyphen. The club's vice president looked super handsome with his mohawk freshly trimmed, the sides of his head shaved smooth, wearing brand-new black jeans, and a crisp button down, long-sleeved black shirt under his cut. A new, shiny titanium wedding ring adorned his finger that had a sapphire-colored band circling the center. He said the color reminded him of Kiki's eyes.

Ivy, also now obviously pregnant, leaned back against Jag as they stood near the edge of the dance floor. She swayed along with the music as his arms were wrapped around her, his hands planted on her stomach. They watched the few souls brave enough to be out on the dance floor that had been set up in the center of the tent.

Slade was on one side of the tent while his ol' lady, Diamond, was on the other talking to Axel and Bella. Brooke heard things had been strained between them since the night the truth about Pierce came out. Brooke hoped things worked out between the two, since they not only lived together in a cabin here on the farm, but she'd been told they were perfect together.

Hopefully they could move past what Brooke's biological father did to Diamond at such a young age. Brooke wasn't even sure if Diamond remembered all the details. She hadn't approached Diamond about it, deciding to let the other woman reach out first, if she was so inclined.

As she watched Zak with Baby Z in his arms approaching her and Dex, her hand dropped to her own stomach. Her damn ovaries were acting up again.

Dex leaned closer and asked softly, "You okay?"

His deep voice sent a shiver down her spine. She turned and met his concerned, dark eyes. "Yes. Whatever's in the water here, I'm not sure I want to drink it."

"Babe, you've been drinkin' it for months now."

His warm fingers wrapped around her bare knee under the hem of her dress and squeezed. Even months later, his fingers still sent a shock of lightning through her that landed in her core. That didn't help her screaming ovaries one bit. Nor did the fact that he'd trimmed his beard very short this morning after their rough and tumble early morning sex. Besides the worn cut he wore, everything else was freshly laundered and he looked and smelled good enough to eat.

Unfortunately, they hadn't had enough time this morning to break out any toys, but she would make sure they made up for it later.

"That's what I'm afraid of. I think I'm going to start getting water delivered to both the house and office."

"So, you're sayin' you don't want my kid?"

"I didn't say that. I still have a long way to go before I can hire more employees and get my design team working smoothly together. Until then, I'm too busy rebuilding my business to concentrate on raising a child. I'm not saying never, just not now."

"Got Kelsea helpin' you."

A couple weeks after their initial introduction, Brooke had asked Kelsea if she wanted to come join her business at the ground level and help her get things rolling in the Pittsburgh area. Her newly-found sister had balked at first but then surprisingly agreed.

Brooke had wondered if one—or more —of the club members had convinced her. Maybe even Dex himself. Though he never said if it was him, she wouldn't put it past him.

Everyone was worried about Kelsea. And they should be. Her behavior had been a bit out of control recently. From what Brooke understood, that wasn't anything new with her younger sister. However, the whole Pierce thing apparently made it worse. Brooke hoped to help get her on the right track.

"Yes, and that would be all well and good if she was more reliable." She glanced around and found the subject of their discussion on the dance floor. "Who's she dancing with?"

Dex's neck twisted as he looked for his cousin. He finally spotted what Brooke had... Kelsea plastered against a man wearing a Dark Knights cut as they ground against each other on the dance floor.

He frowned. "Think it's the same Knight she was dancin' with at Z's weddin'."

"Should we be worried?"

"Knights are allies, babe. Nothin' to worry 'bout." Dex lifted his chin to an extremely large Black man across the room. "Magnum will make sure his brother stays in line."

Brooke noticed that this Magnum did have his eyes glued to Kelsea and the other biker from his club. With arms crossed over his broad chest, he was as large as Diesel, who happened to be standing next to him watching the same scenario. Only D had his baby girl in his arms like normal. That man never let his daughter out of his sight.

Out of nowhere, Lily, Emma's daughter, bravely approached both enormous men and tugged on Diesel's cut before lifting her hands in what looked like a plea to hold Violet. D's gaze dropped to the blonde-headed girl and he shook his head, then went back to watching Kelsea's *practically-having-sex-on-the-dance-floor* moves.

Brooke rolled her lips inward when Lily tugged on Diesel's cut again, refusing to be ignored, and held up her hands. D dropped his gaze once more to Dawg's stepdaughter and shook his head.

When she did it a third time, a giggle slipped out of Brooke. The girl was determined. But so was D.

She couldn't tell who was more stubborn. Especially when Lily stomped her foot, tossed her blonde head, and planted her hands on her hips, glaring up at Diesel.

"Jesus fuckin' Christ," Dex muttered in the seat next to her. "She's gonna be a pisser. Dawg's gonna have a hellion on his hands in a few years."

Dawg was too busy talking to his teenaged daughter in another corner of the reception tent to notice. He seemed to be giving Caitlin some sort of lecture. But then the girl was sixteen going on thirty, as well as beautiful, which was a dangerous combination. And there were a lot of men at the wedding and reception today. Almost seventeen years of age or not, she was hard to ignore. Unless Dawg caught them staring, then they suddenly found something else more interesting to look at.

After Z had been stopped multiple times on his journey to their table, he finally arrived and sat in a chair next to Dex with a grunt. He placed Baby Z on the floor between his legs and held both of his son's hands so he wouldn't waddle away.

She twisted toward the club president. "The insurance checks cleared. I'll be paying the club back this week. I'll give it to Ace."

Z turned his stunning blue eyes to her. "Yeah. Good. Glad the loan helped."

"I couldn't have gotten back on my feet so quickly if you hadn't been so generous."

"You're family, so..." Z drifted off, his eyes dropping to his son.

"Not really," she murmured.

"Kels' sister," he stated. Then he lifted his chin at Dex. "His ol' lady. Family."

"Right." She still wasn't sure how she felt about being "claimed at the table" by Dex a couple of months ago. In these biker's eyes, that now meant she was Dex's property.

And both of them knew that wasn't true.

But if it made things smoother for Dex with his brothers, then she accepted the title. Albeit reluctantly.

Suddenly, their attention was drawn to Axel who had a firm grip on Bella's hand as he approached his brother.

"What?" Z barked as Axel stopped in front of him.

Axel gave his brother an answering frown, then asked, "Seen Jayde?"

Z glanced around the tent with narrowed eyes. "Fuck no. Not since earlier."

"Linc's nowhere to be found, either," Axel muttered, his jaw tight, his blue eyes scanning the crowd.

"Doesn't mean they're together," Bella said with a sigh. Both men's eyes landed on her and they scowled.

"Fuck," Z muttered under his breath, then looked at his younger brother. "You gonna kill 'im or am I gonna kill 'im?"

"Neither," Bella said, pulling her hand from Axel and plugging it on her hip, "since they are both consenting adults. Not to mention, Axel's a fucking cop and you already did enough time in a concrete box, Z."

"We'll just hurt him a little bit," Axel grumbled.

Z pushed to his feet, picking Zeke up as he did so. He shoved the baby at a surprised Bella and the two brothers stalked off.

"Oh shit," Bella muttered as Baby Z clung to her, watching his father walk quickly away.

Dex snorted and shook his head. "*If* they're together, sure it ain't the first time."

"*If* they're together," Bella repeated, "Linc's playing with fire since Jayde's father is a cop who doesn't want his daughter with a biker, her brother is a cop and her other brother is his president. It'd be best if he set his sights elsewhere."

"A-fuckin'-men," Dex muttered.

"Well, *if* they are together, I hope they found a good hiding spot," Brooke added. "Because it might be awkward for both of them if her two pissed off brothers came busting through the door when Linc's pants are down."

Dex snorted. "Awkward ain't the word."

Bella sat down with a sigh, settling Baby Z in her lap. Crow joined them a moment later, stopping directly in front of Brooke.

When he held out a hand and asked with his honey-smooth voice, "Wanna dance?" Brooke's ovaries finally exploded.

She was beginning to push to her feet when Dex's fingers wrapped around her arm and pulled her back down in her seat. "She's good, brother."

Brooke pursed her lips as she studied Dex. "Says who? I would love to dance and since I asked you twice earlier and you refused both times, I'm going to go dance with Crow."

Dex ignored her, his eyes pinned on Crow. "She's good, brother. Maybe Bella wants to dance."

Bella gave Brooke a knowing look, then smiled at Crow. "I'd love that. I'll need to drop Baby Z off with Sophie first."

"She can dance with Crow after I do." Brooke arched a brow at Dex. "Unless you've changed your mind about taking me out onto the dance floor? Because if so, let's go."

. . .

Dex stared at his woman. She must have forgotten where they were. And worse, he knew Crow was standing there smirking, enjoying the fact his ol' lady was making demands on him. Dex couldn't wait until the day Crow was dealing with the same shit he was.

Because that day was coming for him, whether the brother knew it or not. One by fucking one they'd all been falling like dominoes. And he doubted any of his brothers would escape their thirties unscathed.

Including smooth-talking, *more-than-helpful, you-can-lean-on-me* Crow. He always seemed to be there when the women needed their ruffled feathers smoothed.

But no fucking way was he letting Brooke dance with him. Fuck that.

He glanced up at Crow. "Think this shit's funny?" He stood up and pulled Brooke up with him. "Let's fuckin' go," he told her, tugging her away from the table.

"Where are we going?"

"To dance. Since you just pulled that little bullshit back there. You're outta your fuckin' mind if you think I'm allowin' Crow rub against you."

She made a noise, but he ignored it and kept pulling her along until they reached the center of the tent. He turned toward her and when he looked down into her face she was laughing.

"Think that was funny?" Because he didn't fucking think any of that was funny.

"Your jealousy is unwarranted."

"Ain't jealous," he muttered.

Brooke rolled her eyes at him.

"Woman," he warned.

"Did you just *woman* me?"

Dex ignored her annoyance and pulled her into his arms, which, luckily, she didn't cause a scene about. He wrapped his arms around her waist and planted his hands firmly on her sweet fucking ass in that even sweeter sexy dress she was wearing.

Aaaaaand now he had a half chub.

He had no fucking clue how to dance, so he just shifted his weight from one foot to the other while standing in place, hoping that would be acceptable.

No, *fuck that*, it would *have* to be acceptable.

"You didn't have to pull that macho bullshit with Crow," she stated, as she pressed her cheek to his and linked her hands behind his neck. Her hips moved back and forth against him, turning his half chub quickly into a full hard-on.

It didn't take much for her to turn him the fuck on. Which made him take a mental inventory of which rooms were left in their house they hadn't christened yet. His goal was to christen them all at least once. She had bought a pretty big fucking house, even against his wishes. But the one she wanted had an addition on it so large that she had turned it into her office space. She said once her interior design company outgrew that, she'd get an office closer to the city.

Knowing his woman, he had a feeling she'd outgrow it pretty damn quickly.

But that wasn't the problem he needed to deal with right now.

"Babe, told you this. It's one thing when you're fuckin' bossy in the bedroom. It's another when you're fuckin' bossy outside of it. Gotta let me be your ol' man, for fuck's sake."

She pulled back a little to stare up at him with narrowed blue eyes. However, her doing that pressed her heat against his already aching dick even more.

"What does that mean, *let* you be my ol' man? Does that mean you get to treat me like D does Jewel? Because that's never going to happen."

Dex sighed and with a jerk to her hips, pulled her tight against him again. She felt so damn good. They might have to duck out early. Or at least find somewhere to hide so she could suck him off quick-like.

"Look," he began, but before he could continue, she pressed her mouth to his. Her tongue slipped between his lips and drew a groan from him. His fingers flexed harder into the soft curves of her ass.

After a minute, she pulled away enough so he could say, "Already sufferin' here, babe, that didn't help."

"I can tell." She smiled and then ran the tip of her tongue across his bottom lip before nipping it hard. Shoving her fingers into the hair at the back of his head, she pulled it enough so he could feel the sting on his scalp, but not obvious enough where anyone else would notice.

Fuck, that made his dick twitch hard in his jeans.

"How about I let you be my *ol' man* when we're at church, around your brothers and family, but when it comes to our bedroom and my business, I'm in charge."

I'll let you be my ol' man.

He snorted. But in reality, there was no point in fighting it so he gave her an answering, "Yeah." Plus, he liked that arrangement. He fucking liked it a lot.

"Yeah?" she echoed.

"Yeah, babe." He slipped his hand between them and grabbed his dick through his jeans. Her talk of being in charge in the bedroom was stoking his fire even hotter. "You in the mood to be in charge right now?"

Her eyes sparkled with excitement. "What do you want me to do to you?"

Well, that was an easy answer. "Love me as much as I love you."

She smiled. "You have that. What else?"

He pressed his lips to her ear and whispered. When he was done, she pulled back and stared at him. After a second, her wide eyes narrowed and a smile spread across her face. "I can do that."

"Know it, babe. Let's go home."

Turn the page for a sneak peek of the next book in the Down & Dirty: Dirty Angels MC series

---

DOWN & DIRTY: LINC

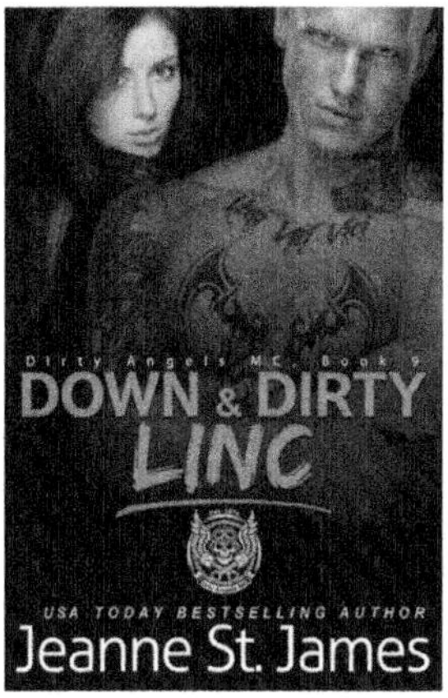

Normally I include the first chapter of the next book in the Down & Dirty: Dirty Angels MC series, which would be Linc's book. HOWEVER, because there are spoilers in the first line of the book, I decided not to include it because I didn't want to spoil that book for anyone. However, on the next page I did include a little taste...

SNEAK PEAK OF DOWN & DIRTY: LINC

Linc's gaze slid to Jayde and he realized she was eyeballing him. Hard. With narrowed eyes.

Fuck.

He tried to swallow the lump in his throat, but it was determined to stick right where it had landed.

Suddenly, all the trepidation he'd been feeling about this meeting, all the dread that had twisted his gut for days, sluiced off him like a cold shower. He shook himself mentally to rid himself of any remaining doubt.

Fuck. This. Shit.

He placed his beer bottle on the floor next to the stool and jumped to his feet. With three long strides, he was at the couch, grabbing Jayde's arm and pulling her from it.

"What—" she squeaked in surprise.

Axel jumped up from the couch, his hand landing on his holster.

Z's stool fell backwards with a clatter as he stood quickly. "What the fuck!"

Linc lifted a palm. "Just need to talk to Jayde. *Alone.*" Then he began to drag her across the room and toward the door.

"No. I've got nothing to say to—"

"We're talking and doin' it right fuckin' now. And not in front of your fuckin' family. No one else's making decisions for us. No one knows what's fuckin' best for us but us. Got me?"

Her mouth dropped open and he didn't wait for her to respond. He yanked open the door and pulled her through it.

"You can talk down in the bakery!" Sophie yelled. "We'll make sure the boys stay up here and leave you two alone."

With a grunt, Linc slammed the door shut and pointed down the steps. "Go. Now."

"But—"

"No lip, woman. Fuckin' go downstairs. Go!"

With a frown and pursed lips, she made her way carefully down the stairs, through the bakery's kitchen and out into the dark shop. He followed closely behind, picking up whiffs of her scent as she moved. Something sweet and light.

She started to reach for something on the wall, but he stopped her. He grabbed her wrist and spun her around, slamming her into his chest. He moved her back until she was pinned against the wall and then he dropped his head until his lips were right above hers.

"You listen to me, woman, and you listen good..."

Get Linc here: mybook.to/DAMC-Linc

IF YOU ENJOYED THIS BOOK

Thank you for reading Down & Dirty: Dex. If you enjoyed Dex and Brooke's story, please consider leaving a review at your favorite retailer and/or Goodreads to let other readers know. Reviews are always appreciated and just a few words can help an independent author like me tremendously!

Want to read a sample of my work? Download a sampler book here: BookHip.com/MTQQKK

BEAR'S FAMILY TREE

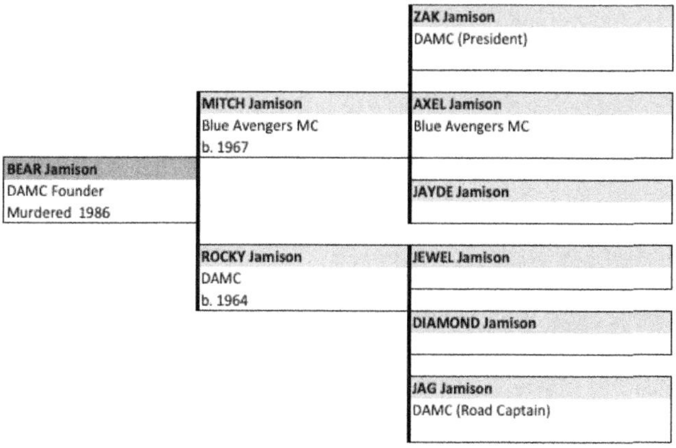
ZAK Jamison
DAMC (President)
MITCH Jamison
Blue Avengers MC
b. 1967
AXEL Jamison
Blue Avengers MC
BEAR Jamison
DAMC Founder
Murdered 1986
JAYDE Jamison
ROCKY Jamison
DAMC
b. 1964
JEWEL Jamison
DIAMOND Jamison
JAG Jamison
DAMC (Road Captain)

DOC'S FAMILY TREE

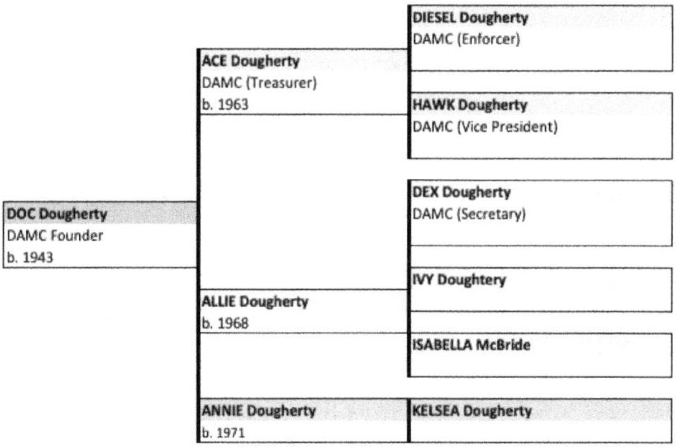
DOC Dougherty
DAMC Founder
b. 1943
ACE Dougherty
DAMC (Treasurer)
b. 1963
ALLIE Dougherty
b. 1968
ANNIE Dougherty
b. 1971
DIESEL Dougherty
DAMC (Enforcer)
HAWK Dougherty
DAMC (Vice President)
DEX Dougherty
DAMC (Secretary)
IVY Doughtery
ISABELLA McBride
KELSEA Dougherty

ALSO BY JEANNE ST. JAMES

Find my complete reading order here:

https://www.jeannestjames.com/reading-order

* Available in Audiobook

Stand-alone Books:

Made Maleen: A Modern Twist on a Fairy Tale *

Damaged *

Rip Cord: The Complete Trilogy *

Everything About You (A Second Chance Gay Romance) *

Reigniting Chase (An M/M Standalone)

Brothers in Blue Series:

Brothers in Blue: Max *

Brothers in Blue: Marc *

Brothers in Blue: Matt *

Teddy: A Brothers in Blue Novelette *

Brothers in Blue: A Bryson Family Christmas *

The Dare Ménage Series:

Double Dare *

Daring Proposal *

Dare to Be Three *

A Daring Desire *

Dare to Surrender *

A Daring Journey *

The Obsessed Novellas:

Forever Him *

Only Him *

Needing Him *

Loving Her *

Tempting Him *

Down & Dirty: Dirty Angels MC Series®:

Down & Dirty: Zak *

Down & Dirty: Jag *

Down & Dirty: Hawk *

Down & Dirty: Diesel *

Down & Dirty: Axel *

Down & Dirty: Slade *

Down & Dirty: Dawg *

Down & Dirty: Dex *

Down & Dirty: Linc *

Down & Dirty: Crow *

Crossing the Line (A DAMC/Blue Avengers MC Crossover) *

Magnum: A Dark Knights MC/Dirty Angels MC Crossover *

Crash: A Dirty Angels MC/Blood Fury MC Crossover

Guts & Glory Series:

(In the Shadows Security)

Guts & Glory: Mercy *

Guts & Glory: Ryder *

Guts & Glory: Hunter *

Guts & Glory: Walker *

Guts & Glory: Steel *

Guts & Glory: Brick *

Blood & Bones: Blood Fury MC®:

Blood & Bones: Trip *

Blood & Bones: Sig *

Blood & Bones: Judge *

Blood & Bones: Deacon *

Blood & Bones: Cage *

Blood & Bones: Shade *

Blood & Bones: Rook *

Blood & Bones: Rev *

Blood & Bones: Ozzy

Blood & Bones: Dodge

Blood & Bones: Whip

Blood & Bones: Easy

COMING SOON!

Double D Ranch (An MMF Ménage Series)

Blue Avengers MC™

WRITING AS J.J. MASTERS:

The Royal Alpha Series

(A gay mpreg shifter series)

The Selkie Prince's Fated Mate *

The Selkie Prince & His Omega Guard *

The Selkie Prince's Unexpected Omega *

The Selkie Prince's Forbidden Mate *

The Selkie Prince's Secret Baby *

ABOUT THE AUTHOR

JEANNE ST. JAMES is a USA Today bestselling romance author who loves an alpha male (or two). She was only thirteen when she started writing and her first paid published piece was an erotic story in Playgirl magazine. Her first romance novel, Banged Up, was published in 2009. She is happily owned by farting French bulldogs. She writes M/F, M/M, and M/M/F ménages.

Want to read a sample of her work? Download a sampler book here: BookHip.com/MTQQKK

To keep up with her busy release schedule check her website at www.jeannestjames.com or sign up for her newsletter: http://www.jeannestjames.com/newslettersignup

www.jeannestjames.com
jeanne@jeannestjames.com

Newsletter: http://www.jeannestjames.com/newslettersignup
Jeanne's Down & Dirty Book Crew: https://www.facebook.com/groups/JeannesReviewCrew/
TikTok: https://www.tiktok.com/@jeannestjames

facebook.com/JeanneStJamesAuthor
amazon.com/author/jeannestjames
instagram.com/JeanneStJames
bookbub.com/authors/jeanne-st-james
goodreads.com/JeanneStJames
pinterest.com/JeanneStJames

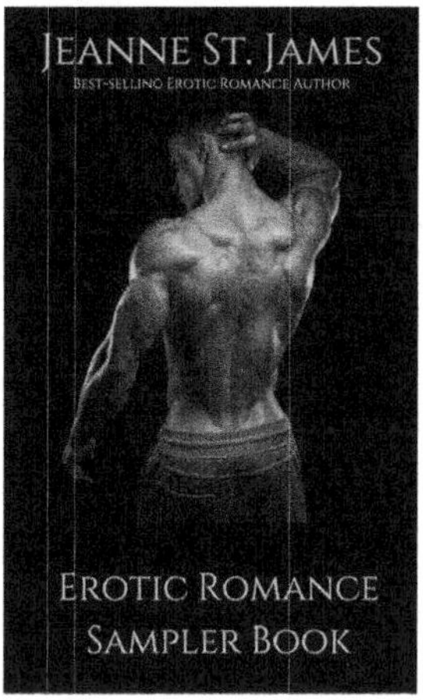
JEANNE ST. JAMES
BEST-SELLING EROTIC ROMANCE AUTHOR
EROTIC ROMANCE
SAMPLER BOOK

Printed in Great Britain
by Amazon

14431536R00150